The War of the Worlds: Aftermath

By Tony Wright

Based on characters created by Herbert George Wells

A Wild Wolf Publication

Published by Wild Wolf Publishing in 2010

Copyright © 2010 Tony Wright

First print

ISBN: 978-1-907954-03-0

www.wildwolfpublishing.com

To my good friend, Rod Glenn, author extraordinaire, without whom this work may never have seen the light of day. Also, thanks to all at my SciFiShocks.com forum for the support and input. Special thanks to Charles Keller for his kind input and advice. Thanks also to Wild Wolf Publishing for their faith in this work. Lastly, but definitely not least, thank you to Herbert George Wells.

AUTHOR'S NOTE

This work began as a short story posted on a now defunct website called The War of The Worlds Online.

I wanted to know what happened after The War of The Worlds. What happened to the Narrator? Did he meet any of the other characters again? Was the rest of his life carried out quietly with his wife in his little house in Surrey? Nowhere could I find the answers to these questions, so I decided to tell more of Wells' Narrator's story myself.

I posted the original first draft in serial form on the aforementioned website, much like Wells did with his work in Pearson's Magazine in 1897. It was a year in the making and was, to my surprise, very well received by those who read it. This version is the second edition.

I hope, reader, that you enjoy this adventure and that it does justice to the original masterpiece that is The War of The Worlds.

I take full credit for any inaccuracies, historical or otherwise, within this work.

Tony Wright

CONTENTS

PROLOGUE

Mr Wells had been most insistent so, as the reader can surely see, I relented.

The story of my adventures has been very well received around the world, and it is due in no small part, to my mind, to Mr Wells' embellishment in his, admittedly highly readable, accounts. It is true that my experiences during that dark time were harrowing but I still fail to see why he chose my reminiscences over those of someone in His Majesty's Government or perhaps a soldier of his armies. In his reedy voice, Wells once told me that the common man would, in some future in which we shall be no part of, be able to feel the horror more than if told from the point of view of some warhorse of a General. What he didn't say was that the military, whilst they fought as bravely as any man in service could, were shown as ineffectual against the monsters within a very short time. So be it.

Wells approached me again, shortly after his work began to create interest.

'A sequel!' he cried as he poured us drinks at his house, 'You have to tell the world the rest of the story.'

'Why?' I asked bluntly.

'Why not?' Wells replied simply. He handed me a glass. 'Look. I know that there is much more to tell. When news of my story about you came out, you were approached to document the subsequent investigations on my recommendation, were you not?'

'I was,' I admitted.

'So,' he said. 'I understand you being reluctant to publish your experiences personally last time. God knows we all experienced the horror of what happened. But I feel that you should set down what happened afterwards for posterity. From what you have told me, it certainly fills in some of the details that people will want to know.'

'I don't know,' I said. 'Much of it was beyond me.'

'Then just give what you do know. Mankind needs to know.'

I sighed. 'Very well, I will give it some thought.'

And so I did.

Later, in the dark of night, with my beloved wife breathing softly beside me, I thought of how I would document such a thing. I was reluctant, still, but the idea had gripped me.

The story of my involvement with the Government is perhaps stranger than that of the war itself, as my esteemed reader will soon see. I also thought of the confidentially agreement I had signed. Could I expect not to feel the full force of the law in telling what I know?

This document, dear reader, is the result of these thoughts. If it is published, I hope it helps to supplement what has been told before.

Note: Whilst my fame, stemming from those who have worked out who I am, is most gratifying, it has somewhat invaded upon my privacy and that of my family of late. Therefore, for that reason, and to facilitate more ease in setting down my tale, I shall here assume the penname of John Smith.

Whilst my readers will doubtless have had their own experiences of the war, before I begin my narrative, I feel it may be prudent to say a little about my own in order to put the following tale into context. The following synopsis briefly covers only my own tribulations. For a more in-depth history of the war, there are other, far more learned, accounts available of events that interested parties can consult.

During the opposition of Mars that occurred in the latter days of the old Queen's reign, observers saw, through their telescopes, strange sights on the red Planet Mars.

First came odd green illuminations, marks on the surface and finally a spurt of green gas ejected into space. Following the last, more jets of gas were seen to erupt from Mars at 24 hourly intervals. The puzzled astronomers had little idea what these strange omens signified. Had they known, much hardship may have been avoided and many lives saved.

My friend, the noted astronomer Ogilvy, showed me a Martian eruption at his observatory one clear night and stated categorically that nothing could live on that barren desert of a world. How wrong he was.

As life went on, as always, on Earth, huge objects sped toward us at tremendous speed through the deep black void of space.

The first cylinder struck, many days later, at Midnight on Horsell Common in Surrey, not far from my home.

Ogilvy was at the site early and by mid morning a large crowd of curious onlookers had gathered. In the afternoon Ogilvy, the Journalist Henderson and Stent, the Astronomer Royal, began to direct men in the task of excavating the cylinder. At Sunset, the cylinder suddenly opened and the crowds moved back, alarmed. Inside the cylinder the gathered people could see the occupants of this vast conveyance; huge grotesque creatures with writhing tentacles and leathery skin.

After much discussion on how to proceed, it was decided to send a deputation to meet these travellers and offer them the hand of friendship. Waving a white flag, Ogilvy, Stent, Henderson and some other hardy souls advanced on the cylinder.

A loud drone emanated from the craft and suddenly, the Deputation were turned to flaming torches by a ray of heat fired by the invaders. The crowd panicked and scattered at this outrage, I was amongst them.

Soldiers arrived and threw a cordon around the Common, whilst, periodically, the Heat-ray pierced the darkness of the night.

Another cylinder fell the next day at Byfleet and the Army moved into place to meet it. That same day, the first of the Martians' Fighting Machines; great metal tripods, one hundred feet tall and carrying the dreaded Heat-rays, destroyed the Artillery at Horsell Common. This diabolical machine marched on and attacked Woking.

I saw my first machines in a storm on the road back to Maybury Hill from Leatherhead, where I had taken my wife to stay with her cousins. The dog-cart I had hired from the Landlord of The Spotted Dog had overturned as the horse reared at sight of the first machine and broke its neck. I watched in awe as the machines stalked away. At home in my study, I saw flames rise in the distance and machines busy at unknown tasks.

An Artilleryman came to my house and told me how his unit had been wiped out and of the destruction that the machines had wrought on the Common.

We decided, at dawn the next day to leave the house; the Artilleryman to report to his unit in London, whilst I would go back to Leatherhead to rejoin my wife.

At Shepperton Lock, more machines appeared and let loose their terrible weapons. One machine fell after a hit from a cannon shell, but the others had their terrible revenge. The Artilleryman and I were separated in the confusion; I barely escaped with my life after jumping into the water to escape the Heat-ray.

Heavy fighting took place South of London and the Martians machines continued their inexorable march towards London, emitting deafening howls – 'Ulla!'

As I carried on my journey, a Curate came across me. He was of the mind that these creatures that had set upon us were doing the Lord's work. Perhaps some terrible holy revenge for all Man's transgressions.

Together, we headed northwards.

Whilst moving on, we saw that the Martians unleashed yet another terrible weapon: the Black Smoke. This was fired from tubes on the machines and loosed toxic gases at anyone, or anything, in its path. When this weapon had done its foul work, the Martians sprayed jets of steam that turned the gas into an inert dust.

My brother, a medical student in London, had joined the exodus from the City after the reports of the carnage the Martians had begun reached the capital's citizens. With the train drivers refusing to return to London, and with the Martians fast approaching, my brother set off on foot. At High Barnet, he came upon two ladies in a pony-chaise. They were Mrs Elphinstone and Miss Elphinstone, her sister-in-law, and, after my brother had helped them to fight off some roughs out to steal their transport, he joined them on their journey to find a boat out of England.

At the Essex coast, they witnessed the well-reported battle between The Ironclad Ram *Thunder Child* and some of the Martian machines that appeared to threaten the fleeing shipping. With many other onlookers, he experienced the exultation of the initial success of this plucky ship in bringing down a metal monster, then the crashing despair as she was sent to her doom beneath the waves by a counter attack from the machine's companions, taking another of the machines with her as she expired.

As the smoke of battle cleared, my brother saw a great black shape soar overhead. This was the Martian's Flying Machine.

The Curate and I had now sheltered in an abandoned building. Suddenly, a cylinder landed on the house burying us in the cellar.

We stayed there for many days, hungry and thirsty with the Curate's rantings become more and more desperate and incomprehensible.

On seeing Martians feeding in the pit – feasting on the warm blood of living human beings – the Curate's fragile mind had snapped and he invited death by screaming out his anguish and horror. I, in desperation, knocked him out and he, to my abject horror, was pulled out right before my eyes by a claw a curious Martian had probed the cellar with.

I spent many more days in that pit until I could stand it no longer and I left my prison when signs of Martian activity seemed to cease.

I continued my weary journey toward London where, at Putney Hill, I again met up with the Artilleryman.

The soldier had taken refuge in a house there and had decided that Mankind's best hope was to take to the sewers and to begin anew down there. He felt that we could perhaps capture a Fighting Machine one day and even learn how to make them ourselves. He had begun digging a tunnel, which he showed me. At seeing how little he had done and how wide was the gulf between his dreams and his powers, I resolved to leave him and continue on my way.

London was deathly quiet. In a moment of extreme loneliness and anguish, I decided to end it all. I would throw myself at the mercy of the Martians! I approached one of the machines that stood stock-still and silent. I was not sent to my maker by this thing; the Martians were dying!

In a strange twist of fate, bacteria had attacked the creatures as soon as they had landed amongst us. Defenceless against these insignificant organisms due to their eradication on their home planet, the Martians had literally rotted from the inside.

As they fed on our blood, their fate had been sealed.

The invasion was over!

Now you are appraised of the facts of my experiences so far, dear reader, I will continue with my tale.

CHAPTER 1
The Appoach

Perhaps a month had passed since the great disillusionment. I trust my esteemed reader will perhaps forgive me using one of Wells' phrases for that terrible war that cost so much, but I always found it most apt.

Plumes of smoke still rolled lazily over some parts of London and the South East. Great metal machines stood silent and unmoving here and there, glittering in the sun, like huge chess pieces carelessly dropped by the gods. Weeds, of a green and entirely earthly nature, already grew around the parts that touched the ground.

In the capital, bridges engineered by some of Mankind's most brilliant minds lay broken, their once proud arches snapped and torn, scattered like piles of toy bricks kicked by some petulant child in a nursery. The top of the Clock Tower had been sliced off cleanly, as though by a surgeon's knife, by a Heat-ray and stood, oddly intact and upright, a short way away as if the tower itself had sunk into the ground. Clumps of brown sludge still floated serenely down the river along with other debris. From time to time, the authorities, grim faced and muttering in hushed tones, patrolled in police launches fishing pale and bloated bodies from the murky water of the Thames.

My house in Surrey, unlike so many others, had escaped most of the destruction, barring a few displaced roof tiles and a smashed garden wall, and was quite habitable. The only real sign that something was amiss was a faint but omnipresent smell of burning inside that we could not disperse, no matter what we tried.

The noise and bustle of humanity was at full pace as I sat staring from the window of my study. Across the road I saw men swarming over houses, rebuilding. People rushed to and fro with carts containing building materials and furniture. A mangy, flea-bitten dog scurried nervously past. The so recently dead and black wreathed streets were alive with activity as man once again stamped his mark on the landscape that had seemed so surely lost. I imagined this was happening everywhere. The newspapers were often found calling the public to arms in the fight against decay and disease and despite the heavy death toll of the war, thousands had returned from their flight and were, sometimes unwillingly, being tasked with the rebuilding of the damaged areas. Grubby children chased each other noisily amongst the ruined houses and clambered over the fallen Martian machines like primates in the jungle whoop and jump amongst the trees.

The door to my study opened to reveal my wife's sweet face, disturbing my reverie.

'John? There are some men here to see you.'

'Who are they, my dear?' I asked, puzzled.

'Well, that's the odd thing. They say they represent the Government.'

'Very well,' I said. 'I will be in presently.'

Opening the sitting room door, I saw two men, to whom my wife, ever the gracious hostess, was handing steaming cups of tea. As usual when we had visitors, she had taken out the best china and the gleaming silver service and was offering sugar from a small bowl when I entered. A warm fire burned in the grate and the Grandfather clock ticked solidly in the corner.

My first visitor was an important looking fellow of around sixty years. A great handlebar moustache was draped over his lip and chops like a snowy white banner. His portly frame barely fit into the chair he was perched on and his small watery eyes regarded me as I entered.

'Ah! Here's our man,' he said in a gruff, but friendly, voice.

The other man looked up from stirring his tea. He was around thirty with dark wavy hair and a goatee. He was slight in frame and dressed impeccably in black.

'Indeed,' he said quietly. His eyes showed no emotion at all.

'Sir,' said the portly man, standing with some difficulty. 'Allow me to introduce myself. I am Sir George Cavendish and my assistant is James Horton. We are representatives of His Majesty's Government.' The man offered me a pudgy hand, which I shook. His grip was firm but his palms clammy.

The younger man nodded slightly, his blank eyes never leaving mine. His hands stayed firmly, I noticed, behind his back.

'Pleased to meet you, gentlemen. May I ask, to what do I owe this honour?' I found a chair and my wife handed me some tea, gave me a small nervous smile and then quietly left the room.

The portly man sat on the chair again and was answered with a small wooden creak of protest.

'Yes, of course. Well, you know Mr Wells, do you not?'

'Herbert? Why, yes I do,' I replied.

'He is an acquaintance of mine, also, and I have heard that he plans to publish your memories of our recent troubles.'

'Yes, he was most insistent. I think he wished to put forth the 'ordinary man's' view of events.'

'Quite so,' said Cavendish, his eyes fixed steadily on me. 'Most admirable.'

'Although, why his own memories are not enough is beyond me,' I continued. 'He is not forthcoming on the matter.'

'Well,' Cavendish explained. 'We have seen the drafts that you wrote for him and we were most impressed. On Wells' recommendation, we would like you to join us and document our further investigations.'

'I hardly think I am qualified,' I began.

'Please, let me finish. We very much need the 'man of the street's' view of things. We are not short of scientists, nor of military men. They will write their own reports. Whilst we expect that we cannot make much of what we may find public, we need a representative of the people, who will write in a way that they will understand and you would seem to fit the bill admirably. Your original draft shows a remarkable grasp of things. It's a pity we have had to ask Mr Wells to excise some of the finer details in the work he is undertaking based on your experiences.'

'You have?' I was shocked. Perhaps I should not have been, on reflection, but it came as a surprise at the time.

'Indeed. It would not do for some of the more ... technical ... aspects to be known.'

Horton, who had been silent until this point, spoke.

'It is for the good of the country, Mr Smith. Surely you must understand that.'

'Of course. What do you have in mind?'

'We will need you to pack some things ...enough for a week or so, initially. You must not tell anyone where you are going, which is why I will say no more for now. Can we rely on you?' Cavendish asked, setting down his cup.

I thought for a moment. The trauma of my experiences during the war was still very much with me. I awoke sweating and screaming every night as I remembered what had happened to my friend Ogilvy, and what the terrible consequences of my actions with the Curate had been. Not to mention the horrible fate that befell so many of my fellow men and women. Without my wife's succour, I would surely be in some institution, like so many other poor wretches who had been found wandering the countryside, aimless and without hope or reason, after the carnage had ended.

Would this help exorcise those demons that lurked in the darkest reaches of the night, waiting to trouble me?

'Would I be free to leave at any time?'

Cavendish nodded his great shaggy head. 'We should like you to submit to a confidentiality agreement. You can only publish that which is cleared by either myself or Horton. Other than that, there are no restrictions.'

Curiosity had ridden rough shod over my doubts now. If only I had known what was to come.

'Yes, then.'

'Splendid!' Cavendish beamed and both men stood. 'You will be collected at 8 o'clock sharp tomorrow. Until then.'

With that, my strange guests said curt goodbyes and left, leaving me alone with my thoughts.

CHAPTER 2
An Old Companion

I slept little, and such sleep as came to me was, as usual, haunted by huge, glowing saucer eyes and the bloodcurdling screams of the dying.

Somewhat bleary eyed and deep in thought, I was sat before an untouched plate of kedgeree in my dining room when the cab arrived to take me to London at eight sharp. I took a swig of cooling tea and made my way to the front of the house to collect my bags.

My wife sobbed quietly as I left. She held me as passionately as she had when we found each other again on my return to the house weeks before and she trembled a little as I gently stroked her hair and muttered comforting words in her ear. We had lost each other once before and she was reluctant to let me go again. I whispered to her that I would be perfectly safe and that I would be back within a week. Both, as it turned out, were false.

Outside, a black cab sat waiting, the horse, steaming in the cool morning air, pawing impatiently at the ground with a hoof. The driver jumped down from his perch atop the cab and shambled toward me.

The cabbie, a rough-looking, red faced fellow of the city, unceremoniously threw my luggage, and me for that matter, into the transport and, with a sharp 'Hyah!' roused the horse into a trot towards London.

In normal circumstances, a train would have been the best mode of transport, but engineering works were still underway to clear debris and repair the tracks in many areas, making rail travel impractical. Resigned, I settled back into the cracked leather of the cab's interior, amid the smell of stale sweat and tobacco, and tried to make myself as comfortable as I could against the chill.

So on we went, but I remember little of the first part of the journey. As the cab clattered through the Surrey countryside, the driver swigged every so on from a flask. My tiredness and the rocking motion of our conveyance finally overcame me and I drifted off into sleep.

Primal dread and darkness surrounded me. A wet shuffling sound quickly turned my head. I peered fearfully into thick impenetrable gloom, trying to see what approached me.

I found myself powerless to move as the Martian lurched toward me. The huge eyes glowed like burning embers and the thing's lipless mouth was coated with a viscous drool. Thick cable-like tentacles rippled and powerful muscles under its glistening, grey-brown hide bunched as it came. Very close now, I felt the monstrosity's foul, stinking breath on my face and I could see every pore in the tough leathery skin.

The creature regarded me balefully for a moment and then it flourished a horrifyingly familiar instrument in one tentacle. I had seen this thing in a pit under a ruined house what seemed like years ago … and in my dreams ever since. The monster hooted softly as it pushed the spiked end of the apparatus closer and closer to me. I could only watch, paralysed, as my flesh was finally and inevitably pierced by the cold, sharp metal. As my blood began to flow, I cried out from the icy pain and I heard in the distance that dreadful howl.

'Ulla!'

With a start, I awoke again. A hulking shape loomed over me and I started. It was no foul beast from the stars regarding me but the cab driver. He stared at me curiously for a moment then shrugged.

''Alf hour,' he drawled and shambled away, muttering under his breath.

I unfolded myself from the cab, body aching from the rough journey, and stretched, taking a moment to absorb in my surroundings and shake off the disorientation that the nightmare had left.

We had stopped, I found, by Shepperton Lock under a cloudy sky, and immediately memories of the battle I had seen here before swamped me. I remembered vividly my flight into the water and the horror as I had waited for the Heat-ray to strike me. A light drizzle fell from the heavens as if in memory of that terrible day.

The church tower was still ruined, but scaffolding had been erected and piles of stone and other materials were ready for the rebuilding. Looking around, I saw the Inn was nearly unscathed and open for business, so I headed toward it, my mouth suddenly dry.

The Inn was busy but I managed to find a table and sat down. A young, rosy-cheeked woman came and cheerily took my order … a stiff drink. I suddenly missed my wife terribly. In the Inn, hushed whispering was punctuated occasionally by loud laughter or gruff exclamations. A thick haze of tobacco smoke hung in the alcohol-soaked air like fog.

As my drink arrived, raucous laughter from the corner of the room drew my attention. A loud, somehow familiar, voice was raised.

'We beat the blighters! Oh yes, my boys! They came and they couldn't take the pressure! They thought they had us, but they were no match for the human race!'

A small, drunken cheer came from the orator's companions.

The landlord glared from behind the bar at them.

'Landlord! More drinks, if you please! We wish to toast the human race!'

I tried to place the toastmaster's voice. Where had I heard it before?

I caught a glimpse of the man's back as he lurched to his feet and staggered to the bar.

The Landlord whispered harshly to him and the man dug into the pockets of his army uniform and, dragging out a heap of change, slammed it onto the wet bar. The Landlord shook his head despairingly, but took the coins and began pouring more drinks.

That was it. The man was wearing a very familiar uniform. Surely not?

As he turned round, I realised that it was indeed the Artilleryman. The very same man I had met twice before as calamity threatened the Earth. At the moment of that realisation, his eyes met mine and he started.

'You!' he mouthed silently. The startled look on his face changed slowly as a great grin broke onto his handsome face.

I found myself smiling.

His motley band of companions in the corner temporarily forgotten, he wandered over to me.

'It's you, my friend from Maybury Hill!' he exclaimed. 'Good lord!' Reaching me, he pumped my hand eagerly.

'Hullo!' I said simply. I could think of nothing else better as surprise was still on me. I had met this man twice before, during the war, but I had not expected to see him again after our last meeting.

'Landlord! A drink for my friend here! Champagne!' he called as he sat next to me. 'Just like old times, eh?' He winked conspiratorially.

Two glasses arrived with a bottle and the Artilleryman poured for us. Taking up a glass, he proposed a toast.

'To us, survivors!'

I waved my glass vaguely at him and sipped the drink. I remembered my old disgust at our last encounter and gave the bubbling drink a bitter aftertaste.

'So, how have you been?' the Artilleryman asked. He swigged his drink down and wiped his mouth on his sleeve.

'Very well,' I replied. I was increasingly aware that the gulf between this man and I was wider than ever.

'I thought you lost once again,' he said. 'You had that wild-eyed look I saw much during the war. Those others with it generally ended up as Martian fodder, I found.'

I smiled, I was only too aware, unconvincingly. 'Well, I am all right, as you can see. I went home and found my wife. All is well.' I did not mention that I had thought, like others it seems in that dark time, to sacrifice myself to the Fighting Machines and their hideous controllers.

'Good for you,' the soldier beamed. 'I continued with my plan. You remember?'

'I do,' I said grimly.

'It was going well too. But the monsters died and that was that. I had such great plans for getting back at them.' He suddenly looked unhappy.

'I remember. What are you doing now?'

'Well,' he said, smiling again. 'Soon after those things started to die off, a unit of soldiers came through mopping them up. Finishing them off. I joined up with them.'

'Finishing them off?'

'Yes. Helping them on their way,' he grinned. 'We showed them what English steel tastes like as they breathed their last.' He mimed stabbing at something on the ground and the gleam in his eyes disturbed me, somehow.

For some reason, despite all the Martians had done and what fate they had in store for us, I found the whole idea distasteful. It must have showed on my face.

'What?' His visage darkened visibly. 'You think we should have shown them mercy? They were as good as dead anyway. In a way, we did them a kindness. Stopped their suffering. More than they did for us, eh?'

Somehow, I doubted that kindness was in his heart as he skewered the creatures as they lay dying.

I was confused by these new feelings and changed the subject.

'I cannot stay long; I am again heading for London and my transport leaves soon.'

'Really?' The Artilleryman brightened again. 'Business?'

'Yes, something like that.'

He raised his glass which he had filled, again.

'To business!' I had the idea that this man would toast anything.

I sipped again from my glass and stood up.

'Well,' I said, extending my hand. 'It was very good seeing you again.'

He grasped my hand and shook it. 'And you too. Look me up if you are in this area again. I believe we are to be stationed here for some while yet.'

'That I will.'

Turning as I left the Inn, I saw the Artilleryman wander back to his friends and I wondered vaguely if fate would bring us together again in the future.

CHAPTER 3
A Brave New World

The final stage of the journey was fairly uneventful. The only incident came when a motor-car careered, screaming like a banshee, around a blind corner and made our horse rear. The cabbie snarled curses at it as he fought to control the frightened horse and he was answered by the shrill parping of the contraption's horn, which did nothing to lighten the man's mood.

We travelled on through countryside scorched and black in places. Through towns busy with activity and ringing with the laughs and good humour of the saved. Here and there, birds perched on the remnants of the great titans that had so threatened to destroy all.

We arrived, after some time, at our destination.

So unlike the dead, silent wasteland I had wandered in the last days of the war, wishing only for death myself, London was breathing strong and sure once again. Like a living creature, it had fought against the invading alien organisms and was healing once more. Through busy streets we weaved for a time, the cabbie expertly steering us amidst the throng and bustle, the calls of street vendors and newspaper boys following us.

To my surprise, we eventually stopped, not at some Government building, but at South Kensington Underground Station. People and vehicles passed us, rushing to and fro, as the cab halted. I stared at the ornate frontage of the station for a moment uncertainly.

'Is this the right place?' I leaned out of the window and asked the driver finally.

'We are to wait here,' he replied simply and sank into his cloak until only his hat showed.

Soon, I spied Cavendish and Horton emerging from the Station. Horton's face was as impassive as it had been the day before, but Cavendish was radiating warmth like a small sun.

'My dear fellow!' he cried shaking my hand as I stepped out of the cab. 'A pleasant trip?'

'Pleasant enough' I replied, rather grumpily. 'The train would have been quicker.'

'Yes,' Cavendish said, non-committally, and motioned me towards the station. 'Don't worry about your things, I'll have them sent on.'

'Where are we going?' I asked, curious now.

'Underground,' Cavendish winked and marched off into the station building. I followed and Horton fell in behind.

I was extremely puzzled now. Underground? What could he mean?

A small grizzled man, dressed in a dark uniform with no visible markings, appeared and whisked us through the concourse and we found ourselves on a platform. It was quite deserted. I felt, rightly as it turned out, that this was not a platform for the public use. The small man left us.

Cavendish made small talk while we waited and presently a train arrived. It had only one carriage and we boarded and sank into plush seats.

'Don't get too comfortable,' Cavendish said. 'It's not far.'

The train screeched along a dark tunnel for a short while then began to slow. We stopped at another station.

This one gleamed as if quite new and was kept in very good order indeed. A couple of men in dark uniforms stood to attention on either side a short distance away. Hobbs Lane was the name of the station, a sign informed me.

'Hobbs Lane?' I said. 'I've never heard of this station.'

A small smile touched Horton's lips.

'That, Mr Smith, is because it is not a public station. It is for His Majesty's Government use only. Simply put, it doesn't exist.'

'I see,' I said, but I didn't.

We alighted from the carriage and walked across the platform. The men on the platform looked straight ahead as if we were not there. A gate opened and an officious looking man in yet another plain black uniform cast suspicious eyes over us.

'Ah. You are expected, Sir George,' he said and held the gate open for us.

At the end of a short brightly lit corridor was a gate. This opened to reveal an ornate gilt lift. The lift operator tipped his hat in our direction and shut the gate behind us. He pressed a small red button and the lift lurched down the shaft.

My curiosity was running rampant now.

'What on –?'

'Please have patience, my dear fellow. All will be revealed soon,' Cavendish said.

The lift gate was opened once more and we entered into a small lobby. Two great steel doors were before us. As we approached, a small slot in the right hand door slid aside to reveal two grey eyes that regarded us carefully for a moment. The slot slid back again with a snap and there was silence. Then, a minute or so later, a rumbling whine and the sound of great pistons started up and the doors slowly parted.

'Hydraulic,' said Cavendish, as if it explained everything.

Another man in black was waiting behind the doors and we were ushered respectfully into an unexpectedly cavernous space. Looking around, I could see, far in the distance above, small pin-pricks that could only be electric lights. They looked, to me, like the aloof stars in the night sky. What was the purpose of such an enormous space beneath the feet of the unsuspecting public, I wondered, awe struck. We walked upon a smooth, dry surface and the air was pleasantly warm and I could not help but marvel at what a feat of engineering the excavation of this place must have been. A low hum and whir of distant machinery hit my ears from all around.

Here and there in the huge space were things covered with scaffolding. Huge shapes, some smooth, some more angular had enormous tarpaulins draped over them. I instinctively had the impression of machinery of some sort. White coated men were looking at charts and swarming over the scaffolding, busily writing notes on clipboards and chatting animatedly amongst themselves.

Men in army uniforms brandishing rifles watched the scientists intently, for that is what the men in white obviously were.

Cavendish gently steered me toward a great glinting shape. I approached but jumped back as I saw a small puff of green smoke.

My mind racing, I stared harder at the thing. I saw a great bulk of metallic body with something protruding from it. Disbelievingly, I watched as the protuberance moved.

'Here we are, Smith,' beamed Cavendish proudly and gestured grandly at the thing. His look of satisfaction quickly changed to alarm at my reaction.

As the hood of the Fighting Machine swung round to regard me with what seemed like huge, dead eyes, I screamed.

CHAPTER 4
Explanations

As light pierced the darkness and my consciousness returned, I caught muffled voices which slowly became clearer.

'… should not have brought him!' a voice hissed.

'Now, now, Horton, I am entirely at fault. I should have explained to him beforehand what we are doing here. The man has had a long day and was quite unprepared for what he saw.' As my vision cleared, I saw the second voice belonged to Cavendish.

I caught the vague reek of smelling salts and saw a white –coated man standing over me.

'Gentlemen!' the man said.

Cavendish marched over to my side and his concerned face peered at me.

'How are you, my dear chap?' he boomed. 'You gave us quite a fright.'

Panic gripped me as I remembered what I had seen before I had, evidently, fainted. I sat up on the couch I had been laid on.

'The machine!' I breathed. 'What-?'

'Calm yourself,' Cavendish said gently. 'I will explain presently, when you feel a little better. I can assure you that you are in no danger here.'

Despite Cavendish's promise, I felt alarm bells ringing frantically within my head again. Nevertheless, I sank back into the couch.

Horton appeared next to his colleague. His face was as impassive as ever as he studied me, but I thought that, for a second, I saw something flash across his eyes.

The white-coated man handed me a small glass of brandy, which I sank with one gulp. The liquid instantly spread warmth through my body.

'A fine way to treat my exquisite Napoleon brandy,' Cavendish chortled. 'How do you feel?'

'A little better, but, I must confess, perplexed,' I said. 'A Martian machine is loose in this ...place and you appear not the least bit concerned.'

'Not loose. Everything is entirely under human control.' Cavendish flashed the same proud smile that I had seen before. Yellow teeth glinted in the dimly lit room. Looking around I caught glimpses of ornate brass fittings and acres of leather upholstery. A large wooden desk stood before a large bookshelf stuffed with books and papers. The couch in which I lay creaked gently when I shifted.

'You mean to say that you can control those things?' I was amazed.

'Some of the finer details elude us for the moment, but we are making great strides on that front daily.'

'But how did you get them in here?'

'Magic!' he said, grinning like a schoolboy again. 'Seriously, it was not easy, but there are more ways into this laboratory than the way we entered.'

'I see,' I said nodding, but I did not see at all.

Horton stepped forward. 'Mr Smith must be very tired and hungry.'

Cavendish glared at him, suddenly quite at odds with the jovial figure he had thus far portrayed to me. It was if this man greatly objected to having his boasts interrupted.

Then, as if remembering himself, he turned back to me, the ever-present grin back on his chubby face.

'Of course. You must go and refresh yourself. I think we shall have dinner soon.'

An orderly was summoned and I was ushered out of the room down a long corridor of whitewashed stone. My guide turned a corner and opened a door for me.

I found my luggage already in the extravagantly decorated room and, still puzzled, I took in my surroundings. The bed was covered with thick blankets and the plush carpet was thick and springy underfoot. Polished brass lamps stood on small tables and a chestnut writing table stood to one side laden with clean, watermarked sheets of paper and writing implements standing ready for use. A large richly upholstered wing chair stood in a corner. Pictures of sea and land battle scenes from history covered the walls here and there; Nelson sailed at Trafalgar and Wellington spurred his troops on at Waterloo in vivid colours.

I was slightly baffled to find that there were curtains hanging on one wall of the room but I did not know why. Closer inspection revealed the reason for my puzzlement. There were no windows behind them. Of course windows deep underground would have been superfluous to say the least and I momentarily found the whole situation vaguely ridiculous. I was surprised to hear a guffaw and it took a few seconds to realise that it came from me, not some interloper. Suddenly deflated, I lay down on the huge comfortable bed and tried to clear my mind.

Dinner was excellent. It appeared that the Government spared no expense in making its workers and guests comfortable in this facility. We dined on the finest beef I have ever tasted, washed down by expensive red wine in a spacious, yet cosy, dining room. I ate my meal in the company of Horton and Cavendish but was vaguely surprised not to see others there. I supposed that the workers ate elsewhere.

After the huge and satisfying dinner, eaten with gold cutlery off finest bone china, we all retired to a panelled library and sank into comfortable leather armchairs. We each clutched a glass of port and huge cigars.

'So, Smith,' Cavendish said at length. 'It's time I filled you in on a few details, what?'

I nodded silently, contemplating the dark liquid in my glass.

Cavendish puffed on his cigar briefly as if deciding where to start.

'You know all about the war, of course and how it ended. Without our allies, the bacteria, we would have been finished.'

'Quite,' I said. 'A lucky escape.'

'Exactly!' Cavendish pointed his cigar at me. 'You are quite right. The Martian fiends were bent on destruction and slavery. They planned to use their machinery to take what is rightfully ours and feed off us like so many cattle. We had no chance; our soldiers fought bravely, but many who resisted were wiped out like ants by the Heat-ray and the sheer power of the Fighting Machines.'

'Yes,' I said. 'But they failed.'

'Of course! But it was by accident, not design. We cannot assume they will not try again.'

This made me sit up in my chair sharply, my mind racing as I considered this. The port sloshed around my glass like a miniature tidal wave.

'Good God!' I exclaimed. 'Do you really think that's possible?'

'They made a mistake,' Cavendish said gravely. 'They will surely learn from it.'

There was silence as that sobering thought hung in the air. I sank back into the chair.

'So,' Cavendish continued after a moment. 'His Majesty's Government wishes to be ready for such an eventuality.'

'You mean to learn how to use the machines?' I asked.

'We do. We have made great progress, even in this short time, but we still have much to discover. The operation of the machines is not as complex as we first thought but HOW they work is still very much a mystery. Many of the machines left behind are wrecked or partially inoperable. We have to discover how to build them ourselves.'

It made sense to me. If the Martians concocted some form of antidote to their weakness, we would have to be ready to fight. I sipped at my drink distractedly.

'We are watching Mars closely, obviously. Telescopes worldwide are trained on Mars, looking for activity. We are lucky also to have other means.'

'Other means?' I was again curious.

Cavendish grinned. 'Yes. Finish your Port, I have something I'd like you to see.'

CHAPTER 5
Observations

Cavendish rummaged in his pocket for a moment and pulled out a set of keys.

'Ah, here we are,' he said, advancing on a huge walk-in safe at the corner of his office.

Horton took folded himself into a wing chair in the corner of this plush, yet functional, room and sat quietly watching, his fingers steepled under his long chin.

Inserting the keys, Cavendish dextrously twisted the number dial this way and that, stood back and yanked the handle. With a solid sounding clank, the door was pulled open.

Cavendish's large frame disappeared into the darkness within for a moment, then re-emerged holding a large, ornately carved wooden box.

Placing it carefully and reverently on his massive oaken desk amidst a jumble of inkwells, blotters and writing implements and papers, as if it contained a relic of the Lord himself, he spoke.

'This box, my friend, contains one of our most important finds. This device could give us the warning we need in the event our erstwhile conquerors resume their plans.' He took a small key on his key ring, inserted it into a small golden lock in the box and slowly lifted the lid.

Inside the box, on a cushion of blue-black velvet, was an ovoid shape covered in a cloth. Cavendish pulled this last away to reveal an egg-like object.

'Beautiful, is it not?' Sir George breathed. Horton, as usual, remained quite silent.

'It is not a Faberge,' I said with authority. I had an acquaintance who had shown me one of the Imperial Eggs.

Cavendish regarded me for a moment with his watery eyes. 'Indeed it is not. Those trinkets cannot touch this in terms of beauty, nor rarity.'

The Crystal Egg was beautiful. But somehow it seemed to me beautiful in the way Nature at her most cruel can be. The thing was eerie to behold.

It was like a giant cut diamond. Not a flaw could I see within its fabric. Its facets shone in the electric lights of the study. I looked closer. Within, as I watched, small flecks of light appeared to play. The lights almost instantly held a slight mesmerizing sway over me. If Cavendish and Horton had left me, I may well have stared into that strange device forever.

'You see them, eh? Not everyone can.' Cavendish grinned proudly at me as if I were a promising pupil. My trance was broken by his voice.

'What is it?' I asked tearing my eyes away. 'Who made this?'

'Who made it is unclear,' he admitted. 'But we have every reason to believe it is of Martian origin.'

'Martian?' I was surprised.

'Horton came upon it quite by chance. It had sat for some time in a little antique shop run by a queer little fellow by the name of Cave and Horton learned about it from a friend of his at St Catherine's Hospital. When Mr Cave died recently, Horton 'acquired' it. Blind luck we found it at all, really.'

I glanced at Horton, briefly, but he merely returned my gaze with those unreadable eyes of his and said nothing.

'If it is Martian, how did it get here? Did they bring it with them?' I asked.

Cavendish shook his head. 'It was here before they landed.'

I was more baffled than ever. 'How can that be?'

'I wish we knew,' the man seemed uncomfortable with his lack of knowledge. 'What is important is what it can do for us.'

'What is that?' I asked.

'Sit in this chair before the egg.'

I moved to the chair that Cavendish indicated and sat down with, I admit, a little apprehension.

'That's it,' Cavendish continued in hushed tones. 'Now look into the Egg. No, move your head up a little. There, that should be about the right angle.'

I, shifted my weight on the chair a little and, feeling as comfortable as I could be, stared into the Egg once again. The lights danced before my eyes once more then seemed to home in on each other. There was now one soft light that slowly grew brighter. I began to see pictures.

I saw odd-looking buildings, domes and spinnerets; buildings that reminded me of the mosques of the East. They stood next to canals in which murky water flowed sluggishly, choked, seemingly, by a familiar plant. I saw this vegetation everywhere. Red Vegetation.

'My God!' I breathed.

Bulky, grey-brown shapes bounced and leaped on thick tentacles around this surreal city. A five-legged, crab-like machine stalked by, the sun glinting off its metallic surface. Pale biped figures sat passively in a great basket on its back. More bipeds were being led, like docile cows, across a vast city square by other brown shapes.

Other machines stalked by as I watched, familiar and yet different, their uses unfathomable.

The scene changed, suddenly, to a large, desert-like area. I could see buildings in the distance so I assumed that this was outside of the city. I saw a huge black bulk lift ponderously off the arid ground, blowing up huge clouds of red dust. A crowd of the brown shapes beneath the machine danced around excitedly at this.

I tore my disbelieving eyes away from the somehow nightmarish sight.

'Is this Mars?' I asked finally.

'It can be nowhere else,' Cavendish replied simply.

'Well,' I said after a moment. 'Now I see what you meant by other ways of observing. Incredible!'

Cavendish nodded. 'We can observe much of what happens on the planet. Any undue activity and we shall spot it.'

A thought sped into my mind. 'Can they not see us through this thing?'

'We don't know,' Cavendish answered. 'They seem to peer into it from time to time. It is most disconcerting to look into it and see the eyes of a Martian seemingly look straight back at you, I can assure you. We have guessed that they have similar devices on Mars but they show no sign of actually seeing us looking at them. The view in the Egg changes periodically, but we have no idea why and how.'

I could think of nothing else to say. This thing was truly one of the strangest devices I had seen yet.

Cavendish stood. 'I think that's enough wonders for one day, Smith. It is late and we have a full day ahead of us tomorrow. We should all get some rest.'

Back in my room, it took me some time to quiet my thoughts and to try to make sense of all I had seen so far. I wrote a rough account of this first most amazing day in my journal. When I had finished, still confused and utterly exhausted, I went to bed.

I was asleep the moment my head touched the pillow.

CHAPTER 6
The Tour

I awoke at around ten the next morning much refreshed. I had not dreamt of the Martians or their machines for the first time, perhaps, since the war had ended.

Perhaps, I think, the massive sensory overload of the previous day had prompted my weary mind to protect me from further depravations. Whatever the reason, I felt much better and ready to face whatever new amazements the day might hold.

As I was washing, an orderly in black trousers and a white jerkin rapped on my door and, opening it, peered into the room.

'Breakfast, Sir?' he said and, when he had seen I was awake, disappeared the way he had come.

When I had dressed, the orderly, who had waited for me outside my door, escorted me to the dining room where I found Cavendish and Horton waiting for me. They had evidently eaten long before and sat nursing steaming cups of coffee.

'Did you sleep well, old man?' Cavendish asked, placing his cup on its bone china saucer.

'Like a top,' I answered. 'I'm ravenous. What's for breakfast?'

The orderly appeared again, as if by some unspoken command, and placed before me a plate of freshly caught Scottish kippers, accompanied by scrambled egg and a pile of hot buttered toast. The smell instantly made my mouth water and I jumped into a chair and set to the repast with gusto, washing it down with good, strong coffee.

As I devoured the meal, Horton watched me silently whilst Cavendish made small talk.

'When you are ready, Smith,' the older man said at length, 'we shall take you on a tour of our facility. To write properly of our work you will need to see it for yourself.'

Pushing my empty plate away and finishing the last of my coffee, I stood satisfied.

'Then there is no time like the present.'

We walked together down another long, sloping corridor, Cavendish chatting animatedly, as was his way, and Horton bringing up the rear like some silent shadow. I found myself feeling disorientated as there were no signs and one corridor looked much alike another. Unlike the extravagantly decorated rooms I had seen so far, the walls were rough, bare stone and the smooth floor was painted a dull, battleship grey.

Electric lights were fixed to the walls at intervals and we cast strange distorted shadows around us.

I had the idea that, as the slope of the corridor got slightly steeper, I thought I knew how Verne's Professor Hardwigg and his party must have felt as they started on their journey into the bowels of the Earth. Unlike those intrepid explorers, though, we had no runes to guide us.

Soon, we came to a dog-leg in the corridor and Cavendish pulled and held open some large wooden double doors.

I went ahead and found myself in another cavernous chamber. In this one, my ears caught a dull throbbing sound and in front of me, a large metal stand held something bulky. It was a large, matt black, rectangular box with a tube protruding from one end of it. I realised quickly that the sound was emanating from this thing.

'Do you recognise that?' Cavendish asked from over my shoulder.

'Dear God! It's a Heat-ray, isn't it?'

'It is,' Cavendish confirmed, grinning. 'Soon, we hope to be able to fire it and perhaps even make our own.'

I was astounded. 'You mean to fire it? It's too dangerous man! I've seen what those things can do!'

I glanced at Horton and caught him gazing at me once more. I thought I saw a glimpse of a look of curiosity pass his eyes, but it was gone as soon as quickly as it had appeared.

'I'm assured it will be quite safe under the right conditions,' Cavendish said dismissively. 'It is apparently quite undamaged and we will take every precaution possible.'

'Do you know how it works?' I asked. 'The papers said that its workings were unfathomable.'

'Putting it extremely simply, we are coming to the conclusion that it works using energy created at an atomic level. We cannot be sure how this happens, though, and we continue to investigate.'

'You understand it so little and yet you think to fire it?' It struck me as madness.

'We will,' Cavendish answered determinedly, 'when the time is right. These devices could be our best defence. Imagine being able to use the Martian's own weapons to defeat them! We must continue our research'

I said no more but I thought of the Artilleryman, who had made a similar plea in a different and more turbulent time.

There was no more to be said on the subject, it seemed and our group fell silent. I turned to see a small group of scientists, that were gathered around the Heat-ray tube, watching us, but they glanced busily at papers and clipboards when they saw me observe them.

We continued the tour.

The next area I was shown contained another Martian machine, or part of one anyway. It was a Fighting Machine, without doubt, but the legs had been severed, whether by design or accident I could not say, about ten feet from where they joined the body of the machine. The body of the machine had dark, rusty-red splashes on it, which, I realised with some dismay as we grew closer, appeared to be blood. Elsewhere, a large scratch and scuff-marks covered the side of the device, as if this machine had fallen heavily as its occupant perished. A large dent in the metal toward the rear seemed to confirm this.

As I watched, a young man in a one-piece suit clambered up a ladder into the hood and disappeared from view.

'The controls, as I suggested before, are quite simple,' Cavendish explained. 'There are a system of levers in the hood which move the thing around. The machines are, essentially, driven by way of a sort of artificial muscle. It really is quite something. You will, of course, have seen the green smoke that emanates from the machines as they walk and we are analysing this substance to see if it can be replicated. At the moment, we can only drive machines that have been left operational, but we hope to be able to create our own if we can unlock their secrets.'

Fascinated, I watched as the hood of the machine swayed from side to side, then up and down. Suddenly, the machine lurched forward uncertainly as the driver struggled with the controls, the truncated legs making sharp clanks as they impacted with the stone floor. It was a disturbing sight, even if the being at the controls was human.

I glanced at my companions. Horton looked as impassive and unimpressed as ever, Cavendish was making small clapping motions with his hands. He reminded me of an oversized schoolboy spying his first steam engine.

The Fighting Machine jerked forward a little more and then stopped. Suddenly, there was a whine and one of the legs swung violently and unexpectedly out to the side. Nearby scientists scattered. The whole machine wobbled slightly and the hood flailed around like the head of a wounded snake. Then the device slowly toppled over onto its belly with a resounding crash that echoed like the report of a cannon around the huge space. White-coated scientists rushed into the resulting cloud of dust to help the stunned driver out, whilst others, with dismayed faces, inspected the machine. A scientist walked quickly over to us and whispered something into Cavendish's ear. Cavendish whispered harshly back and the man disappeared again.

'Problems?' I asked. To my surprise, I imagined I saw a smirk, ever so briefly, flicker across Horton's face.

'Teething troubles,' Cavendish grumbled. 'It's to be expected. Come, Smith, I think it's time you saw our biggest secret.' As we left, the driver of the Fighting Machine, shaking his head as if in a daze but seemingly otherwise uninjured, was led away, supported by two soldiers.

After traversing more corridors, as blank and featureless as before, we wandered through a kind of airlock fronted by a huge steel door, not unlike one you would see in a bank vault, into another room. This place was smaller than some of the other spaces I had thus seen and was dimly lit. My nose was assailed by a sickly sweet smell that I knew but could not place, as I entered, and the air felt thick and oppressive. It was very warm in this room.

At one end I saw a great steel door with several locks on it. Huge rivets dotted its surface and it gleamed as if highly polished ... or new.

An army sergeant with cropped salt and pepper hair and a neatly trimmed moustache, stood up quickly from behind his desk near the door, his chair squealing on the floor, and hurriedly dropped a copy of Pearson's Magazine to the, otherwise empty, wooden surface.

'Stand easy, Sergeant,' Cavendish said, amiably. 'How is our guest?' Who was he talking about? I was puzzled.

'Restless, Suh!' barked the soldier, evidently, from the drawl, a Scotsman. 'Made a helluva din earlier. I don't think he likes the food, Suh!' He winked, almost imperceptibly, at Cavendish and neither seemed aware that I had seen it.

'Well, he'll have to make do won't he?' Cavendish said. 'Come, Smith, meet our friend.'

I walked forward, uncertain. The Sergeant, with great care I noted, unlocked a slot in the door and Cavendish waved me forward, a slight smile on his ruddy face. I glanced at Horton. He nodded almost imperceptibly but, for a second, I thought I caught a look of concern cross his face. A slight hissing and the sound of something heavy shifting suddenly emanated, it seemed, from whatever lay in the room beyond.

Taking a deep breath and steeling myself, although I knew not why, I put my eyes to the slot.

Hooting softly, the Martian stared steadily and menacingly back at me.

CHAPTER 7
Exorcising Demons

Physiologically speaking, the Martians are far more complex and hard to fathom than my friend Wells ever imagined. This fact was proved by the presence of that thing before my disbelieving eyes.

'Surprised?' Cavendish smiled. This smile had none of the usual warmth and I suddenly felt that cruelty, not unlike the cruelty of the schoolboy who delights in pulling the legs asunder from a helpless daddy-long-legs, lurked within this man.

'I ... how?' I could say no more.

'You're quite safe. It cannot escape.' Cavendish's small eyes gleamed with barely concealed excitement.

I turned to face the man and felt the Martian's eyes bore into my back. I fancied I was bathed in the stare of that loathsome creature, as if bombarded by the rays of some malignant sun. I felt very uncomfortable but endeavoured to ignore the feeling and satiate my curiosity.

I gathered myself together a little. 'How is it alive? Did they not all die?'

'We found it within the pit in Horsell Common. The first landing site, as you will no doubt know. I believe you were there upon the opening of the cylinder, were you not? Terrible business, I am told. Anyway, our friend here was in the cylinder surrounded by its dead comrades. Barely alive then, but it appears to be doing well at the moment. '

'Yes, but why is it alive at all?' I felt the question was being avoided.

Cavendish was not smiling now and he sighed. 'We think that some, certainly this specimen you have just seen at any rate, were immune. Not many are thought to have survived but that is not the last of it. We think they were working to combat their demise.'

My God. This latest news caused a flutter of panic. I flopped into a chair next to the guard's desk.

The guard appeared by my side with a glass of water so quickly that I had the idea that he had seen the reactions to the imprisoned monstrosity before, but I ignored the glass he offered me and simply stared at Cavendish. The guard placed the water carefully on the desk next to me and melted back into the shadows.

'How?' I continued. 'An antidote? But that means—'

'Yes. Which is why our work here is so important. It is almost certain that they will return.'

'The people must be warned!' I demanded. 'Not only could they return, but there could be more survivors out there.'

Cavendish shook his head slowly. 'This is not possible. No, no. Would you see another panic? Civilisation was taken to the brink of destruction, could our society survive if mankind took flight again? I think not. We must find out more before we act further. We have troops searching high and low for any other surviving Martians. They cannot stay hidden for long.'

'This really is too much, man!' I stood again, my cheeks burning with anger. 'We cannot keep this from the people! We must prepare them for the worst.'

'No, we must NOT!' The Knight of the Realm fought for control of his temper, his already red face a crimson storm. 'You must understand. We do not know if and when they will try again and news of this will certainly create a panic, perhaps needlessly. We are watching Mars using both our telescopes and the Egg device. We must prepare unimpeded and we WILL be ready!'

I sat slowly down into the chair again and thought for a moment. Horton leaning on the wall on the other side of the room, watched throughout this exchange, his brow furrowed.

'How much time do we have?' I asked quietly.

'Weeks, months – perhaps even years. We cannot say,' Cavendish had won his battle with his anger and he even tried to offer a comforting smile. 'We are working around the clock. We will find the answers.'

My mind went back to the monstrosity in the cell and a thought occurred to me.

'That thing,' I said quietly pointing toward the cell. 'What do you feed it?'

'Would you like to see?' Cavendish asked and glanced at his pocket watch. 'It's about that time'

I don't know why I nodded. I suppose now that my curiosity had to be satisfied. Perhaps I felt that observing the thing would help me face my fears. It seems strange now, this morbid curiosity, but I had seen so much and I just had to know everything.

We went through a small door and I found myself in a room next to the cell. In the wall a large window had been cut.

'The glass is very thick,' Cavendish explained. 'We use this room to observe it.'

'Does it not know?' I asked.

'Oh yes. But it seems not to care. It does little, except at meal times.'

As we watched a steel panel at the back of the cell moved aside by some unknown means. I could just see a soldier, bearing arms, standing beyond.

The Martian turned lazily and glared at the opening as a cow was pushed, none too gently, into the cell.

'Not their favourite food,' Cavendish muttered, his eyes fixed on what was unfolding.

The panel at the end of the cell slid closed and the Martian slithered, slowly like a beast of the Serengeti stalking its prey, up to the hapless animal. As if from nowhere, it quickly flourished a long tube with a spiked end, I had seen this before.

The Martian regarded the cow for a moment and then with a dextrous leap, thrust the pipette into the cow's neck, its other tentacles wrapping themselves tightly around the poor animals body. As the startled cow lowed pitifully and struggled to shake the creature off it's back, the Martian inserted the other end of the tube somewhere out of sight on it's own body and drank its fill.

As the bloody spectacle of the circus must have transfixed the Romans, the sight now before me held a horrid fascination. Horrified as I was, I could not look away. The Martian drank and the cows lowing became weaker.

I finally managed to tear my eyes away, glancing first at Cavendish and then Horton. Cavendish was staring thoughtfully at the scene, a strange smile twisting his features. Horton, to my surprise, looked as shocked as I. Evidently this was his first view of the prisoner's eating habits, as well.

The Martian had finished. It withdrew the pipette and turned slowly toward the window in the wall, its eyes burned like coals. As quick as a flash, it grasped the head of the now prone cow and, with a quick flick of a tentacle, tore it clean off. Hooting happily, it flourished its prize then, flicking the tentacle again, threw the head at the window.

We jumped back as one as a red stain covered the viewing window and the cow's head fell with a thump to the cell floor.

'Not their favourite food,' Cavendish repeated grimly.

CHAPTER 8
Alone

When the orderly called me at nine the next morning, I had, much to my surprise, enjoyed another night of deep, dreamless sleep. I felt sure, as I had laid my head on the pillow the night before, that my dreams would be haunted by Martian terrors once more after the terrible things I had witnessed.

After the incident at the Martian holding area, Cavendish and Horton had been called away on some unknown business and had not returned. As I was still unsure of the way around the facility, I was escorted to my room and deposited there unceremoniously, but ever so politely, like so much left luggage. Meals were brought to me in my room by the orderly, whom I discovered went by the name of Johnson, but he was my sole human contact for the next few days. I tried to strike up conversation with him on a number of occasions but, though he was always polite, he pointedly avoided all but the most necessary of intercourse. Whether this was down to orders or a lack of social skills I could not say.

On the third day, the Johnson appeared again at nine thirty with a laden breakfast tray. The man informed me that my hosts were away still and asked if I would like to see the library. Needing to occupy my mind, I agreed.

The library was not too far from my room. Like much of the living area of the facility, it was as if it had been lifted from some country pile, all panelled wood and elaborately woven Persian rugs.

I spent some hours perusing the books on offer: rare works by the great philosophers, scientific texts and contemporary fiction all rubbed shoulders on the many shelves. I was astonished to see works by Dee, 'The Discoverie of Witches', the 'Malleus Malificarum' and other obscure and rare books there. The library even boasted a copy of the mad Arab Al Hazred's 'Necronomicon' in a glass case, a rare tome indeed. Many of the books were priceless and my mind boggled at the sheer weight of knowledge in this room and I marvelled at how Cavendish had managed to pull all of these rare works together into one place.

I chose a work by Verne, the Frenchman whom possessed an imagination I much admired, and sat in a wing chair beside the fire that roared in the grate at one wall.

The book did not hold my attention, though, and my mind drifted back to the Martian that would, at that moment, be sitting seething, and perhaps plotting, in its cell.

Intellectually speaking, it is obvious that these creatures are as far apart at least from us as we are from the apes. Yet, I had seen this creature, consisting mainly of brain and, seemingly, part of a remarkably ordered and sophisticated society, petulantly play with its food and throw a tantrum not unlike a human child in the nursery.

They seem to us a war-like race, bent only on destruction and conquest, but I wondered then if perhaps we are too ready to impose human qualities onto them and this is why we find their behaviour difficult to fathom.

It seemed to me, I concluded, that the Martian psyche was as complex as their machinery and I found myself eager to know more about them.

I was given dinner, slices of beef that melted in my mouth and fresh vegetables, after being led to the dining room this time, and Cavendish and Horton joined me as I began to tuck into my meal.

'Sorry we left you alone, old chap,' Cavendish said sitting down and eyeing his food greedily. 'We had pressing business with the PM,'

'Quite alright,' I replied, around a mouthful of delicious beef. 'I made use of your excellent library.'

'Ah yes. I chose all the works there myself. Had the devil of a job finding some of them. It's a bit of a hobby of mine, not that I really have time for such things now.'

Horton spoke, then. 'We would appreciate it if you don't wander alone too far in the complex, Smith. As you can imagine there are some areas that could be highly dangerous if you don't know where you are going.'

'Of course, I fully understand.'

Horton simply nodded.

'Anyway, tomorrow we have to go on a recovery party,' Cavendish said. 'We would be pleased if you would come with us. It should be an interesting trip.'

'Recovery?' I asked, curious. 'Recovering what?'

'Martian artefacts, machinery, anything we can find. Our friends can still teach us much.'

'Why yes, I should be glad to come along.' A chance to get out of this sumptuous, yet stuffy, place and into the fresh air appealed to me very much.

'Good man. Warm clothes will be the order of the day, we will provide you with rain gear. The weather is atrocious today and will apparently be no better tomorrow.'

'May I ask where we are going?'

'Tomorrow,' Cavendish paused dramatically for a moment and then continued, 'we shall be investigating a Martian cylinder.'

I was just about to drift into slumber when there was a soft knock at the door.

Momentarily disorientated, I assumed it would be the orderly calling me to breakfast.

'Come,' I mumbled and sat up in bed rubbing my eyes.

The door opened and a dark figure slipped into the room.

'I cannot stay long here,' Horton said, his voice almost a whisper.

'What? What is it?' I fumbled for my spectacles on the dresser, but putting them on allowed me no better sight of the room.

'Smith, I have to warn you. You are in grave danger, we all are. There is more going on here than you know. I hope you never find out.' I peered at him, to try to catch his expression, but the gloom in my windowless quarters was too impenetrable and I could only vaguely make out his dark outline facing me.

'What do you mean?' I demanded.

'You must leave. You are free to go, if you wish, whilst you know so little. Use that freedom. Leave.' Unease gripped me now. Why was this man who had barely spoken to me before, but was part of my recruitment in this endeavour, suddenly trying to warn me off?

'Horton, what are you babbling on about? There is so much—'

'If you value your life, just go!' Horton hissed.

I went to speak again but the door closed quietly and Horton was gone, leaving me alone in the dark to puzzle over this strange and unexpected behaviour.

CHAPTER 9
An Explanation

The next day, my curiosity of the Martians and all their works was still in me, but I also had a strange heavy feeling in my stomach. Horton's words of the previous night echoed around my head and, at breakfast, I caught him looking at me surreptitiously from time to time.

As I sat, deep in thought and chewing toast in the dining room, Cavendish exhibited his usual schoolboy enthusiasm for all that he expected of the day.

'It's going to be an exciting day, what?' he said through a mouthful of scrambled egg. 'We have done some preliminary investigations on the cylinders but we hope to have some more wonders to bring back with us before the day is out.'

"Wonders", I had learned, was how Cavendish referred, in a rather childish way, I thought, to the Martian technology he had ordered, salvaged and utilised.

'I am surprised that the people have not taken souvenirs,' I said, feigning a little more enthusiasm than I now felt, due to the strange warning the night before. Still, I had decided that it would not do to arouse Cavendish's suspicion and I would sit tight, for now, and see what emerged. I was now on my guard and I hoped that that would be enough to alert me to any trouble, should it arise.

'Ah,' Cavendish continued. 'Well, we have guards posted at most of the major landing sites against just that eventuality. We did not waste any time on that front. The wonders therein are too precious and we are sure that not just the ordinary man on the street would like to get their hands on such treasures.'

'What do you mean?'

'Spies, man!' Cavendish exclaimed. 'We have word that at least one foreign government have people on our soil sniffing around. They have asked for information through diplomatic channels, of course, but we are reluctant to share whilst we know so little.'

'Would we share at all?' I asked. I was beginning to see how having such advances in our possession would mean a great advantage in many ways.

'Of course,' said Cavendish. 'When the time is right.' But I felt that he was not telling the whole truth and he would say no more on the subject.

Later, wrapped up in warm, waterproof clothing and boasting stout walking boots on our feet, we were ushered into the lift back to the surface. A short trip on the private underground train took us to an overland train waiting at Kings Cross.

It seemed that the problems with the rail services had been overcome, enough, at least, for us to be able to travel to Woking in the comfort of a plush carriage: myself, Cavendish, the ever-present Horton, who pointedly avoided my attempts to catch his eye and three other men whom I had not met before.

So, we were headed for Horsell Common! A slight feeling of dread lurked in the pit of my stomach, not just because of Horton's words, but also because I was to revisit the place where I had stood with my late friend Ogilvy and observed at the cylinder that was to cause so much strife to humanity, in a time that seemed so long ago.

Shortly into the trip, Cavendish fell asleep, snoring loudly and with his chubby hands crossed over his considerable girth. Horton engrossed himself in some papers he had taken out from a valise and periodically scribbled notes on them with a pencil.

The weather that day was indeed as miserable as Cavendish had predicted. The rain poured from leaden skies and clattered noisily against the roof and windows of the carriage as I regarded the newcomers to our excursion.

As I have intimated, as well as Cavendish, Horton and myself, our party consisted of three others. The men who shared our carriage, I learned after one, Peters, struck up a conversation with me, were scientists at the apex of their fields. Baxter, a small, grey, bearded man, was involved in Biology. He sat nervously twitching his fingers and muttering under his breath. Peters favoured physics and was a tall black haired man. He chatted amiably to all and spoke a little of some of his work so far. His talk was, of course, mostly beyond my understanding. Carter, a young Engineer with a swept-back mop of blonde hair and long, bushy sideburns, stared quietly, through the rain dashed window, at the countryside as it passed.

We were not travelling unguarded. In the next carriage travelled ten troops, armed to the teeth and led by a grizzled Welsh Sergeant by the name of Jones. Even from the next carriage, the Sergeant's barked orders reached my ears from time to time. Quite what trouble was expected on this trip was unclear, but I felt better for the presence of these men.

At Woking, a town like many others, still showing scars from the war but with re-building well underway, carriages and a few motor vehicles waited. Some were full of bulky looking equipment under tarpaulins, some obviously meant for our transportation. We climbed aboard one of the latter and travelled on still pitted and rutted roads to Horsell Common.

The inclement weather reminded me of the first night I saw a Martian machine, as I stood terrified next to my overturned dogcart. In my mind, the machine's ghostly howl reverberated once again.

As our vehicles rattled up to the Common, my feelings of unease evidently became more apparent. Horton looked concerned at me.

'Don't worry,' he said quietly, 'you're safe for now.' This man was quite an enigma to me.

The bushes and trees around the common still stood blackened and charred, pointing at the dark sky like the accusing fingers of the dead. Great swathes of the area showed the scars of what had occurred when the cylinder had opened. Mounds of churned up earth lay here and there along with the wreckage of guns and other equipment. The horrible memories of those early battles were again fresh in my mind.

Here now was the cylinder, glistening in the wet and like some great misshapen metal cathedral. An edifice dedicated entirely to the engineering of our destruction, once ringing with the howling prayers of our persecutors, now silent and deserted. A Fighting Machine loomed, like some giant unholy priest, on guard close by.

As we approached, I noticed that there was a small encampment near to the entrance of the cylinder. Soldiers milled around, smoking and talking in low voices. I saw none of the usual soldierly bravado and humour here. The gaping maw of the Cylinder entrance exuded some sobering influence. I felt it only too strongly as I stood nearby.

We were shown to a large marquee, which was crowded with wet soldiers and smelled accordingly. As the wagons containing the equipment were unloaded we were given battered mugs containing hot, sweet tea. Cavendish wrinkled his nose a little at the lowly appearance of the drinking vessel he was handed, but the rest of us gratefully supped the warming drink as if we drank from the best bone china.

Cavendish called for quiet and the chatter in the tent lessened.

'Today gentlemen,' he boomed, 'we will be looking for more equipment to take back with us. I know our scientists are anxious to learn more about the workings of the cylinder and we have only scratched the surface here. Please be careful. There is still much we do not know and we can't afford to lose any more of you because of some silly mishap. After all, there are none of our Martian friends here to cause the trouble, are there?'

This off-colour comment was met with a little nervous laughter from some. I thought the joke, if it were one, in very poor taste indeed. One or two evidently agreed as one or two men near the back scowled and muttered to one another.

'Anyway,' Cavendish continued, 'please ask if you have any concerns or questions. Are we ready, gentlemen?' He led the way out of the tent as the chatter from the people inside began again, Horton, as always, shadowing him.

I set down my, now empty, mug, fastened my coat close about my neck and followed.

Once outside, we scrambled down the walls of the pit and approached the cylinder opening. At the entrance, planking had been laid in an effort to cut down on the amount of mud created by the comings and goings of the soldiers and scientists. The group assembled for exploration of the Cylinder consisted Cavendish, Horton, the three scientists from the train carriage and myself. For a moment, we glanced nervously at one another; the cylinder aperture was exuding that malign influence once more. A group of four soldiers, including the Sergeant, Jones, joined us and we entered.

CHAPTER 10
In the Belly of the Beast

It was warm inside the cylinder. Much to my surprise, it was also not as dark as I expected. No earthly light source illuminated our progress, but the metal walls themselves glowed with an eerie, blue-green luminescence. Once my eyes had accustomed themselves, I could see quite clearly.

Nothing could prepare me for the smell, though.

'My God, what is that smell?' Carter asked covering his nose, evidently noticing it as I did.

'Putrescence,' answered Baxter grimly. 'Death, call it what you will. Sir George, have the bodies been cleared from here?'

'We have penetrated little into the cylinder's mysteries,' Cavendish said. 'We have, until now, not ventured much farther than the openings. Some soldiers have been further looking for survivors but that is about all. I am as new to much of this as you.'

'You don't know what is in here?' I asked, incredulous. Some of the others looked vaguely queasy and not a little concerned.

'We have the stories of the soldiers, of course. Many other things have occupied our time. Guards were posted at the opening until we could spare the time to investigate properly.'

'What did the soldiers find?' asked Baxter, twitching nervously, his hands fluttering with his obvious agitation.

67

'Well, we shall soon find out if the gossip is correct, eh?' Cavendish said and strode off.

The space inside the cylinder was cavernous, but oddly without echoes. It was if this vast space greedily swallowed our quietly spoken words and our soft footsteps almost as soon as they sounded. Walking through, it seemed impossible that such a huge thing could fly through space at many thousands of miles an hour, as this must have done. It seemed to me like finding that an Ironclad could soar up into the sky as lightly as a bird. But here it was, as if to prove just how little our civilisation knew about the mysterious laws of the Universe.

The floor of the cylinder was a sort of metallic mesh that our feet sank into slightly. As our feet rose again, the surface reshaped itself and was as flat as before. Carter, the Engineer, found this especially interesting and jumped up and down experimentally.

'This is astounding,' he enthused. 'I must test some of this substance. Fascinating!'

The walls of the cylinder had been bare near the entrance, but as we walked, on either side, dim shapes became gradually apparent. We moved in our group towards one of the shapes.

A partially built Fighting Machine squatted there, or at least the hood. Leg sections, which must have constituted parts of the same Machine, were stacked neatly and securely against the gently curving wall, along with what looked like some kind of engines and other parts, the use of which I could not fathom.

Further we went, past more of these partly built machines. The smell of death grew stronger as another shadowy shape loomed.

As we drew closer we saw that it was an enormous basket. A surge of horror from deep within me reminded me that I had seen such things before. The Handling Machines had carried such baskets on their backs and had stored human beings in there for their diabolical needs.

Inside this cage were bodies. Twisted human bodies. Men, women and children, in death, acting out grotesque tableaux of terror and fear.

Perhaps these poor souls had seen their captors start to die and thought that they were saved. But fate, or more properly the Martians, had dealt them a cruel hand.

'Poor devils!' breathed Jones.

'How did they die?' I asked.

'See the black powder scattered around?' asked Baxter pointing. Small drifts of the dreaded substance were indeed all over the floor.

'Bastards!' breathed a young soldier, horrified. 'They gassed 'em! They were helpless and they killed 'em like insecks!'

'Steady, lad,' said Jones resting a calming hand on the boy's shoulder.

It appeared that the Martians in the cylinder had, in a last act of defiance, unleashed their most horrific weapon, the Black Smoke, on their defenceless captives when they had started to die themselves. Was this an act of sheer spite? It appeared we would never know.

Cavendish led us away from the carnage and further into the depths of the cylinder. Along the way, we saw the putrefying bodies of Martians here and there. Even in the cold depths of this unearthly machine, a place where no earthly laws seemed to hold sway, nature was taking her course and flies buzzed around the stinking remains. The young soldier kicked at one of the prone creatures as we passed.

'Please, don't do that!' Cavendish said, eyes wide. 'We may need the bodies for testing later and we cannot have them damaged any more than they already are.'

'That's enough, lad,' Jones said quietly to the boy, but his face spoke of the possession of as much anger boiling inside him as the boy was venting.

The boy glared at Cavendish as he continued on.

Soon, we came upon a large area of wall with a sliding door, which was open. This led into another smaller space.

'The control cabin?' asked Peters glancing around.

'So it would appear,' said Carter. 'Those look like controls to me.'

The engineer was referring to a panel on which were many levers and switches. A set of three portholes sat in the centre of the panel, each with a switch next to it. The portholes were blank and they appeared to be closed.

Carter reached towards one of the switches.

'No don't!' Cavendish said. It was too late though, and the switch had been pushed.

To our surprise, the porthole next to the switch lit up and we could see a rainy landscape.

'Look! That's outside!' exclaimed Peters.

It was indeed outside. The scene was of the encampment at the cylinder opening.

We could see soldiers standing around shivering, capes slick with the driving rain.

Carter pushed the other two switches, this time Cavendish did not try to stop him.

The other portholes lit up and more scenes appeared. On one was what I took to be the other side of the cylinder and I could see a wooded area and the wreckage of a fallen Martian Digging Mechanism. The other showed stars. Only stars. Was this outer space? The open mouthed expressions of the others told me that they had similar ideas.

'Incredible!' breathed Peters, rather unnecessarily.

We turned our attention to the rest of the cabin. On the other wall we saw a row of large tanks, not unlike large upended metal horse troughs fronted with glass. A complicated array of tubes and wires left each tank and entered into a large console.

'What are these?' I asked.

Baxter answered. 'I have an idea about these. They may actually go someway to explain how the Martians managed to survive the journey here at such terrific speed.'

'Go on,' I said, intrigued.

'Well,' Baxter continued. 'In the terms of the Layman, I think perhaps the Martians were suspended in some kind of liquid in these tanks. Somehow it kept them being crushed by the forces that the speed of this conveyance must have put them under.'

It was a mystery to me as to how he reached such conclusions, but it seemed feasible to at least some of the party, so I asked no further questions. I had a feeling that more answers might muddy the water for me somewhat, anyway.

There were more panels around the walls with dials and switches on them. The scientist agreed that it must have needed a crew of three or four to pilot this vehicle. Would this vessel have had a Captain directing operations, like our own, seagoing, ships?

It has been supposed by some that this first cylinder was the 'flagship' of the fleet, as it were. Perhaps this is just because it landed first. It certainly appeared to have given directions to the cylinders that landed elsewhere, but was this just a case of imposing human qualities on an unknown race once more?

There were no indications, to me, that this was a special vessel. No insignia, no writing of any kind, just those glowing metal walls.

We left the cabin for now and went deeper into the cylinder. Another room opened up before us and we, to a man, almost gagged at the smell. Handkerchiefs were quickly raised to mouths and noses at this latest violation on our senses.

Inside the room were more bodies scattered carelessly around. I thought at first that these were more of our unfortunate fellow humans, but further investigation proved otherwise. My eyes watering from the rancid, cloying air in the room, I saw that these were biped figures, but they were very pale, almost white. The creatures had protruding foreheads and prominent jaws and they looked, even to my untrained eye, like some strange hybrid of human and ape. Their arms were long and their naked bodies were almost completely hairless.

I realised that these were the food that the Martians had brought with them, possibly denizens of the Martian's home world, bred, like we breed livestock, for our own needs. Or perhaps, it suddenly occurred to me, they were harvested from some other world that we knew nothing about: a world that had also felt the fiery touch of the Martian Heat-ray. I had, along with many of my fellow man I assumed, never before considered that the Martians might have visited other worlds apart from ours, before finally setting their sights on Earth. It was a thought that I pondered on, but kept to myself. After all, as I have stated before, I am no scientist.

A glance around this foul-smelling room told me that this was some kind of feeding area. Complicated looking machines sprouted from the walls and from these came spiked tubes, ending in instruments that looked like the pipettes the Martians used to drink the blood of other creatures. Everywhere, the smell of corruption mixed with the coppery reek of putrefying blood pounded at our senses and I felt oppressed and claustrophobic. Several of the party were looking increasingly shaken and unwell and it was decided that we should not stay in that room for long.

CHAPTER 11
Deeper

On we went into the depths of the cylinder, the eerie light within the walls showing us the way.

We passed more compartments, all containing more machinery and unfathomable instruments. Cavendish was like a child in a toyshop and did not try to hide his glee at each new discovery.

'Such wonders!' he would exclaim periodically. He and the scientists would coo over each new thing like a flock of pigeons over crumbs.

Horton stayed silent as usual but still cast glances at me now and then, the look in his eyes spoke volumes. What danger did he foresee for me? Was I not safe with our armed guards? Once I went to question him, but I saw that Cavendish was looking over curiously and Horton waved me away with a small flick of his hand.

Finally, we appeared to come to the end. A great wall faced us with another of the sliding doors set into it. This too was half open.

We entered into a final cavernous space. A dull thrumming sound came from the black machinery that took up a great part of the room. The vibrations and enormous power evident in this strange machinery literally shook my body. I felt strangely weightless, as if I would float away, should I push myself up from the floor. Some of the others looked around themselves curiously, almost as if they felt the same thing. Small green puffs of smoke hissed from joints in the black metal, as the machine worked at some unknown purpose.

'The engine room!' Carter said reverently, casting quick, excited glances around him.

'Magnificent!' exclaimed Cavendish. 'Can you imagine the power? I'll warrant one of these could produce enough energy to power all of London!'

'At least,' said Carter.

We stared at the engine for a short while; the dull thrumming had an almost hypnotic quality.

'We must discover how this works,' Cavendish said finally. 'Can you do it, Carter?'

'I couldn't say,' the engineer answered. 'To even try, I will need a team of men under my direction and access to funding.'

'You shall have it,' Cavendish said. 'As we discussed before, anything you need, you shall have. We must discover the secrets!'

'Very well,' Carter nodded his agreement.

Cavendish turned to address the whole group.

'Gentlemen, we have many discoveries here to be made. I would suggest we move back outside and plan the extraction of these items. Obviously, the engine will have to stay in situ for the present; it is obviously far too unwieldy to move. Carter, you and your team will set up a workshop here at the back of the cylinder.'

Carter looked decidedly nervous by this prospect, but nodded once more.

This decided, our group shuffled out of the engine room and began the arduous trek back to the outside. I, for one, was not looking forward to passing some of the horrors we had seen on the inward trip again.

The journey back was without incident. The soldiers seemed nervous, but I could not blame them for that. I wondered how many of them had seen friends in the service scattered to the four winds by the Martian Heat-ray, or choked by the black smoke. I actually felt better that they were wary; as it seemed to me that they would be on guard and ready to face any eventuality.

One of the soldiers, Perkins, began to chat cheerily with his comrades as we walked. Perhaps he was attempting to raise their spirits in this sinister place but eventually Jones, the sergeant, hissed at him to be quiet.

I turned my eyes away as we passed the charnel houses of the feeding room and the baskets. I had no wish to see those poor wretches within again.

From time to time as we travelled through this strange monument to destruction, the soldiers muttered, but Jones silenced them with harshly whispered words. The scientists, for the most part, whispered excitedly amongst themselves, while Cavendish strode ahead like the proud, strutting Drum Major of a military band.

At length we saw the fading light of the sky in the opening. Had we been inside that long? It didn't seem possible. I realised that we hadn't even stopped to eat all day. It was probably just as well.

As we left the cylinder, I felt like a great weight had been lifted from me. I took a great lungful of chill evening air and let the slight breeze gently blow the foul odours that had clouded my senses away.

The rain had stopped and clouds scudded like ships across a rising moon. As darkness fell, we retired to the mess tent for refreshment. Despite my lack of food for the day, I did not feel like eating.

That night, I lay in a folding bunk within a tent that had been provided for me. It appeared we would be staying on the Common for at least another day whilst Cavendish directed operations.

I could not sleep, at first, so I lay and tried not to think of the horrors I had seen. I thought of my wife and better times. Times before the Martians came.

Occasionally, the low murmurs of our guards and the pop and crackle of their campfire drifted to me.

Finally, sleep began to take me and my eyelids grew heavy. I drifted away.

A scream woke me almost, it seemed, as soon as I had fallen asleep. I jumped like lightning from my bunk and fumbled for my clothes. What was happening?

Angry shouts now, then a clanging of an alarm bell.

I left my tent to be confronted with a scene of utter confusion.

CHAPTER 12
Sabotage

Soldiers rushed here and there whilst Jones stood, dressed only in his under garments and uniform trousers, in the middle of it all barking short, sharp orders and pointing quickly in all directions. The pungent smell of smoke assailed my nostrils and, looking around, I saw that a couple of the tents were aflame. A man throwing water at the tent got too close and his coat caught fire. A soldier wrestled him to the ground and rolled him before the flames could take proper hold.

The action stopped at the sound of a single gunshot. Buckets full of water were held in still hands as all eyes turned to the far edge of the camp, where a soldier, Perkins I saw, was standing looking down the sights of his rifle. Another shot pierced the, suddenly deathly quiet, night.

The ruckus resumed as the other soldiers dropped buckets and other fire-fighting materials and ran to grab their weapons. Weapons raised, these men made their way cautiously to where Perkins stood.

'What are you shooting at lad?' the Sergeant bellowed at the top of his lungs as he ran to join his men.

Perkins did not look round, nor lower his weapon. He merely carried on firing at something we could not see.

The other soldiers got to within a few yards of Perkins, when they fell back suddenly. It was as if something invisible had swept past and knocked them over like skittles.

With horror, I realised what it was. A Heat-ray!

Perkins stood stock still for a moment then, silhouetted against the flames that now surrounded him, arched his back and screamed. Although I could not see clearly, I knew that his skin would now be peeling, blackening and cracking. His eyeballs would be turned to liquid in their sockets and his hair would have been ablaze. A small pop sounded as, I assume, his ammunition ignited. Mercifully, the torment would not have lasted long for him.

In a moment, his still burning remains fell to the ground.

A shocked silence fell on the camp. Then, the chaos resumed as people ran towards the remaining soldiers.

A few, who had nearly reached the young warrior, were quite badly burned but would live. The others were winded but otherwise unharmed. Jones picked himself of the ground and looked around with a practised eye to see where the ray had come from. Bushes and patches of ground in the area that had been touched by the Heat-ray smouldered, just like poor Perkins. The trees where the ray seemed to have come from hissed accusations at one another in a rising breeze but no further attack came and there was no sign of any assailant.

Jones swore mightily and assembled a small group of unhurt soldiers to make a thorough search.

As the soldiers left to scout the surrounding area, the rest of us set to putting out the fires and bringing back some semblance of order to the camp.

We gathered in the mess tent an hour or so later.

Cavendish looked around the assemblage grimly but said nothing until the search party returned.

'Nothing, Sir! We could find no sign of anyone … or anything,' Jones said, breathlessly entering the tent.

Baxter spoke next. 'Sir George, who do you think attacked us? Martians?'

Cavendish thought for a moment. 'Perhaps. We cannot say for sure that there aren't roving bands of Martian survivors somewhere out there. Of course, this information is not to leave this camp.'

'Well who else could it have been?' I asked. 'They had a Heat-ray!'

'Anarchists, foreign governments – we cannot rule out anything. Many people want to get their hands on the machines we are discovering. This was some kind of sabotage, but who instigated it, I could not say.'

'The Martians will want their playthings back, too,' observed Peters stroking his chin thoughtfully. 'Their numbers may be severely depleted but they can still cause us a lot of bother, I am sure. Keep us busy until their comrades arrive, perhaps. If they arrive.'

'Is anything missing? Any of the captured weaponry?' Carter asked.

Cavendish shook his head. 'We don't think so. We have checked the lists and all appears in order.'

'So where did whoever it was get the Heat-ray from?'

'This was a Heat-ray, alright,' Cavendish answered, 'but a portable one. Did you notice that the effect was much more localised than usual and only claimed one victim.'

I saw Jones kick the ground and grit his teeth a little at the casual manner in which the death of one of his soldiers was described.

'Something new?' Carter wondered.

'No. We have found Heat-ray rifles before. We think they were putting the finishing touches to them when they met their demise. They were experimenting with many things.' This last reminded me of the Flying Machine my brother and his companions had seen. I made a mental note to ask Cavendish about that later.

'So I suppose they have raided some other cylinder or some such to get weaponry, whoever they may turn out to be,' Peters said.

'It's not impossible,' Cavendish conceded. 'But we have had no word from the other camps that this is the case.'

There was little else to be said for the moment and, with that, we retired to our tents to snatch what little sleep we could.

CHAPTER 13
A Warning

A few hours later, I was awoken, un-refreshed, from a restless slumber by the sound of activity in the camp. I made use of the washing facilities provided and then wandered over to the mess tent.

The weather had taken a decided turn for the better and the sky was a bright blue. Small, fluffy clouds meandered across this airy landscape like lazily grazing sheep. A bright sun gently warmed and dried the earth and was reflected dazzlingly off the cylinder and the sentinel tripod that stood nearby.

The three scientists were poring over some artefacts that had been placed on trestle tables near the mess tent. I heard disjointed snatches of conversation coming from their little huddle.

'... powered by some kind of atomic power ...'

'... possible applications in the Empire ...'

'... our own machines!'

I stood a little way off trying to catch more but Carter saw me and muttered something to the others. They took to talking more quietly after that. It appeared that I was not to be included in all that occurred in these investigations.

In the mess tent, some soldiers sat soberly sipping tea. One had a bandage on his hand and his hair was singed. I nodded to him. I understood his pain for the loss of his brave comrade Perkins. If it wasn't for that man's thoughtless actions, we could all have fallen prey to the same horrible burning death as befell him. We owed him an un-repayable debt of gratitude.

Cavendish was talking animatedly to Horton as I took a seat near them. He looked up.

'Smith, that was a terrible business last night. We must get the artefacts back to the laboratory. We have much more control over security there.'

I felt exposed here out on the Common, despite our guards, and could not disagree.

'We hope to leave by noon. Carter will, of course, be staying here to work on the engine of the cylinder and we have more soldiers on the way to subsidise the forces already here. I have business outside now; I will leave you in Horton's capable hands for the moment.' With that, he shuffled out of the tent.

Horton regarded me for a moment with his black eyes and then he stood.

'Shall we take a walk?'

We left the tent and walked silently for a while. I found myself superstitiously avoiding burnt patches of ground as if they were cursed. It occurred to me that perhaps, with the Martians still a possible threat, the whole of our Planet Earth was cursed.

When we were out of immediate earshot of the main camp Horton spoke. 'Smith, I know you are suspicious of my motives, but I assure you I mean you no harm. On the contrary, I wish only to save you any more trials. I ask you again to leave as soon as you can.'

'I have too many questions. I must know what is going on,' I replied.

'I can understand that.' Horton stopped and faced me. 'However, you have seen the danger that lies around our work. For Heaven's sake, man! We were all nearly killed in our beds last night. Whoever it was that attacked us meant to sabotage our operations. If it hadn't been for that soldier, we might not be speaking now.'

'What do you know of the sabotage attempt last night?' I asked, suddenly suspicious.

Something flashed behind Horton's eyes but was gone as quickly as I noticed it.

'Nothing I can divulge with any certainty,' he said. I could detect no untruth in his voice or manner, but something still felt wrong. Horton continued.

'All I can say is that I have information that this will not be an isolated case. Last week a strange turn of events began.' He paused for a moment, as if wondering how much to tell me. 'Scientists who have recently worked on various projects for the Government started to disappear. A few days ago one reappeared but he had been killed. In fact, he was horribly burned and mutilated. We were only able to identify the man through personal effects that were with the body.'

'Why?' I asked. 'Is there some conspiracy afoot?'

'Yes, I believe so. I am working hard to find out what this is about and who is responsible but I fear that the danger will deepen. That is why I wish you to leave.'

I regarded the man for a moment. I could see no reason why he would wish me ill. I was not even a pawn in this game. I was here only to report on the investigation and offer explanations to the public, was I not?

My mind was now made up.

'Horton, I thank you for your concern but I cannot leave now. I have seen too much and I was asked to do a job. I will follow it through.'

'I think you are a fool,' Horton sighed. 'I cannot guarantee your safety and you stay with this project at your own risk.'

I nodded. 'Understood.'

'Your misplaced sense of duty and adventure could well get you killed, Smith. I hope you don't have cause to remember my words.' Shaking his head, he led us back to camp.

Work continued apace and wagons were being loaded with Martian weaponry and machinery whilst some soldiers watched curiously. Other military men stood on guard at the edges of the camp, much more wary than before.

Cavendish directed all this activity like a true maestro conducting an orchestra.

The man looked up as Horton and I approached.

'Ah. We are nearly ready for the off. Gather your things.'

We finally left the camp in our convoy of wagons and carriages at one p.m. Soldiers and orderlies ushered us on our way us like fussy nannies and the journey back to the laboratory went by uneventfully.

CHAPTER 14
I, Spy

Cavendish, my steward informed me the next morning, had to leave again on urgent business. I assumed Horton would have gone with him and was resigned to another day of boredom, so I was surprised when there was a sharp knock at the door, a little after ten, and Horton entered.

'Good morning,' he said and strode over to where I sat at my desk writing notes in my journal.

'And to you,' I replied. I still had in mind the Government man's previous visit a few nights before and I readied myself for more warnings.

'May I?' he asked, indicating my notes with a raised eyebrow.

'Of course.' I settle back in my chair and watched.

He picked up my sheaf of papers with a well-manicured hand and sat lightly on the arm of an easy chair. There was silence for some minutes as he thumbed his way through my notes. He gave little sign of what he thought of my work, barring a frown or a slight nod from time to time, until he had finished.

'Does my work meet your satisfaction?' I asked finally.

'Splendid!' he said and placed the sheaf of papers carefully back on the desk.

He regarded me for a moment from his perch on the chair like some great black bird and I fancied I could see that he was thinking hard about something. His hooded eyes gave away nothing but I felt a question coming.

He slapped his knee after a moment as he obviously came to a decision.

'Have you anything planned today?' he asked.

I fought back ironic laughter at this. Without my hosts around I was shepherded around like a spring lamb and, I sometimes felt, penned up like one.

'Well no,' I said, a little too straight faced.

'The missing scientists trail seems to be paying off. I have to go topside to do some sniffing around.'

'Really?' I asked, but said no more.

'Indeed,' Horton took on that look of intense thought yet again for a few moments, then spoke again. 'How would you like to accompany me?'

Now that was more like it! A trip outside into the real world, away from strange machinery and stranger people.

'Of course I would!' I exclaimed.

'Make no mistake, Smith, this could be dangerous. I have no idea what we shall find.'

'I think I have seen enough danger in my life to be able to take care of myself,' I answered.

'Very well, we leave at five,' Horton said, getting up and smoothing down his trouser creases. 'Warm clothing, Smith.' The Government man left the room.

As we left the facility, at five sharp, Horton dug into the pocket of his coat.

'Here,' he said handing me a metal object. A revolver. 'Do you know how to use one of these?'

'Point and shoot?' I said with a grin.

Horton glared at me for a moment as if disapproving then a small smile turned up the corners of his mouth.

'Yes,' he said. 'Something like that.'

I stashed the weapon away in the deep pocket of my overcoat.

'Come along, the train leaves in two minutes,' Horton said, his smile fading as quickly as it had come, and stalked away. I followed quickly.

The journey was monotonous, once over-ground, a cab was waiting for us. I saw the driver was the same man who had brought me to London. He cast a surly nod at me and gee'd his long-suffering horse along.

The weather was cold and foggy. Great dark clouds loomed over the city like a damp blanket and the streetlamps were burning brightly.

The hooves of our horse and the wheels of the cab disturbed patches of mist that lay here and there on the road as we rushed through the busy city streets.

I sank a little further into my coat trying to gain what warmth I could.

'Where are we going?' I asked Horton.

'Whitechapel,' Horton replied. 'I had a tip that someone may be being held in a house there.'

'A scientist?' I breathed.

'A local saw the man being bundled roughly into an abandoned property and he seems to have fitted our man's description.'

'I see. Do you mean to try to free him? If it is your man, that is?'

Horton eyes peered at me from the dark shadows beneath his hat brim. 'If the opportunity arises. You, my friend, will likely not be part of any such action, though. We will see how the land lies, in any case.'

As we made our way, now silent, I pictured all kinds of secret agent derring-do taking place before my eyes. This appealed greatly to the schoolboy within me. But, as a man, I was less full of bravado.

Presently, the cab stopped.

'Thank you, Nichols,' Horton said to the cabman as we left the comparatively warm interior of the cab to feel the force of a cold breeze. 'We shall be walking from here.'

Whitechapel was a ruin, although not due to Martian intervention. In fact, the invading forces had hardly touched this area. No, this place was purely the victim of the East End nemesis – neglect.

The Commercial Road was bustling, but the lost souls scurrying here and there had a look of desperation that was not brought on by the hardships of war. Their plight was poverty.

Surly looking men in threadbare clothes eyed us as we walked the murky streets avoiding piles of refuse heaped and rotting here and there. Hard-faced, drunken women lurked here and there on corners and in doorways and shouted out lewd comments and offered promises as we passed.

Horton and I waded through this tide of sad humanity like dogged rats swimming through a sewer.

The street lamps grew less and less frequent as we progressed and the streets quieter and darker. Nerves set in as the fog grew thicker and looming shapes of passers-by came and went.

'Keep your wits about you,' Horton muttered. 'At the first sign of trouble run back the way we came.'

At Dorset Street we passed the bright windows of a public house. Loud singing and raucous laughter floated in the damp air from the run down building. A man careered out of the door as if thrown, narrowly missing me as I passed, and fell with a thump to the floor. A loud cheer came from the pub as if this man being thrown out was universally approved of and the door slammed shut again. I went to the man but he lay still muttering and dead drunk.

A little blood oozed from his mouth where teeth had broken on the hard stone of the pavement.

'Leave him,' Horton said sharply and marched off again.

A little further up the street, I saw a youth leaning against a lamppost whistling. As we made to pass, he spoke.

'Pardon me, gents, but where do you fink you is goin'?'

The youth must still be in his teens but he was, I now saw, holding a nasty looking club. He tossed it up and down meaningfully.

'Get out of our way, or you shall regret it' Horton hissed, his hand in his pocket.

'Shall I now, your 'ighness?' the lad said. 'Boys!'

Suddenly, we were surrounded.

At least eight more youths appeared, all dressed in the same scruffy way as their leader and armed with blunt weapons, standing around us.

'Y'know,' the leader said. 'We don't see many of your sort round here, these days. Not so long back, there was thrill seekers as would come dahn from the West End and look round where old Saucy Jack did the Devil's work. Used to make a pretty penny, showing 'em around, I did. Very good business!'

'F'rinstance,' he continued, gesturing grandly further up the road, 'over yonder a little ways is Millers Court where pretty Mary Kelly got a necklace and some rouge wot finished her. She wasn't so pretty then, I can tell yer. Saw it meself. 'Orrible! Then the Marshuns came along and put a stop to my 'onest little trade.' The lad stared at his club for a moment.

'So,' he continued, doffing his dirty cap mockingly. 'If you fine gents would be so kind as to part with your valuables, we can all be on our way.'

CHAPTER 15
The Irregulars

Horton glared at the young faces before him.

'I say again,' he said quietly. 'You don't understand. It would be in your best interests to get out of our way this minute.'

'No,' the leader said, prodding Horton's chest with his club. 'You don't understand, M'lord! Hand over the loot and I'll let yer go. If not, you'll know how poor Mary felt as that Devil made his mark on her.'

The boy, despite his outward bravado, began to look a little nervous now. Perhaps he was used to being obeyed immediately in the face of such odds. This worried me more. A frightened criminal can be like a cornered tiger when provoked.

I saw Horton begin to draw his hand slowly out of his pocket. His eyes were like ice as he glared at the youth. I began to feel for my weapon. If it was all going to start, I had best be prepared.

Suddenly, there was the sound of someone clearing their throat.

The leader of the gang of ruffians looked around sharply, peering into the foggy air.

'Wiggins, has it really come to this?' a cultured voice said. 'I had such high hopes for you.' The voice had a note of genuine sadness in it.

The youth dropped his club immediately as if it wasn't his and motioned for the others to do the same.

'Sir?' he said incredulously to the shape approaching out of the murk. 'Is that you?'

'Indeed it is. I am very disappointed in you.' A match was struck and the flare lit aquiline, refined features. The face was somehow familiar. There was a moment's silence, barring a sucking noise, as the newcomer used the match to light a large pipe. Presently, smoke drifted away to join the fog in the air.

'Sir, I–' the lad began.

'Sir, nothing, Wiggins,' the man said. 'I should think the least you owe these gentlemen is an apology.' This man obviously held some kind of power over these young men.

Wiggins hung his head and muttered something unintelligible.

'Not a moment too soon,' Horton said marching up to the man. Then, I suddenly recognised him.

Not so long before the war, a consulting detective had been the toast of the world. Solving puzzling cases for Royalty and the masses alike, his fame always preceded him. News of his exploits sold papers by the ton, all written by his accomplice, a Doctor. I had read several of these exploits and thought them acceptable if taken as fiction, but a little too much to take as fact. I often told my wife that I thought his adventures were probably embellished beyond all recognition for the benefit of sensationalism. To the Detective's credit, I had heard that he was supposedly uncomfortable with the way that some of these stories were told, but indulged his old friend who had written them.

So, here he was. The slicked back hair had a touch of salt and pepper that had not been present in the likenesses I had seen of him and deep lines cut across his strong features, but the icy eyes were as sharp and piercing as those in the images.

'Smith, this is–' Horton began.

'Yes, I know,' I said stepping forward and taking the great man's cool hand in mine. 'It's a pleasure.'

'It's all mine, I assure you. I have heard much about you, Mr. Smith. How is Wells?' the Detective asked.

'He is well,' I answered. So this man knew Wells, too! Wells, whom I thought to be an intimate friend, was turning out to have hidden depths.

'Capital!' the Detective said around his pipe. 'Now, Horton, I think we should be off. The Inspector should be around here somewhere in this soup with a few of the Force's finest.'

'Was the tip correct?' asked Horton, all business now.

'Ah, that is what we are about to find out,' the Detective said. 'We have cabs on the way to take us on.'

'Will the Doctor not be joining us?' I asked.

A look of genuine sadness flickered across the Detectives face at this.

'I fear not. My friend was killed during the invasion.'

'I'm sorry, I didn't know.'

'Why should you?' the Detective asked with a small sad smile and said no more on the subject.

'Now, Wiggins,' the Detective said, turning to the young ruffian. 'I have a job for you and your scoundrels should you wish to begin to travel the right road once more.'

'Of course, Sir!' Wiggins said, his dirty face a picture of genuine gratitude and adoration.

The Detective nodded, placed an arm around the youth's shoulders and walked away a little with him, muttering instructions. A few moments later, the conference was over.

'Very good, Sir! Come on, lads!' Wiggins shouted excitedly. A cab, at that moment, clattered up. The boys clambered, like a small group of monkeys, onto and into it.

The overloaded cab careered crazily off again, the horse whinnying in protest.

The Detective watched them go, another small smile on his face. When the cab had disappeared into the fog he turned back toward us.

'Are we ready? Let's see if we can find your man, Horton. Ah, Inspector, how kind of you to join us.'

A man, flanked by two uniformed men had arrived in another cab and was just disembarking. The Inspector, a short, rotund man with a moustache and a balding pate jumped heavily to the pavement and looked wearily at the Detective.

'Well back in your cab, man!' the Detective said. 'We must be off!'

The Inspector, without saying a word, shot off an annoyed look and climbed back into the conveyance.

CHAPTER 16
On the Trail

We did not have far to travel. Our cabs pulled up outside a dark, crumbling building a few streets away. The windows facing the street were quite dark.

'Ready, gentlemen?' the Detective asked, pulling out a revolver from within his overcoat.

'Smith, you wait outside until I deem it safe for you to enter,' Horton mumbled to me.

I nodded and, as I exited the cab, I put a hand on the revolver in my pocket. The metal weight of the weapon gave me some small comfort.

The Detective, the Inspector, the two uniformed officers and Horton carefully approached the building carrying lamps turned low. A figure was waiting in the doorway.

One of the Bobbies braced himself and began, at a signal from the Detective, to put his shoulder to the door. At the third heave, the door gave way with a loud crack and the policeman nearly fell to the floor. The group quickly entered the building with the unknown figure following hesitantly. I could see the jogging lights of the lamps flitting across the walls as the men made their way through the building. I glanced nervously around my surroundings, but there was not a soul about.

My grip on the revolver in my pocket tightened a little.

After what seemed like many long minutes, Horton appeared at the door and nodded his head toward the inside.

'It's safe,' he said, his manner somewhat dejected.

I followed him into the place and a strange, sickly smell that almost made me gag, instantly intruded upon my senses. At one end of the hall, a rotten staircase ascended into impenetrable blackness. Somewhere in the house, I heard the squeak of rats.

The walls, I could see from the dim lamps now placed here and there, were covered with huge patches of black and silver mould and the wallpaper was peeling off on great swathes. Heaps of plaster lay here and there on the damply carpeted floor and, looking up, I could see that the ceiling had collapsed in places. In one area I could see right through to the night sky and, although I may have imagined it, amongst the few stars I could see through the clouds, was the red eye of Mars mockingly winking at me.

The sickly smell became stronger as I followed Horton through the rotting house.

In a room towards the back, with great black curtains draped across the window, I assumed, to keep out curious eyes, the Detective was bent over a shape on the floor. A poor looking old woman, probably a local, was quietly sobbing in the corner. She must have been the figure waiting outside the house as we arrived, and the original informant.

'It was like I said, Sir!' the woman gasped at the Detective between sobs. 'I saw some grim lookin' fellows bundle this poor man into this 'ouse. I didn't get a good look at 'em seeing as 'ow they was all wearing big cloaks. Just shapes really, Sir. I lives next door an' this place 'as been empty for a few years now.'

'Thank you, Madam,' the Detective said distractedly, without looking up. 'I don't think we need deter you any longer.'

The woman shuffled away wiping her face with a filthy handkerchief.

I went to where the men were gathered around to see what interested them so.

The shape was a man, or the remains of one, and the smell was more intense than ever in his immediate area. I pulled out my handkerchief and held it over my nose and mouth, my eyes watering a little. I noticed that one of the young Bobbies was hunched over in a corner, quietly retching.

As I took in more detail, the horror of the man's situation hit me. He was quite dead, for in his grim state he could have been nothing else. One of his legs was missing from the knee down. The place where the severance had occurred was literally melted. Half of his face was black and his chest had a great hole burned in it through which I could see charred and shrivelled internal organs and the blackened bones of his ribcage. A pair of twisted spectacles hung off his one intact ear, the lenses darkened and cracked. One arm was twisted around unnaturally over his head. Above him, on the ceiling, was a large patch of soot and a large smear of yellow, sickly looking grease stained the wall upon which his motionless body leaned.

'Spontaneous combustion,' the Inspector said sagely, a grimace of disgust on his face. 'I've seen it before, twenty years back—'

'Nonsense!' the Detective snapped, springing to his feet. 'This was no supernatural event!'

'Why, many scientists think it is worthy of investigation,' the Inspector retorted stiffly. 'Sir Arthur Conan-Doyle himself says that some things like this are proven fact.'

'Quite so,' the Detective replied. 'The great, but gullible, Sir Arthur also believes, I have it on good authority, that children talk to fairies!' The Inspector looked at him sulkily but said no more.

The Detective turned to Horton.

'Is this unfortunate fellow your man?'

Horton nodded slowly, his eyes still fixed on the stinking corpse.

'Then, alas, we were too late. But we may still catch the culprits! My unruly troops should return presently and I think that we have not long missed those responsible.'

The grim faced men left the building and I followed.

We set foot on the damp street just in time for the return of Wiggins and his clamorous mob. Their cab clattered to a halt outside, the horse panting and steaming in the cold air, and they spilled, en mass, out of the vehicle like a swarm of rats.

Wiggins presented himself immediately to the Detective.

'We found them all right, Sir! Seems you was correct as you always are,' the lad beamed. 'They is holed up down Limehouse way. The old warehouse next to the opium den, if you knows which one I means.' A strange look passed between the boy and the Detective.

'Good man,' the Detective said, after a moment, tossing him some coins casually. 'Get yourselves some lodging for the night, you have done well. And stay out of trouble!'

'Thank you very much indeed, Sir,' Wiggins said and made to be off.

'Oh, Wiggins,' the Detective said. ' I may have more work for you soon so I will be in touch. It appears my retirement will have to wait.'

'Very good, Sir!' the youth said and the rabble disappeared into the night.

'Well gentlemen,' the Detective addressed us. 'If we mean to catch these villains we should be off. The cabs are waiting.'

CHAPTER 17
Peril in Limehouse

Our cabs clattered noisily through the London streets once more as we attempted to capture those responsible for the terrible death of the scientist.

As we went, thoughts flashed through my mind. Who were these mysterious assailants? Terrorists perhaps? Foreign spies trying to get at the British secrets so far discovered with regard to the Martian machinery? Or worse, were these shadowy figures Martians who had survived the destruction of their brethren, just like the creature I had seen held in the underground facility? If they were Martians, why had they holed up within the city?

Certainly all of these entities might have reason to mean harm to Government people. The description given by the old woman helped little. Strange figures wreathed in cloaks. That did not sound like a typical Martian trick to me, but perhaps in their desperation they were now going forth into the human world. Perhaps they had decided to hide in plain sight. The death of the scientist seemed to fit a hurried Martian attempt at silencing an enemy and the apparatus used to burn the man must have generated incredible heat. The knowledge, that it was now all the more likely that there were Martians skulking around using Heat-rays on British citizens once more, worried me greatly.

Horton looked at me with a look on his face that mirrored the one I felt I had. Perhaps he had come to similar conclusions.

The cabs soon slowed and the Detective peered through the window into the fog.

'We have arrived,' he declared. 'Mr Smith, I should be grateful if you would wait outside should assistance need to be called.'

'Very well,' I said, in no mood to argue.

The huge building we were now halted outside was a rundown warehouse. A large painted sign, illegible due to the battering of the elements was fixed above the doors. On the other side of the dock I could just see, through thick drifting fog, black, inky water. The sound of small waves lapping the dock sounded, in this darkness, menacing.

To the right of the building was another smaller edifice. Dim lamps burned in its few windows and there were a few men slumped, in a stupor, by the door. This must be the opium den.

The party of police and Government sponsored people carefully approached the warehouse. The two uniformed officers, at a gesture from the Inspector, skirted the building and headed towards the back, the others heading for the huge front doors.

As I watched from the comparative safety of a few yards away, my hand again in my pocket on my revolver, the deep, wounded animal bellow of a foghorn from some distant vessel sounded across the dark water. I thought instantly of one of the Martians huge machines and started, my heart racing. I, with no small effort, pulled myself together and tried to concentrate on what was happening before me.

Horton and his companions reached the doors and the Detective gingerly pulled at a smaller door inset into one of the larger ones. It swung open with a loud squeak. The party of men raced inside, revolvers at the ready. The small door swung shut behind them.

There was no further sign of any life then and deathly quiet set in, making me feel more nervous.

Then, after a few moments, shouts from the building became audible then a shrill human scream pierced the night.

Three shots were fired then there was more shouting. I shuffled a little closer to the doors. There was silence once more. I strained my ears trying to hear any other sign of what was happening.

Suddenly one of the large doors exploded outwards in a shower of wood splinters. I put up my arms instinctively to shield my face and fell to the floor.

A large, black shape burst at incredible speed from the hole in the door and rushed, it seemed, headlong at me. I cried out and cowered on the cold floor, fearing this thing would be upon me. More shots followed the dark shape and one appeared to bounce off it with a metallic clang.

I saw a brief glint of what seemed to be metal and the thing, just before it reached me, launched itself into the air right over my head. This was followed a loud splash as the thing hit the water beyond the dock and sank quickly out of sight.

My companions ran out of the warehouse at full pelt.

Nichols, the cabman, was standing on the dock next to his cab, scratching his head.

'What in the Devil was that?' he breathed.

'Can you still see it?' Horton shouted as he ran up.

I shook my head shakily. No words would come.

The Detective went to the edge of the water and peered out.

'No sign. It has made good its escape,' he said, a note of anger in his voice.

'By God it was fast!' the Inspector exclaimed unnecessarily as he puffed up behind the rest. One of the Bobbies, I noticed, was missing and I knew then it was from he whom that awful scream had come from.

'The other policeman?' I asked. Horton shook his head slowly.

'It ran him down. He had no time to react.'

'Did you see what it was?' I asked. 'It nearly ran me down too, I could not see it, it moved so fast.'

'It was too dark,' the Detective said.

'I could swear it was – no,' I began.

'Go on,' Horton prompted.

'Well, I am sure I saw metal on it. A shot hit it and bounced off, I am also sure of that.'

The Detective looked thoughtful.

'I fear Smith may be right,' he said.

'A metal man?' the Inspector scoffed, then instantly regretted it after the look the Detective gave him.

'Inspector, where have you been this past year or so? We have seen metal machines a plenty on our fair land of late. Indeed they were almost our undoing, or had you forgotten?'

'Yes, but the Martians is all dead,' the Inspector said defensively, great droplets of sweat standing out on his brow.

'Are they now?' the Detective said. 'However, as far as the public are concerned this is definitely the case. Perhaps for the time being at least, you should leave such flights of fancy out of your report?' He glared at the bristling Policeman meaningfully. The man did not reply.

'This does not bode well at all,' the Detective muttered, absently filling his pipe.

Horton gave me a glance that spoke volumes.

More police soon arrived and the dead officer, who would leave a young widow and two little ones, was carefully placed into an ambulance carriage. The sheet that covered his remains was stained red with blood. The other constables muttered darkly amongst themselves and swore to catch the killer of their comrade.

We did not dare, nor wish to, intrude upon their grief and point out the unlikelihood of that occurrence.

The Detective spent a few minutes talking quietly to the Inspector and Horton. Presently he came over to me.

'Well Smith, it was good to meet you. I believe you and Horton are now to head back to Hobbs Lane.'

I shook his hand.

'We will, no doubt, meet again,' he said. 'Meanwhile, there is much to do. Farewell.'

'Are you ready, Smith?' Horton said coming over, a troubled look on his face.

'Yes,' I said simply. In truth, tiredness had hit me suddenly and I wished for nothing more than a comfortable bed. Nichols was atop his cab and, as soon as we were in, we were carried off into the fog.

CHAPTER 18
The Flying Machine

The next few days I passed in compiling notes and pondering my experiences. I often thought of my wife and whether she worried about me. I wrote a letter to her, that I was promised by my Steward would be delivered, which I filled with calming phrases and implications of a fictional banality of my situation so that she would not fret. I think that had she known what had already happened to me since my arrival in the underground laboratories, she would have set out to find me and take me back home herself. I, for myself, was still full of curiosity as to how this whole affair would play out and wished to see it through, despite my gut feeling that I had not yet seen all of the hardships I would face before I could return to my old life.

Cavendish was gone on one of his missions in the City and Horton was mostly absent, I assumed in his further investigations on the sabotage attempt and the disappearances of the scientists. Horton did not ask me to accompany him on any subsequent expeditions.

Horton did, on the third day after the adventure in the East End, conduct for me a tour of other areas of the facility, mostly huge laboratories where white-coated men worked at studying some of the artefacts we had brought back with us. Horton warned me of my perilous situation no more. Indeed he acted as if nothing had happened and we had never spoken of the danger that my presence here posed to me. Even when he was not there, though, I had the strangest feeling that he was watching me. Was he a sort of guardian angel or was he keeping his enemy close? Time would tell, I thought.

On that day, for some reason I do not understand, I asked if I could see the live Martian again. Horton seemed reluctant to allow it but finally he relented. Why I wished to go back and see that monstrosity again, I could not say, but I felt that I had to.

So, Horton and I stood at the observation window. The Martian was squatting faced the other way at first, swaying like it were in some reverie. Perhaps it was dreaming of its home world or scheming as to how to escape. But after a short while, it wriggled around on its tentacles and faced us. Slowly, it slithered across the floor of the cell until it was almost at the window. The great glowing eyes locked onto mine and it stared.

'Careful, Smith,' Horton muttered. I ignored him.

All I could see were the great glowing eyes like twin burning suns. They burned into my mind and, my mind began to wander. Suddenly, I saw images in my head.

I saw Mars with many of these creatures moving around the streets, just like I had seen in the Crystal Egg. I saw a scene inside a cylinder, the Martian crew in the tanks full of liquid we had seen in the cylinder. I saw Martians pouncing on pale bipeds and feeding. I saw a group of these creatures sitting in some kind of council chamber hooting excitedly at each other.

I felt something probing at my mind. It was reading my thoughts!

I heard a voice, far away: 'Smith! Smith!'

These strange mind pictures were stopped abruptly when a sharp pain on my cheek was the result of a slap from Horton. I stared uncomprehendingly at the man for a moment.

'What happened?' Horton asked. 'Are you all right?'

'It was talking to me. Showing me things,' I answered distractedly.

'Hmm. It has tried that with a very few. We order the guards not to look at it at all. Perhaps some people are more susceptible. Come, we must go'

I was starting to wonder how long I was to be at the facility. When I had agreed to document events there, I had not envisioned the length of my stay as being so long as it had so far. I did not seem to be performing any function at this time and I intended to ask Cavendish, when he returned, if I could visit my wife. The Knight returned two days later, his usual ebullient self.

'Ready for a trip then, Smith?'

'Where to?' I asked rather grumpily. I felt I knew how a neglected and forgotten child might feel.

'How would you like to see the Flying Machine tested?' Cavendish had a glint in his eye.

'The Flying Machine? You have it? Of course I should like to see it!' I said brightening. I remembered my brother's account of having seen the machine that had, as he put it, rained darkness upon the land.

'We leave in an hour,' Cavendish went to leave but turned back to me at the door.

'Oh, I should appreciate if you did not visit our Martian friend any more. You have had, I gather, a taste of the powers that those beasts possess. Until we understand more, please stay away.'

We went via overland train to the Essex coast, I am not entirely sure exactly of our destination. I asked, during the journey, how they had secured the Flying Machine. Cavendish answered simply that they had found it abandoned in a field near a cylinder. The station that our train stopped at appeared to have no signs and I neglected to ask my hosts of the name of the place. Perhaps this was yet another unmarked station for use only by my Government hosts.

We were conveyed from the station by carriage and travelled a short way on windswept and pitted roads to a rural area with no sign of habitation around. In a large field, a tall fence had been erected and I could not see what lay beyond. The fence stretched for a goodly number of yards either way.

Our carriages pulled up at some great wooden gates in the fence and two soldiers, after checking our identities, let us through.

Beyond were more soldiers, all armed, and the machine.

It sat in the middle of the fenced area like a huge, squat black bird. It was a matt black, not shiny and it appeared to absorb light rather than reflect it. If this thing was metal, I had not seen it's like before.

The machine was shaped like a massive 'V' and had little in the way of surface features. I could see a small window at the pointed front end and a pale green light could be seen within.

A little knot of men stood chatting animatedly nearby and we headed in their direction.

Cavendish shook hands enthusiastically with a tall uniformed army man and made introductions.

'Smith, this is Frederick Roberts, Commander-in-Chief of His Majesty's Forces. He has come from London, like us, to watch this event.'

The man nodded curtly and introduced the various men he was with. They were all minor dignitaries, there to represent their various governmental and forces departments.

A scientist went to Cavendish and muttered something. Cavendish seemed pleased. He jabbered something to Horton, then addressed the assembly.

'Gentlemen, we are ready to start. Now we are all aware of the advances that the Wright brothers in America, and others, are making in the field of manned flight. If this test is successful, we will push those advances far ahead and will re-write history. Shall we begin?' He nodded at the scientist.

There must have been a man in the machine already for the scientist waved a finger and there was a coughing report from the huge contraption then a deep throbbing noise. Small green puffs of smoke hissed from vents in the wings and the noise gradually became higher in pitch.

After a pause, the whole thing began to lift, slowly, straight up in the air.

I saw that the air under the thing was rippling and it reminded me of the heat haze on hot pavement. As the thing rose into the air, a small ripple of applause came from the gathered dignitaries and the guarding soldiers craned their necks to watch, open mouthed. The machine had gone up, perhaps twenty feet or so when there was a commotion at the gate. Shouting floated toward us, just audible over the hum of the machine's engines. Heads swung round, en masse, from the majestic sight before us to see what the trouble was.

Soldiers ran this way and that then there was a tremendous explosion. The gates had imploded scattering splinters and chunks of wood every which way. Then, all that could be heard was the machine. Everyone stopped dead as if time had been frozen.

'NO!' Cavendish exclaimed suddenly. 'Not again!'

Roberts started marching towards the gates barking orders. Soldiers rushed to obey.

Through the smoke at the gate came four glittering metallic figures. They made strange whining, whirring noises as they walked and I was struck with the odd appearance of them. Thinking back, the closest approximation I can come up with is of two-legged dogs. Six feet tall two legged dogs, to be precise. The legs both looked much like a dog's rear legs and they sprouted from odd, rounded bodies topped by a small head thrust forward on long necks.

They marched steadily through the ruined gates and onwards towards us.

'What devilry is this?' someone gasped. No one answered.

Roberts barked again and the soldiers again moved quickly. Raising their rifles, they fired off volleys at the strange intruders. Bullets bounced off the shining metal bodies and on the things marched.

'What are they doing?' Cavendish asked, then realising where the machines were headed, his face took on a look of horror.

'Stop them!' he screamed at the top of his lungs, his face a livid red.

Then, with an escalating sense of dread, I spotted the small funnels that protruded from the heads of the machines. The first soldier that was hit by a miniature Heat-ray did not know what hit him. Others dropped their weapons and ran only to be picked off by this vile death regardless. The dignitaries and I ran blindly away as the machines came close to where the Flying Machine was hovering. They stood stock still for a moment, then loosed their rays, as if by some unspoken command, on one of the wings of the floating giant.

The Flying Machine wobbled slightly from the impact of these blasts then, as more rays were unleashed, tipped over onto one side. A wingtip churned the grass as the machine performed a slow, graceful pirouette then crashed the ground.

Green smoke poured out of the machine then there were muffled explosions deep within its belly. Bits of black metal flew through the air and I ran faster, terror filling my mind. I was now a being of pure instinct, survival was all I could think of.

Horton, who was running beside me, shouted a sharp warning. I looked around but Horton suddenly pushed me hard to the floor. I looked up to see his face turn pale, then there was a whistling sound through the air and he toppled over, a large piece of metal wreckage sticking out of his body. I momentarily forgot the danger and went over to the prone man. He looked at me with pain filled eyes, opened and closed his mouth a few times as if trying to say something to say something.

'Don't try to speak, Horton,' I said. Another explosion rent the air. 'We have to get you some help.'

Horton coughed wetly and black blood issued, in a gout, from his mouth. His eyes glazed over and he was suddenly still.

Filled suddenly with rage at this new waste of life, I went to stand up.

Something hit my head and there was blackness.

CHAPTER 19
To Hell and Back

It is hard, in many ways, for me to describe how the next year of my life passed.

Anyone who has suffered the deep darkness and despair of madness may understand, for those who have not it may be more to comprehend. I shall endeavour to piece together events as coherently as I am able.

In that field when the strange machines had attacked the captured Flying Machine, as I stood over the body of poor Horton, I had myself been hit on the head by a piece of flying metal. The wound was not serious, but I had been knocked for six for a moment or two.

I next remember standing with blood trickling down the side of my face, quite dazed and disorientated.

The mighty Flying Machine was a useless, smoking pile of metal scrap in the middle of the field and the cries of the wounded drifted on the wind. Here and there, blackened piles of bones and ash marked the last stands of the brave soldiers who had tried to defend us.

A whirring sound made me turn my head slightly. To one side, one of the strange new machines was regarding me curiously.

Again I felt something like fingers probing my mind. I saw more images.

Water, a huge stretch of water. White capped waves. Dark, rainy skies.

More Martians at work at some machinery I did not recognise. Dextrous tentacles flourishing tools. A huge dark insect-like shape I could not see clearly.

My head began to throb. Green flashes tore across my mind.

I saw more Martians grouped around a metal table. A struggling shape strapped down.

I could now see clearly what was happening. A terrified man was being dissected by those vile creatures. Alive!

As the Martians hooted triumphantly, a human scream started and grew louder and louder.

I realise now that it was not the man at the table screaming. The keening wail was coming from my own throat.

The last thing I remember in that field is hearing an odd, stifled version of that nightmarish howl, 'Ulla!', coming from the odd machines as they stalked away.

This final assault on my mind had torn at the already silk thin threads that held my mind together. Weakened by all I had experienced over those months, my mind had no defence left and gave. Those last threads snapped under the strain, and that is all that I remember fully for a long time.

Time had no meaning from then on. I spent many days beneath crisp white sheets, being tended by white-coated doctors and brisk nurses.

From time to time, I would be wheeled out in a bath chair to some fragrant gardens and I would sit staring, without seeing, out at the distance.

My wife came to visit me often, but in the early days, I do not think I even recognised her.

A jolly looking man with big, white side-whiskers would also appear before me and say things to me that I cannot remember. I am told I would think him an orderly or doctor and open my mouth, like a hungry chick in the nest, for food or medicine. This man would shake his head sadly, pat me on the shoulder and go away.

The days and months passed in this sorry state. I lived as if in an impenetrable fog. My days passed in a world which I was not part of and the nights, I am told, I spent, screaming and sweating, tortured by memories and dreams of all the terrible things I have witnessed.

Gradually, though, my tortured soul began to heal, and with the diligent care of the Doctors, the fog that clouded my mind slowly lifted.

I began to speak coherently to my wife. I could enjoy the fresh air in the garden, the bright colours of the flowerbeds and the feel the warmth of the sun on my face.

Nearly a full year after I had lost myself, I was declared fit to leave the institution and I went home to my beloved wife. We spent a few happy weeks rebuilding our life together.

Until the day that Cavendish reappeared.

Cavendish perched on the edge of a chair in my sitting room, a cup of tea lost in his big hand.

'We were very worried about you, Smith,' he said with a concerned expression. 'I trust you feel better.'

'Much,' I said. 'I gather I have you to thank for the care I received.'

'Least we could do, old man. Only the best for those who work for us, you were in very safe hands.'

'Quite. Alas, I can remember little of my time there. One thing I do remember, with hindsight, was your visits. I fear I did not recognise you at the time.'

'Bah!' Cavendish said with a wave of his hand. 'Think nothing of it. I quite understand. One thing I must ask though.'

'Yes?' I asked warily.

Cavendish stared me straight in the eye. 'They spoke to you again, did they not? Those machines.'

'Yes,' I said slowly. 'It was quite horrible. Cavendish, those things … were they Martians?'

My visitor nodded.

'But they are so much smaller than any machine we have seen so far,' I said baffled.

'When I say that they were Martians, I mean that they were of Martian origin. Horton had been looking into reports of such things being seen. Your adventure with him in Limehouse: it is possible that you saw those things then.'

Horton. A wave of sadness washed over me as I remembered how he had sacrificed himself to save me.

'Horton was a good man,' I said.

'Yes he was,' Cavendish agreed. 'He is sorely missed.'

There was silence for a moment.

'Smith,' Cavendish said finally. 'Those machines were unmanned Martian machines. We think they could be controlled remotely to create havoc without causing any loss of Martian life. We call them Remote Walkers.'

'Where do they come from?'

'That's the thing. We believe we have found out their origin. A Martian base that we never knew existed. We are going to try and find them and when we do, we will destroy them all.'

'Where do they come from?' I repeated.

'I cannot tell you as a civilian. To announce this would cause panic. Smith, I want you to join us again.'

I was afraid of something like this as soon as Cavendish had reappeared. 'Why me?'

'I cannot think of anyone better suited to observe this endeavour,' Cavendish said. 'You have seen much of our work and have proved yourself trustworthy. Not only that, but you seem to have some sort of a link with the enemy that is rare to find. Of course, should you wish to decline, I will respect your wishes. I do not want to put you through any more hardships unless you feel up to it'

He paused and absent-mindedly stirred his tea with his spoon.

'But,' he continued, finally. 'It would be a good opportunity for you to see those things eradicated, once and for all.'

My mind whirled again. I had been through so much and yet I had an idea that seeing the Martians destroyed could be the best medicine I could have. I thought for a moment.

'I will come with you. I wish to see this ended.'

Cavendish nodded but said nothing.

'So now, tell me,' I said. 'Where are we going?'

Cavendish looked at me evenly,

'The North Sea,' he replied.

CHAPTER 20
Returning to the Fold

Much had changed in England whilst I had been held, captive and despairing, in my cage of starched cotton sheets and wicker.

Many buildings damaged in the war had been rebuilt along with the lives of those who returned to reside in them. People again worked, slept and ate, going about their little human affairs as if nothing had happened.

Industry once more filled the sky with smoke and the trains again ringed and grumbled, ferrying the swarm of humanity about its business.

Not all was well, though.

As we travelled, on comfortable seats in a Pullman, back to the underground laboratories, Cavendish explained events so far.

'The terror attacks have continued,' he said, puffing on a great wooden pipe. Oddly, I couldn't remember him having had that habit before.

'And the perpetrators, I assume you mean Martians,' I put in.

'Yes, that is correct. The Remote Walkers have been spotted all over the country, seemingly trying to cause as much disruption as possible. They appear, as if out of nowhere, destroy targets and disappear again just as easily. Upwards of forty targets – mostly industrial and Government related – have been hit.'

'Are they trying to soften us up? For another invasion perhaps?' I wondered.

'It could be, although there appear, at the moment, to be no signs of activity on Mars. We have been watching the Egg very closely.'

'Have you traced the exact origin of the machines?' I asked.

'We have a fairly good idea of where they come from,' Cavendish said from behind a cloud of fragrant pipe smoke. 'We engaged the consulting detective, whom I believe you have met, and he was of great assistance to us. Helped to collate reports of sightings of the machines and we were able to gain an approximate location. Alas, we could not persuade him to accompany us on our mission; he would have been a valuable asset.'

'So you really think they come from the North Sea, as you said before?' I asked.

'Yes. Extraordinary, I grant you, and we would never have guessed that our friends would actually think to land a cylinder under water. But it seems to be so.'

I shook my head in wonder. 'Indeed. So what is the plan?'

'We go and destroy their base. Stop this nonsense once and for all. We have to give their comrades on Mars reason to think again about coming here for another visit.'

'That I have to see,' I said. 'But how can we touch them underwater? Some new weapon?'

Cavendish grinned, 'Exactly so. We have some new toys to play with.'

The laboratories were, as before, a hive of activity.

'We have made great strides in our work on the machines,' Cavendish said as we walked through the cavernous testing areas. I soon found out that he was not exaggerating.

I was amazed to see a new Fighting Machine being put through its paces in one area. A prototype of a human machine!

I gathered, from what I understood of Cavendish's excited chatter, that the makeup of the Martian metals was still causing some problems for our scientists and the prototype Fighting Machine was heavily armoured with steel, like an Ironclad, and its dull battleship-grey surface was dotted with rivets. The legs were thicker than those on their Martian counterparts, to take the extra weight I assumed, and they ended with sprung gripped feet. The engines were based on those of the Martian machinery, but, apparently, so far, much less efficient. Cavendish informed me that they were working flat out to remedy these problems.

So, a year after I had last been here, I saw our own human Fighting Machine clatter and thud jerkily across the rock floor, steam hissing noisily from the joints of its legs.

'Marvellous, is it not?' Cavendish beamed. 'Soon we will be able to take on the Martians on their own terms. Who knows, perhaps even on their own world!'

'We could go to Mars?' I asked shocked.

'Why ever not?' Cavendish said. 'We have been experimenting with various things, not least that marvel Cavorite'

'The metal from Wells' book?' I said. What he was talking about was pure fiction.

'The very same. Well, the real metal, anyway,' Cavendish affirmed, chuckling. 'Our friend Wells knows more than he might perhaps let on.'

I could get little more from him about that.

'You still haven't told me how you mean for us to travel to the Martian base in the North Sea,' I reminded Cavendish. 'Do you have some new kind of Ironclad?'

'We have something much better,' the Knight said, winking. 'A submersible.'

That night I had lucid dreams of machines floating gracefully across the sky, land Ironclads clanking around the Earth and great ships that could cross the black gulf of space and carry men to other planets.

CHAPTER 21
What Really Happened at Kensington

Preparations had begun for the expedition to the North Sea in earnest. Weaponry and other equipment was already on the way to our sea base, although I knew not where it was apart from the fact that it was somewhere on the West coast of Scotland.

The consulting Detective, visited me one day and, much to my surprise, greeted me warmly. I had heard that his reputation was that of a bit of a 'cold fish' but I was treated like a long lost friend.

He walked now, with the aid of a cane. He had sustained some injury during his investigations and this was why he would not accompany us on our mission.

Apparently, the Detective was here only to impart final intelligence and to wish us 'Bon Voyage'. Cavendish seemed very disappointed that this man would not be with us for the duration, as was I.

I asked Cavendish, over dinner that night, what had become of the Martian in the holding cell.

'Martians,' he said grimly.

'What ever do you mean?' I asked.

'It's the strangest thing,' Cavendish said. 'The thing reproduced! More of the blighters popped off it like peas out of a pod! The scientists call it 'budding'. Apparently, the young ones just grow out of the parent. An extraordinary sight!'

'How many?' I asked incredulous.

'We now have 5 of them in there. Quite a handful they are. We have had to put them in separate cells as they were causing our guards a lot of trouble. They grow very quickly.'

'I can imagine,' I shivered, not entirely comfortable with the thought of having that many of the creatures in close proximity.

It later appeared that I was right to be worried.

Two days later, I was with Cavendish watching the last of the supplies being loaded ready for transport.

A soldier ran up to us.

'Sir, we have to leave,' the man said, trying to catch his breath.

'Why? What is it?' Cavendish asked, visibly confused.

'They have found us.'

Cavendish's ruddy face paled as a horn began to bellow out a hoarse warning.

'I was afraid of this,' he said. He hurried to his office with me in tow and began to gather up papers and documents.

'Cavendish,' I shouted, as the rumbling of an explosion sounded. 'Leave those!'

The man looked at me blankly for a moment, dropped the papers and grabbed the box that contained the Crystal Egg.

'We cannot leave this!' he exclaimed. I grabbed his sleeve and dragged him away clutching his precious cargo.

We were hurried out in a small group, just in time to see five of the Remote Walkers stalk into the testing area, Heat-rays blasting everything, and everyone, in sight. Small fires raged in areas of the room.

'Get out of here!' someone shouted, somewhat needlessly.

The machines steadily progressed through the base leaving wreckage in their wake. We came upon a dirt-streaked and bleeding soldier as we entered the lift to the surface and he informed us that the walkers had freed the captive Martians.

'Cavendish,' I said, dismayed, as the lift rose to the surface. 'How did they find us?'

'I do not know,' Cavendish replied. 'I suppose it was a matter of time. Luckily, we have moved much of our machinery to other laboratories and to the sea base. They cannot do much harm here.'

A terrifying thought occurred to me. 'Do you think they are following me?'

It suddenly seemed to make sense. How many times had disaster and carnage happened when I was present?

'I do not think so,' Cavendish brushed some dust off the shoulder of his jacket. 'Make no mistake, they do seem to be able to communicate with you in some way but you are not alone. Take heart from that fact. If I thought you were a danger to our mission, I should never have asked you along.'

Still, I was unsure and the thought echoed around my head.

We reached the underground train just in time to see the machines stalk quickly out into the tunnel. Explosions boomed deep in the bowels of the Earth and smoke poured out of rents in the walls. The liberated Martians clung on to the machines with their tentacles like nightmarishly deformed new world cowboys. The glittering machines, seemingly unencumbered by their joyously hooting riders, gathered speed and we soon lost them from sight.

As we left the train at the station there was another tremendous explosion and a huge fireball came at us at a tremendous pace down the dark tunnel.

'Run!' I shouted.

As we made the street, just in time, the glass blew out the windows of the station showering passers-by outside. There were more deep booms and the ground heaved. The station building and some of those around it began to crumble and dust clouds flew into the air. Rubble flew this way and that knocking running pedestrians off their feet.

Pedestrians screamed and ran as there was one last terrific report, a rippling of the pavement and some of the buildings finally, slowly toppled over.

As the dust cleared, we stood dazed in the sunlight, staring at the great pile of rubble that had been caused by the end of the underground laboratory at Kensington.

CHAPTER 22
Jealousy Abroad

We did not linger long in Kensington. We found a large group of soldiers had been waiting for us, very much on edge, outside the station. It turned out they were barracked in one of the buildings nearby as a precautionary measure in case of just such an attack as befell the laboratory. They had not seen the Remote Walkers enter, a captain told us, but the machines had been spotted racing away toward the Thames as the soldiers arrived to investigate the explosions coming from the Station area. Some of the men had apparently given chase but despondently joined us a short while later, having finally lost the attackers somewhere along the embankment.

When a roll call had been taken of people who had escaped the attack, we found that somewhere around thirty souls has been lost. Cavendish took comfort in the fact that the toll could have been larger, had not operations already been largely transferred elsewhere, but I was appalled and was eager for retribution. Any basic thoughts of empathy with these creatures I may once have had were draining away at each new outrage. Where once I had pondered over our right to exterminate them, I now wished only for their eradication.

The injured were taken away to hospital and our group, in a motley convoy of carriages and motorcars, made our way to the railway station. We only had a short wait until the train arrived.

The train that clunked into the station was quite unlike any I had seen before. It was armoured like an ironclad and was bristling with turrets. The wheels were covered in great metal guards and a large scoop, like the American 'cowcatchers', was fixed to the front. It looked like some great metal fortress that moved.

'Are those Heat-rays?' I asked Cavendish, pointing at the turrets.

'Of a sort,' he replied. 'I admit that they are not quite as effective as the Martian Heat-ray, yet, but much more so than conventional weaponry. We have all sorts of toys we have developed. Quite extraordinary in such a short space of time, would you agree?'

This man's pride in the minor successes with this wholly alien technology was quite unflappable. I would believe how well these things worked when I saw it for myself.

'Just think of the applications for atomic power,' Cavendish continued. 'We have made great leaps in that field thanks to the Martians. We have a lot to thank them for in actuality. They have unwittingly given us the means to not only fight them, but also to improve ourselves.'

I had my doubts. Would the usage of this new technology drive us forward to enlightenment or would it change us in an altogether more unpleasant fashion?

'Other governments still wish to get their hands on this stuff, you know,' Cavendish said. 'We have managed to keep them from infiltrating so far through strict border controls and the like. We will not share until we are ready. You have heard that there have been warlike rumblings on the continent, of course.'

I had. It seemed that some of our European neighbours were getting impatient and their jealousy was getting the better of them. France and Germany, in particular, were openly demanding in public that Britain share the findings in regard to the technology we were discovering. There were public demonstrations in these countries, which were spreading to others, and some of our less reputable newspapers had already taken to using jingoistic rhetoric in their defence of our Government's stand. I wondered how much worse matters would be if it were generally known how far Cavendish and his scientists had advanced. It was only a matter of time before we would find out.

Despite the fearsome outward appearance of the train, it was quite comfortable inside and we settled into our seats for the long journey to Scotland. I doubted a Pullman car could have been fitted out less extravagantly. We had a carriage to ourselves but the whole thing was spoiled somewhat by the fact that there were only slits for windows. The air soon became warm and, with Cavendish puffing on his pipe, somewhat smoky. I tried to engross myself in a newspaper but the reports of unrest abroad began to depress me and I tried to stare out at what countryside I could see through the narrow window.

Soon, it became dark and even this diversion became impossible.

I retired to the sleeper car and tried to sleep.

At some unearthly time before dawn, with the moon riding high in the clear, cloudless sky, the train screeched to a halt. A great tree trunk had fallen across the track and men got out to move it.

As this task was being completed, a shout went up and the men ran back to the train. I gathered, from the excited chatter of others on board, that Remote Walkers had been spotted moving across a clearing in a nearby wood and I strained to see, without success, what was happening. I did think I may have seen the glint of metal, momentarily, in amongst the trees, but I cannot be sure. There was a thrumming and a whoosh from above my head as a Heat-ray turret spoke and some of the trees in the wood burst into flame. I think I might then have heard that odd, strangled 'Ulla' cry of a walker, but it could just have been wind rushing through the branches of the trees.

The train moved off without further incident.

CHAPTER 23
Holy Loch

The base at Holy Loch had its own railway station not too far away. The armoured train was unloaded quickly and efficiently and we soon found ourselves at the gates of the sea base complex.

The defences here were quite impressive. Huge metal gates topped with spikes and barbed wire. The fences themselves were electrified and any interloper would, if they passed these, have to cross a mined no-man's land only to face tall, smooth walls of plastered brick, topped with broken glass. At intervals along the fence and either side of the gates, stood tall towers with Heat-rays mounted on them.

The base itself was full of uniformed men dashing this way and that at various tasks. In the compound I saw some human Fighting Machines standing in a row like grotesque metal soldiers on parade. Technicians in one piece coveralls swarmed over one machine that had smoke pouring out of its hood, another machine was twitching fitfully like a sleeping dog and I wondered if Cavendish's faith that these clumsy-looking machines would be an effective defence, or indeed offence, against the Martians was entirely misplaced.

We were shown to our quarters and left to unpack. My room was small but very comfortable. Gleaming brass trim framed everything and I felt as if I were in the first class cabin of a steamer. Another example, I'm sure Cavendish would have stated, of the taxpayers money well spent.

There was a knock on the door and Cavendish appeared.

'Would you like to see our transport for the mission, old man? She's just coming back from testing at sea.'

'Very much,' I said throwing some clothes in a drawer. 'I'm ready.'

I found myself, a short while later, in a cavernous building. This was an enormous boatshed and there was a large docking area in the middle. I looked carefully over the edge of the decking into the water and it seemed very deep. My undulating reflection looked back curiously at me from the dark, cold water.

'Ah, this must be her,' Cavendish said and I looked up.

A klaxon sounded and an amplified voice boomed out from speakers that I could not see.

'All land crews prepare for docking.'

The water in the huge bay was churning now as bubbles rose to the surface. Then the water suddenly parted as a tall black tower began to rise up and out. More and more of the black shape became visible and I began to get an idea of the sheer size of this thing. Now, the deck cast off water and rose up. A minute later, I could see the whole thing. It was easily wider than any vessel I had ever seen before and was certainly longer. The smooth black surface contained no visible joins and few features, much like the Flying Machine. The design was so obviously of the same origin I gasped. I realised that this thing could not be human!

'Smith,' said Cavendish grandly. 'Meet Nautilus!'

Cavendish cut into my stunned thoughts and confirmed what I thought about this new machine.

'Yes, she is a Martian vessel,' he said. 'We found her adrift off the South coast, all her crew dead. We took her and adapted her for our needs. It was decided that she was, by nature, so fantastic that she should have a name to suit.'

'Most fitting,' I agreed. Verne, I felt, would have approved.

'She possesses enormous power, Smith. I believe that we can defeat the Martians utterly with this machine and the weapons we have developed. She is a submarine like no other!'

I knew that the submarine vessel was not a new concept … many nations were already deploying these stealthy and dangerous machines. But, although I had never seen a human one 'in the flesh', I could clearly see that this vessel before me was something else entirely.

'I hope you are right,' I said, 'When do we go aboard?'

'Later, old chap, first, I think I shall introduce you to the people we will be sailing with.'

The barracks were not quite as opulent as my cabin, but seemed clean and functional.

Five men lay around on bunks reading or chatting amongst themselves. They stopped talking and looked up as Cavendish and I entered. Before Cavendish could say anything, another door opened and another man entered.

'Squad, shun!' one of the men said. The other men stood to attention.

'Ah, Lieutenant Churchill,' Cavendish said to the newcomer. 'This is Smith, would you be so kind as to introduce the men?'

The Lieutenant nodded.

'Of course, Sir. This is Corporals Jameson and Glenn, and these gentlemen are Thomas, Dawson and Wayne.' The soldiers tipped their heads as they were introduced.

'Is this it? I asked disbelievingly. The men by the bunks looked at me curiously.

'No,' said Cavendish. 'These men are the best His Majesty's Forces have to offer, specially trained to do a particular job. There will be another one hundred men going with us.'

'I apologise,' I said sheepishly to the men. 'I meant no slight to anyone.'

'Don't worry about it, old man,' Cavendish said. 'Churchill, could you outline the plan for Smith?'

Churchill, a gruff looking man somewhere in his thirties, looked at me doubtfully.

'Smith is along for the mission as my guest,' Cavendish prompted. 'He can be trusted completely.'

Churchill nodded and told me what they had planned.

CHAPTER 24
How it Would be Done

Churchill, I later discovered, had been an MP before the war. He had become disillusioned with his party and was on the verge of changing allegiance when the Martians had landed.

He had immediately decided to spring to his countries defence and had taken up arms. As a war correspondent during the Boer War before his career in politics began, he had seen battle before and slipped into the military life with comparative ease.

He stood now, puffing on a cigar and speaking of the plan for the assault on the Martians undersea lair. I did not wonder at his previous vocation, as his voice was steady, clear and confident. This was a man well used to oration.

'Our plan is to use the larger force as a diversion. When we locate it precisely, these men will attack the cylinder from several sides whilst our little force of commandos here slip in quietly and enter the base separately. Of course, we know little of what we will be facing and much will need to be decided on the field. At any rate, our smaller force will, if possible, set charges within the Martian base and slip away again. With luck and the grace of God, we will blow the blighters to kingdom come!'

I thought this plan a little vague and said so.

'But there are so many unknown factors, are there not? The Martians are not to be underestimated.'

'Indeed,' said Churchill looking me squarely in the eye. 'But the basis of the plan is sound and the rest will come as we discover more. The truth is, we do not know just what we will face down there and we must be prepared to improvise.'

'What weapons do we have?' I asked.

Cavendish stepped in.

'All in good time, Smith! For now we are keeping our cards closely to our chests. Needless to say, we will not be embarking on this endeavour half cocked. We feel sure we can defeat these creatures and win the day.'

This show of confidence brought murmurs of approval from the men. I sincerely hoped that this bravado was not misplaced and wondered what poor Horton would have thought of this plan.

'So this small group of men will destroy the cylinder?' I said. 'Again I mean no offence, but it still strikes me as suicide! Why there are only six of them.'

'Seven, actually,' said a familiar voice from the doorway.

Many times, incidents in my life have taken me by surprise. In times of war, perhaps, this is not so unusual. Events in war themselves are far more unusual than in peacetime. However, since the war began, my life had been composed of an unending succession of bad luck, horror and coincidence. It is little wonder, perhaps that I fancied, at times, that some bored god was using me as some kind of plaything.

The man standing at the door was another reason for my mind to reel once more with the pure strangeness of it all.

'Ah, Sergeant!' Cavendish said. 'Come in.'

'Good Lord!' I spluttered finally as the man sauntered into the room. 'The Artilleryman!'

'Sergeant, actually,' said the man grinning and pointing at the stripes on his uniform. 'Done well for myself haven't I?'

The man came over to me and pumped my hand just as he had so long before.

'Don't look so shocked, my friend,' he said. 'I find the fact that we keep meeting, and in one piece, to be a good sign.'

'Yes, of course,' I said, simply. I was not so sure that I agreed with his thoughts but I saw his point. We had both lived through much and continued to survive to meet again.

'So what do you think of this motley bunch?' he asked sweeping a hand grandly at the men seat around the room. 'A finer lot I couldn't wish to see. We'll show the Martians a thing or two, eh?'

The men around the room gave a small cheer and I was reminded of when I had last seen this man in the public house.

'Thank you, Sergeant,' Churchill rumbled. 'We were just informing our guest of our plan.'

'Ah,' said the Sergeant. 'I take it you are coming with us?'

'I am,' I said.

'Excellent. It will be like old times, eh? This man, Lieutenant, is a survivor. Just the sort we need with us.'

'He will not be fighting. Sergeant,' Churchill said levelly. 'Smith is here purely to observe.'

'It doesn't matter. It's good to see him nonetheless. He can be our lucky mascot!'

This exchange seems to have quietened the men's suspicion of me and, from then on, they looked at me in a much more friendly fashion. It seemed that the Sergeant vouching for me meant that I was all right by them.

134

CHAPTER 25
Waiting for the Off

The next week was spent in preparing for the voyage. I was escorted around the base and saw the men training. A few times the men went outside of the compound. Many vehicles took them, large wagons, which travelled more quickly than any motor vehicle I had seen before. I gathered these were derived from the machinery that the Martians had left behind and some contained men and the backs of others were covered with tarpaulins. Cavendish told me vaguely that they were going for training that could not be done at the base.

One day, I was allowed to go on one of these expeditions and watching the men running at stuffed target with fixed bayonets and practicing for various eventualities was, I had to admit quite a stirring sight.

I counted ten human Fighting Machines staggering about the compound, as I wandered around the complex, in clouds of steam and noticed that they had odd boiler shaped tanks fitted to their backs.

They also had tubes on either side that looked like some kind of weapons but not like the Heat-ray cannons.

After much questioning from me, Cavendish finally admitted that these human machines had been refitted for use underwater and would be carried on *Nautilus* as part of the assault. He also intimated that there were more 'wonders', as he put it, yet to be seen but would say no more.

I saw Heat-rays being tested on vehicles and other sorts of weaponry being fired.

Seeing the whole force on parade in the middle of the base towards the end of the wait for our mission was a most impressive sight and, despite my misgivings, I felt my spirits lift. I had been assured that these men had all been handpicked from the cream of His Majesty's forces and they certainly looked an army to be reckoned with. They all wore specially made, dark blue, uniforms for this mission. Embroidered patches were carried proudly on sleeves that proclaimed them to be part of the 'King's Expeditionary Force'.

I just hoped that the Martians would be as easy to defeat as everyone seemed to believe.

The Sergeant came and visited me in my cabin, after dinner one night, and we played cards. He regaled me with tales of his exploits since I had last seen him and I, in turn, told him of the things I had seen since I had last seen him.

'Sounds like you have had quite the time of it, mate!' he exclaimed as I finished my tale. 'You are a lucky man indeed to escape so often. Seems like someone is watching over you, eh?'

I was not so convinced.

I, rather tactlessly, reminded him of his dreams of an underground Utopia but he changed the subject. I think he found his behaviour then a little shameful and wished not to talk about it. I, in light of my own hardships since the war, thought I understood him better now than I had before.

Whilst preparations carried on, reports came in of harassment of shipping in the North Sea. Cavendish told me that ships had been attacked and sunk and strange machines had been sighted speeding away in those waters.

There had also been a further two Remote Walker attacks on land; one successful, the other repelled using the Human Heat-ray. The Martians were evidently still trying to disrupt things as much as possible.

I did not escape the training. Even though I was only an observer, I had to be taught how to use the underwater suits that had been developed, from existing and new technology, for this mission. Apparently, even Cavendish had learned this new skill and the thought had amused me greatly.

These strange suits would allow members of the force to be underwater for an extended length of time. I was a very good swimmer but, for my own safety, it was decided that I had to learn how to use them in case of emergency. I was assured that I would be aboard *Nautilus* throughout the mission but was submitted to the training anyway. Just in case, as Cavendish said with a small smile.

The base had a large water tank that was used for training and testing and a soldier was assigned to help me into the suit and show me how to use it.

The suits were lighter versions of the suits that I knew deep-sea divers use and seeing them reminded me of Verne again. The helmet was fashioned out of brass with little portholes around it and there was a large tank, for air, to be worn on the back. I spent some hours learning to control my breathing in the helmet and how to walk in the great heavy boots that were made to allow the wearer to walk on the sea floor. I hoped, sincerely, that all of this was a waste of time.

Soon came time for the voyage to begin. Cavendish woke me at eight one morning and told me we would be off at dawn the next day.

Butterflies fluttered in my stomach that day. I had seen and experienced much but the fear of the unknown still had an effect on me.

I had little appetite for food and I tried to busy myself in bringing my notes up to date.

The rest of the base, too, seemed effected. The men were quiet throughout the day and there was none of the usual joking and raucousness that could be expected in a great gathering of fighting men.

Final tests were carried out on the machines and I heard explosions coming from the far side of the base. I gathered that the weaponry was being taken through last minute tests as well.

The day passed very slowly and I retired early but slept only fitfully.

CHAPTER 26
Bon Voyage!

The next morning, I stood nervously in the docking bay watching the final pieces of equipment being loaded onto *Nautilus*.

There was much light-hearted chatter from the men of the commando squad and the Sergeant turn occasionally to wink or grin at me as if to allay my, evidently obvious, fears.

Churchill stood alone silently watching operations and puffing on his ever-present cigar, but seemed to me like a coiled spring, as ready to get going as his men.

The main body of troops were next stowed away deep in the belly of the huge submersible, through huge doors at her nose, and it soon became our time to board.

The front of the machine was open, like the jaws of some massive undersea beast, and I entered with trepidation. I felt some primal fear that this enormous thing would swallow me whole and I would never be seen again.

Inside, it was not unlike being within the cylinder on Horsell Common. That same sickly glow emanated from the metal walls and no man-made lighting was either needed or in evidence. As Cavendish and I crossed the threshold, the 'jaws' started to slowly close with a high-pitched whine. As we walked inside, our footsteps clattered on the grated floor.

The human Fighting Machines were secured against the walls of the vessel as we passed and there were other bulky shapes covered in tarpaulins. Soldiers and the vessel's crew, who were also dressed in dark blue uniforms but with jaunty sailor's caps on their heads, went busily around the area carrying weapons and equipment here and there.

We were eventually ushered, past a bewildering array of unknown machinery and controls, to our cabins and I saw that the human touch had, unexpectedly, been added. My quarters were almost as opulent as those I occupied in the underground laboratories in Kensington, all wooden panelling, brass fittings and superfluous curtains. This amalgamation of human decor and Martian superstructure struck me as vaguely unsettling.

After a short time of trying to acclimatise to these odd surroundings, Cavendish came to me and asked if I wished to stand on the bridge of the vessel whilst we put out to sea. To get there, we had to negotiate many corridors and staircases which, I was told, had been adapted for human use, as had much of the inside of this alien craft. It appeared she had been virtually gutted, save the machines for her control, of course, and adapted as required for this mission.

The bridge was yet another large space lined with lit up instrumentation. Around twenty sailors stooped over dials or manipulated levers on these instruments. I was, I admit, impressed by how the use of such strange technology had been adapted, seemingly so easily, by man. Cavendish said some things about these controls and such, but much of it, I confess, went over my head.

Cavendish steered me towards a tall greying man who stood barking orders before a large viewing window. I wasn't sure if this window was real or was, perhaps, a projected image like those 'portholes' I had seen in the cylinder. I could see the entrance to the docking bay through it.

'Smith,' Cavendish said motioning towards the man. 'This is the Captain of Nautilus.'

140

'Smith,' grunted the Captain and brusquely shook my hand. 'I have heard much about you. Welcome aboard.'

'Thank you, Captain,' I replied. 'This is a most impressive vessel.'

'Indeed she is,' the Captain said, simply.

Cavendish steered me away from the Captain and we stood a little away as he returned to his duties.

'I have to tell you,' Cavendish said in a low voice. 'The Captain had a special reason for requesting this mission. His brother was also a naval man and commanded a ship you may have heard of.'

'Really?' I said. 'Which vessel is that? I confess to not knowing much about these things.'

'Nevertheless, this one will mean something to you. The vessel the Captain's brother commanded was HMS Thunder Child.'

Again, the odd synchronicity of this struck me. This man was the brother of the man whose ship had battled valiantly to defend shipping during the war, and my own brother had seen that brave vessel sink, with all hands, in that defence.

That so many things could be tied together in such ways seemed impossible to be mere chance.

A dull rumbling deep within *Nautilus* signalled the start of our journey. Through the viewing window, we could see the docking bay slip away to either side and soon we were heading to open sea. Land crews waved and cheered as we passed. I saw that we were being escorted by heavily armed Ironclads, four in all, and they were all seemingly carrying newly added Heat-ray funnels. I hoped that we would not hit trouble this early in the voyage.

If it hadn't been for the distant rumble and whine of the engines and the view through the window, I would have been hard pressed to know if were actually moving at all. I have never before, nor since, travelled in such a smooth fashion. I had expected the vague feeling of nausea or disorientation that had accompanied all my previous sea journeys but there was nothing of that sort on board this vessel. I marvelled at how something so huge could slip through the water like a hot knife through butter.

So now, for better or worse, we were on our way.

CHAPTER 27
Out to Sea

Cavendish never ceased to amaze me with his encyclopaedic knowledge of how all the machinery adapted from Martian technology worked. Although he himself never told me much about his life, in fact he seemed to make a point of not doing so, I do know that he had a background in engineering and other similar sciences. Apparently, he was an advisor in the sciences to the Government, although in what exact capacity I never found out. Our American cousins might have called Cavendish a 'trouble-shooter', although I felt that he would have disapproved of that term.

Whatever his exact origins, he was obviously much in demand in those post-war years.

I was surprised to hear, from overhearing some idle gossip amongst the men, that there was a Mrs Cavendish. Somehow, he had the air of the eternal bachelor about him and he did not seem the married type at all. Thinking about that, and wondering quite how this woman stood his continued absence, brought to mind my own sweet wife who must, I thought, feel a kinship with her. I felt ashamed that I had neglected my wife so, of late, especially as I had already put her through so much, and I made up my mind to return home to her as soon as our task was completed. If I survived.

Nautilus was fitted with an array of the latest developments in technology as I have intimated before, and it seemed that much of this equipment was enhanced by items the Martians had left behind.

Rows and rows of consoles lined the control rooms and the bridge and little lights winked and flashed, like tiny stars amidst the firmament, though to what purpose I could not even begin to comprehend. Young and fresh-faced sailors, some barely out of their teens I guessed, hovered around these banks of equipment. These young men were overseen by a grizzled and bearded Mate who perched, an old, unlit pipe clenched between his yellow teeth, on a raised chair, overlooking all this activity. The Mate reminded me, rather absurdly, of some strange tennis umpire keenly watching a game.

Cavendish proudly showed me the vessel's radio system, again staffed by a boy who I warranted could barely grow a beard had he tried, and I watched as the Captain contacted Holy Loch with details of our course on it. The scratchy, clipped tones of the voice that came from the contraption in answer gave me an idea and I asked if I could talk to my wife on the machine. Cavendish frowned a little at this. Apparently, this equipment was for official use only but he said he would see what he could do. From his manner, I assumed that this request would be conveniently forgotten and I felt a flash of annoyance.

I watched as a crewmember tested out the 'sonar' equipment. The man had his eyes locked to some form of appliance attached to yet another console. The appliance reminded me of the binoculars I had once seen my late friend Ogilvy using. A light from within bathed the attendant's face in a sickly green glow. This 'sonar' was apparently something that was on board when *Nautilus* was found and its usage had been learned since by trial and error. I gathered that it worked by projecting sound waves outward from the vessel, which then bounced back from any objects that these waves hit and the results showed on a display within these 'binoculars'. It was then possible, I gathered, to ascertain what lay ahead of the vessel from quite some distance. Cavendish explained that this would be our most likely method of finding the location of the Martian lair.

In the afternoon, I joined some men up on the huge, flat deck of the submersible. I took in the bracing, spray-filled air and the cries of the seagulls that circled and whirled in the air above us. Our Ironclad escorts steamed along beside us, dwarfed by this great hulk we stood upon. The whoops of the ships' horns sounded periodically and the sailors on board lined the rails and waved enthusiastically at us. I saw the little flags on the masts, buffeted by the light breeze, and heard the cheers of the men on these ships and momentarily felt a celebratory atmosphere. It was like a street party and the men on deck with me seemed thoroughly caught up in it. They waved and cheered at their comrades over the sea, filled with pride at having been chosen to staff this extraordinary vessel. These high spirits were soon dissipated for me, however, when the thought of the unknown that yet faced us elbowed its way roughly into my mind. Cavendish, through all this, stood alone further up the deck, gazing unflinchingly out into the horizon. I wondered at the thoughts that must be crossing his mind.

The weather took a sudden turn for the worse, as it often does in those waters, and we were all ushered back into the bowels of the vessel, as dark, ominous clouds quickly blew in and a sudden heavy rain lashed the deck.

The first sign of trouble came early the next morning.

A loud klaxon sounded and I stumbled wearily from my bed to see what caused this noise. I quickly dressed and made my way, through men rushing too and fro around the corridors, to the bridge and found Cavendish already there. I wondered then if he ever slept.

'What is it?' I asked him, now fully awake and not a little concerned.

'An attack,' he replied evenly. 'One of our escorts has been holed by some sort of small machine that came from the water. I gather she is sinking fast.'

'They do not waste any time,' I said. 'Do they wish to take Nautilus back?'

'They will take her over my dead body,' Cavendish asserted, rather oddly I thought, as if he were the only person who could guard this vessel. 'Captain, I think it is time we submerged.'

The Captain turned and stared at him.

'What about the other ships?' I said. 'Surely we cannot just leave them?'

'We can do exactly that. This vessel is the only machine we have that can help us complete our mission successfully. We have to preserve her for what is to come and cannot take the chance that there is a whole fleet of those things waiting for us at this stage.'

I thought of those sailors that I had seen waving so happily the afternoon before now fighting selflessly to defend us. Through the viewing windows an explosion, some distance away, lit up the darkness outside.

'Captain,' Cavendish said grimly. 'If you please.'

Something flashed across the Captain's eyes then. I wondered if these orders went against his wishes as much as mine. The Captain turned after a moment and shouted orders and sailors pushed levers and flicked switches.

There was a slight lurch, and as another explosion flashed through the viewing window, *Nautilus* began to sink into the cold, black water.

CHAPTER 28
Submerged

The mood onboard *Nautilus* was much subdued. Some men looked grim, and some a little frightened, but applied themselves, with every ounce of professionalism they possessed, to their various tasks. Cavendish stood, hands behind his back, looking as self-important and defiant as ever. From time to time, I caught various crewmembers surreptitiously casting sharp glances at him. The Knight either pretended not to notice or was too wrapped up in his own thoughts. Rather than a penny, if I could, I would have given the Royal Mint for them.

There was little to see through the viewing window but gloom until the Captain gave an order and powerful lamps lit up the sea ahead. Startled shoals of fish glinted as they hurried this way and that in a frantic effort to make way for this huge invader of their territory.

Away from the battle on the surface we travelled, I could not guess at the speed but there was no feeling of movement. I could only gather that we were travelling very fast indeed.

'Captain, small object coming at us ahead!' a sailor cried. He was hunched over the sonar binoculars and the green glow made his eyes appear wider than they perhaps were.

'Evasive action!' the Captain growled. A crewman whirled a great wheel around and there was a slight change in the pitch of the distant engine sound, but that was the only sign I could detect of any change of pace or direction.

'Ready the sonic weapon,' the Captain said.

Ahead, through the window, I could now see a small shape keeping pace with us. As we had changed course, it had raced to follow. This new machine looked like a much smaller version of *Nautilus*, a black shadow in the murk, punctuated with green lights that shone along its length. It was getting closer and it seemed to me that if neither vessel changed course or slowed, there would be a collision.

'Fire!' the Captain shouted.

A sailor pressed a lever and there was a high-pitched whine. From the front and side of *Nautilus* the water seemed to ripple.

The Martian craft chasing us turned and quickly fired off some sort of missile. This small black missile came rapidly toward us but narrowly missed, shooting straight passed us at incredible speed. A young crewman near me breathed an audible sigh of relief and I saw that sweat beaded his brow.

'Fire!' the Captain repeated. Again, the water rippled ahead of us and the nose of the other craft jerked to one side as if it had been roughly pushed by some giant's hand. Our pursuer tried to return to its intercepting course but the water rippled once more and the craft was suddenly enveloped in bubbles as it disintegrated. The torn pieces of the machine began to sink slowly to the sea floor as we sped past.

The bridge erupted in cheers and sailors jumped up and down with glee.

'The sonic weapon works perfectly,' Cavendish beamed at the Captain, who did not seem inclined to join in the celebration. The Captain nodded.

'That is just as well,' he muttered.

The sailor on the sonar instrument confirmed that that there were no more enemy craft in the vicinity so the Captain barked orders for us to resume our original course. Our search for the Martian base began in earnest.

I retired to my cabin after this conflict and tried to concentrate in writing notes for my account. I soon gave this up, however, and lay on my bed to mull over things. Despite my tiredness, my mind was again racing and sleep was impossible.

I felt I could understand, if not agree, with Cavendish's reasons for his orders for us to flee the scene of the Martian attack on the Ironclads, but that understanding did not make me feel any better. It seemed obvious to me that many of the crew, and perhaps the Captain, were wracked by similar doubts. We had left brave men to die and I could not come to terms with that. I wondered if the crew felt as cowardly as I, even if there was nothing I personally could have done and it may have, as Cavendish insisted, ended in the failure of this crucial mission.

I was not left to my thoughts for long, though, as the Sergeant appeared at my door and asked if I would like to join him and the commandos in their mess.

As a distraction from my thoughts was most welcome at this point, I followed him through the vessel to a smoky mess room where the men lolled about laughing and joking. I wondered if they were even aware of the drama that had played out in the sea so recently.

At first, this frivolity in our situation grated on me slightly but it soon became infectious. I allowed my thoughts of guilt slip away and I laughed at times as the Sergeant and his colleagues told risqué stories and sat absorbed as they took turns in telling exciting stories of their army exploits. At a request from Glenn, a stocky red-haired fellow, the Sergeant prodded me into telling of my own experiences and of our previous meetings. The others took up this cry and I stood to address them. Gratified by their rapt attention, I related what had happened to me in the war and the assemblage gasped, cheered and booed, like an enthusiastic music hall audience, at appropriate parts of the story. When I had finished, they clapped and cheered then insisted on toasting me with some rather palatable wine. They even proposed a toast to my wife so many miles away.

Dawson and Glenn were the real wags of this bunch and had us laughing mightily with their tales and horseplay. The camaraderie of this little band of commandos affected me greatly and, for the first time that I could remember since leaving my home to go to the underground laboratories with Cavendish and Horton, I felt myself truly relax in that jolly atmosphere.

We talked long into the small hours until, one by one, the men drifted off, for the most part slightly the worse for wear, to their bunks. The Sergeant and I talked a short while longer and then I myself had to retire or I should have slept were I sat. I went to my cabin, staggering a little in the warm embrace of a cloud of wine, but full of good cheer.

That night came the first nightmare I had had for many months. It was not the usual one of the Martians feeding upon me, this time our mighty vessel cracked and broke open by some unknown means. As I watched myself sink, eyes wide and limbs flailing ineffectually, to the ocean floor.

CHAPTER 29
The Search

The next day, when I awoke with a headache, *Nautilus* had already begun her search of the seabed. The Captain had the vessel steered up and down in a wide grid pattern whilst the sonar swept the sea floor. The sonar device was so sophisticated, Cavendish told me, that it could detect a single ha'penny from miles away if properly tuned. As the Martian base we were looking for was obviously expected to be bigger than this coin of the realm, however, detection this precise was unnecessary. In fact it may have confused the issue. Too sensitively tuned, the device would have picked up every piece of wreckage and any other sea rubbish that had accumulated over many hundreds of years of shipping.

I found the viewing screen fascinating during this time and watched as fish and other creatures of the sea regarded this immense intruder curiously.

The sonar picked up several large targets as we searched, but they turned out to be shipwrecks many years old. One wreck, however, appeared to be of a much more recent origin and had a huge gash in its side. One of her funnels was tilted forlornly to one side and flags and insignia still fluttered, eerily, in the current. Some of the contents of the ship were scattered about her and I somehow knew that this ship had been a victim of our quarry. Cavendish considered sending a search party on board to investigate but, after a moment's thought, decided that it would serve no purpose. He ordered curtly that we resume the search.

There was no further incident until later that afternoon when more, smaller targets were picked up by the sonar device. These objects seemed to be observing us as they came no closer and kept pace with *Nautilus* for a while. They were five in number and appeared to be moving at great speed as the little dots that represented them danced, around and about each other, at the top of the sickly green screen where the sonar returns were displayed. They carried on this strange display for something like ten minutes and then disappeared as soon as they had come. Cavendish took this development as a bad sign and recommended that extra watchfulness be exercised.

I asked again that day about the possibility of talking to my wife on the radio set but Cavendish told me that radio silence was now being observed.

He evidently felt that the Martians, if nearby, may be able to monitor any such transmissions and would get more warning than we could comfortably allow.

I felt sure that, although the reason for this certainty was unknown to me, they already knew we were on their trail but realised the futility of arguing the point. Cavendish barely acknowledged my presence during the search, he merely stared distantly out through the viewing window.

The search continued on and periodically we saw the strange objects come into view on the screen and perform their eerie display. Nothing else of any size was spotted that day, though and, weary of the silent tension on the bridge, I went and joined the commandos in their mess.

The Sergeant was sitting smoking in a chair with his feet up on the table as young Jameson led the men in singing some bawdy music-hall standards. Private Wayne skilfully accompanied this gleeful troupe on an accordion.

I had at first wondered why the commandos did not mix with the other men who were quartered elsewhere in the submersible. As I grew to know them, I felt that perhaps their group's whole foundation was built upon an unshakeable bedrock of trust and experience and, whilst they did not shun fellow servicemen, they were as close as a family and spent their time together accordingly.

The jolly mood in the mess, as before, lifted my spirits and, after a glass or two, I joined in the singing and laughing with great gusto. How different and refreshing was my time in this simple mess in contrast with the staid quiet of being in the company of Cavendish. These times were made further unbearable as the Captain seemed to despise Cavendish, although whether this was purely because of the orders Cavendish had given or there was something else, I did not know. Cavendish, for his part, was as aloof and untouchable as always.

I allowed myself, again to immerse myself in the company of my new friends and I found that my glass was never empty.

An orderly came to find me later and asked if I would be joining Sir George for dinner. I, rather the worse for wine by this stage, told him that I wished him to tell my host that food was for scoundrels and women and I would drink more wine instead. The poor orderly left with the rough laughter of my companions ringing in his ears.

Later that night, alone in my room, I realised I may have gone too far and, with my head pounding and with the room gently spinning, made a mental note that I would apologise to Cavendish in the morning. As it turned out, I had no need to worry, as the orderly had evidently, with the good judgement and discretion typical of such men, told him that I was 'feeling unwell'. I later thanked him.

CHAPTER 30
The Flagship

Two long days later, the search of the seabed bore fruit at last.

There was no chatter on the *Nautilus* bridge save from the Captain muttering new headings and a sailor calling out small targets caught on the sonar screen. The men flitted around like ghosts, pressing this switch or pulling that lever, making course adjustments and checking gauges. The humming and chirping of various instruments working acted as the musical backing to this quiet ballet of activity.

Mid morning, there came a shrill cry from the young seaman with his eyes glued to the sonar console.

'Captain, a target dead ahead! We're coming up fast on it and it's not moving.'

The Captain turned quickly, the excitement in the boy's voice making him instantly attentive.

'A ship?'

'If it is, Sir, it's a big'un! This is like nothing I've seen before on the screen!'

'Any other targets?' the Captain asked.

'No, Sir, not a one.'

As one, the gathered ensemble turned to look through the viewing screen. There was nothing to see there but the usual darkness dashed with small fish that glittered like tiny stars in the night sky. I wondered briefly if I would see a similar view from a ship in the depths of space.

'Ahead slow, ready weapons!' the Captain snapped.

Cavendish breathlessly appeared behind me. A sailor, under some previous order, had fetched him from his room at this latest development.

'What is it, Smith?' he puffed.

'Looks like we may have arrived,' I replied.

'Keep a sharp eye out,' the Captain told the sailor at the sonar. 'Anything else comes along, sing out, sharp and clear!'

'Aye, Sir.'

The darkness in the viewing screen held our attention as we approached this object. Presently, a dim shape appeared in the murky distance and grew larger.

'The cylinder!' Cavendish uttered. 'That's it! We were correct!'

'But where are the Martians?' I wondered aloud, a sense of impending doom growing as we neared this awful thing.

'Inside, perhaps?' Cavendish said. 'Captain! I think we should stop and ready the troops.'

The cylinder was now visible on the screen. It was a glinting black and looked much larger than even the cylinder on Horsell Common. A line of dim green lights went from the nose to tail of it and it sat on the seabed like some nightmarish sleeping sea monster. It was rested with its back to a large hill with what appeared to be a sharp drop behind it.

'It's enormous!' said an awestruck sailor, rather obviously.

'The flagship!' Cavendish said excitedly. 'It has to be!'

Churchill appeared at the door of the bridge now, grimly chewing on his cigar.

'Churchill, the troops?' Cavendish asked him.

'They are on standby; do you wish me to ready them?'

'No time like the present, eh?'

Churchill now sat at his own small console on the bridge. On it he could monitor events as they unfolded.

After a brief conference, it was decided that the original plan for the assault would be adhered to. The main body of troops would approach, en masse, the cylinder from the front, hopefully diverting the Martians attention from the Commandos who would try to enter the cylinder elsewhere and destroy it. The submersibles weapons could have been brought to bear and we could have tried to destroy the cylinder from the vessel without the need for loss of human life, I thought, but Cavendish wanted, he said, to try to take the cylinder intact. This new revelation disturbed me and did not seem to please the Captain either. On hearing this, he cast another malevolent glance at Cavendish before turning back to his duties. Churchill, for his part, looked more grim than usual for a moment but gave no other indication of his feelings away.

I imagined men rushing to and fro, machinery being readied and weapons checked as the tension built on the bridge. The cylinder was still the only target to be seen on the sonar.

I wondered why the Martians did not attack as they surely must have known this huge vessel was so close to them. The feeling of unease in my stomach grew.

There was a radio link up to the Sergeant's men that had been built into their suits. That this technology existed was quite astounding and brought home to me again that, since the war, we were advancing rapidly in our knowledge.

Churchill now called to the Sergeant on this device and I heard my new friend's voice scratchily make a brief reply.

'We are ready,' said Churchill turning in his seat.

'Very well, let's begin,' Cavendish answered.

CHAPTER 31
Spider to the Flies

A high-pitched whine signalled the start of the campaign. The great doors at *Nautilus'* front opened and the main body of troops disembarked. A sailor, at a barked command from the Captain, flicked a switch and the viewing window suddenly showed two different views; one from within the front of the vessel looking out, as before, and another from just outside at the level of the seabed. I assumed that the latter view was generated by some additional device somewhere on the outer hull.

I watched as the human Fighting Machines jerkily stepped out onto the seabed and, bubbles rising from their joints, began to make their way toward the cylinder.

I could just see one of the men in the hood of one of these machines looking nervously around as he drove his vehicle past the device showing this view. He did not seem, to me, to have much faith in the ability of his machine to keep the water out. I could not say I would have blamed him. I had seen the 'teething troubles' that these machines had had.

Accompanying these lumbering machines were the be-suited troops, one hundred in number, walking as if in slow motion and obviously fighting the friction of the water that surrounded them. All carried weaponry of some sort or other and big square packs sat like the shells of crabs on their backs. Little trails of bubbles emanated from the bulky helmets they wore and rose slowly toward the surface so far above.

In the corner of the viewing window another display flickered into life showing what I assumed to be the sonar console. Green concentric circles emanated from a single point at the centre and a paler green 'hand', like that of a clock, swept speedily around the display. Here we could see these soldiers and machines start as a green mass of pale blobs, which then gradually became small individual dots as they slowly spread out.

Churchill sat stiffly at his console muttering orders into the radio set, occasionally scratchy voices answered.

'The main body of troops is underway,' Churchill said, looking in Cavendish's direction.

'Very good,' Cavendish answered. 'Send the Commandos on their way.'

Churchill muttered something into his radio and he turned to watch the sonar.

On the screen, a small green dot appeared at the front of the vessel and headed off to the side of the rest of the men and away.

'Commandos despatched,' the Lieutenant snapped.

'Excellent,' Sir George answered.

The tension was rising on the bridge but I noticed that a small smile played around Cavendish's lips.

The sailor on the sonar screen seemed coiled like a spring, ready to shout out should any foreign targets appear. None did.

'Why don't they come?' I asked finally. 'Cavendish, something is wrong about all this.'

Cavendish regarded me for a moment.

'Calm yourself, man. I expect they are in the cylinder wondering what to do about us. Soon we will have them surrounded and they will not have a hope. I expect a full surrender from them at any moment.'

'Surrender?' I said, incredulously. 'The Martians do not surrender! Have you taken leave of your senses?'

'Certainly not,' Cavendish retorted. 'Have you? These creatures, aggressive as they may be, will surely see that they have no option but to give up. We are holding all of the cards now, Smith, mankind need not fear them anymore.'

I shook my head but said nothing more. The Captain cast a quick glance at me and I again wondered what this man was thinking. Did he think me, or Cavendish, to be the fool?

We watched on as the troops grew nearer to the cylinder. One of the Fighting Machines ground to a halt, barely staying upright. I could imagine the driver in a state of panic, as I would surely have been. There were a few excited conversations on the radio as some men came to the aid of the driver. After a few moments of activity around the stricken machine, it began moving again.

I saw from the sonar screen that the Commandos were now well away from the main group and were rounding on the cylinder from the side. I tried to imagine what it would be like to be one of these men, in a hostile environment and sweating in a bulky suit with the adrenaline pulsing through their bodies. The sheer physical effort of making headway through the freezing water, let alone the feelings of claustrophobia, must have put an enormous strain on these frail human bodies and I did not envy them.

Again, I began to wonder why the Martians did not attack when there was a panicked cry from the sonar operator.

'Sir! Multiple targets approaching!'

Cavendish hurried to the boy's side and I peered at the viewing screen.

'Where?' Cavendish asked excitedly.

'Sir, they're everywhere, all around!'

I looked closer, my heart beating rapidly, at the screen. I could see our soldiers clustered near to the cylinder, which showed as a large pale bulk. Around the rim of the ghostly image appeared many small dots encircling all within the centre. Horrified, I realised that the men were suddenly and completely surrounded.

'My God, Cavendish! They've walked into a trap!' I shouted. 'Get them out of there!'

Cavendish stood frozen to the spot, a look of utter disbelief on his face, as this deadly net slowly and inexorably closed in on our forces.

CHAPTER 32
Disquiet in the Ranks

I grabbed Cavendish's shoulders and shook him. His limp body gave as much resistance as would some overstuffed rag doll.

'Come on, man!' I shouted straight into his now pale face. 'We have to do something!'

'But what can we do?' Cavendish eventually replied in a small voice. His watery eyes met mine like an admonished puppy. I pushed him away from me in disgust.

'Churchill?' I pleaded, turning to the Lieutenant who sat grim faced at his console.

Churchill looked at me steadily for a moment then he flicked a switch on the panel before him.

'Mother Hen to Chicks, Mother Hen to Chicks,' he barked urgently into his radio device. 'Return to nest immediately. Repeat; return to nest immediately. Targets closing in all around you, over.'

A harsh whine emanated from the speaker and then a far away sounding voice answered.

'Chicks to Mother Hen; no visual on targets. I repeat; no visual. Are you sure, Mother Hen?'

'Positive returns on targets. You are ordered to withdraw immediately,' Churchill shouted into the device.

'Returning to nest, Mother Hen,' the distorted voice answered. Despite the scratchiness of the reply, a new note of uncertainty had crept into the voice.

Cavendish seemed to return to himself a little at this exchange. He shook his shaggy head and moved forward a little.

'No!' he spluttered. 'They must fight!'

'What?' I asked incredulously. 'Cavendish, those men are surrounded by God alone knows how many of the Martians. They must get back here or they will all die! Churchill, can we not just destroy the cylinder with the weapons on this vessel? Without a base of operations, surely it would be just a matter of tracking down any surviving Martians then?'

Churchill nodded soberly. 'Perhaps that could work.'

Cavendish shook his head again emphatically. 'Order them to fight, Churchill or I will have you Court-martialled.'

The Captain, who had been silent up until now, stepped forward. His whole frame shook with barely concealed anger and his hands clenched and unclenched by his sides.

'Now look here, Cavendish. I am Captain of this vessel and am responsible for the safety of all aboard her. I will not stand here and watch those men massacred because you wish to save a few more of those Martian trinkets.'

Cavendish eyed the Captain coldly and spat a reply. 'I am in overall charge of this mission and I will not have my orders questioned. Get back to your post, Captain, or I will have you relieved of duty immediately.'

On the sonar screen, the small dots closed in on the mass of men who were now visibly heading back toward the safety of *Nautilus*.

The radio hissed suddenly and a frantic voice could be heard.

'Mother Hen, Mother Hen! Targets sighted. They are Martians all right! I think we are going to have to fight our way through them, they are coming at us too quickly.'

Those of us on the bridge turned our gazes to the viewing window. I could see the men returning, walking as quickly as they could in their bulky suits. I could not see the Martians yet. A Fighting Machine came into view amongst the men and headed jerkily backwards toward the submersible, covering the retreat. Some seaweed was caught in one of its legs and flapped behind it like pennants in a strong breeze.

Then the men and machines suddenly stopped dead and all appeared to be looking frantically around them, weapons ready. I soon saw what gave them pause.

Out of the murky gloom to the right and left came Martians. There must have been at least a hundred, perhaps more. They wore strange bronze coloured helmets and skipped along the seabed on their tentacles with an amazing turn of speed. Accompanying them were numerous Remote Walkers, small hoods swaying to and fro as they came.

'My God!' Churchill breathed.

The Martians slowed as they neared our force and brandished strange looking weapons. Some of our men knelt and took aim. Then nothing happened for a moment.

For what seemed like hours, but must have only have been seconds, this standoff continued. Man facing Martian in a hostile wasteland.

The conflict between us on the bridge was momentarily forgotten as we all stood breathlessly transfixed.

The radio hissed to life again. Somebody yelled one word.

'Fire at will!'

With the utterance of this one small word, there was no turning back and chaos ensued.

CHAPTER 33
A Fight for Survival

It has never been never discovered who started the battle with that fateful cry. The military analysts who have studied the more technical aspects of the carnage are, to a man, of the mind that it little mattered. Conflict was unavoidable and one single creature, be it Man or Martian, was all it took to begin the fight.

As it was, our forces were first to begin firing from their position in the middle of a closing circle of enemy creatures and deadly projectiles headed with lightning speed towards their targets.

The weapons used were of the harpoon type, small, wickedly barbed metal arrows fired, by pressurised air, from a specially adapted type of rifle.

Some of these projectiles bounced harmlessly off the Martians helmets, doing little more than knocking the recipients back a little. Others, however, found their mark and the creature hit would thrash about wildly as their lifeblood billowed out into the water around them like dark smoke.

Almost as one, the Martians raised their own weapons and, with the twitch of their tentacles, fired. The enemy had their own harpoon weapons and groups of our men fell back screaming and bleeding as the enemy harpoons pierced their suits.

The human Fighting Machines hurriedly took position surround, as far as possible, the panicked soldiers and brought their own weapons to bear. They too were armed with harpoon weapons and soon the water was filled with deadly metal death.

Churchill screamed into his radio.

'Fall back in groups! Those not moving lay down suppressing fire!' Despite his best efforts to regain control of events, panic and the instinct of self-preservation had set in too deeply with the retreating troops and they continued firing wildly around themselves.

The carnage continued.

The Remote Walkers came forward from the Martian ranks and began to target the Fighting Machines. Trails of bubbles marked the progress of the projectiles these machines released.

I saw, as the view on the screen panned around the battle, the horrified driver of a Fighting Machine frantically pulling levers in the hood of his machine as he tried to get out of the way of this onslaught. He had no time to scream as a black missile ruptured the glass in front of him letting in the freezing water under enormous pressure.

The machine staggered around drunkenly for a moment then its legs splayed out in three different directions. As its body hit the floor, it suddenly exploded in a huge cloud of bubbles, almost knocking another nearby machine over and ripping a small group of unlucky soldiers around it asunder. A man staggered away from the explosion with air billowing out of his ruptured helmet. He made it a few steps toward us, then fell slowly to the seabed.

Another human machine targeted the walker and fired a hail of harpoons at it. Most of these missiles were easily deflected by the hard metal, making the machine stagger a little but not penetrating its armour. One missile, though, tore right through its thin neck, decapitating it. It ran crazily away like a headless chicken, knocking the Martians in its path this way and that. Clouds of blood bloomed in the murky water.

Another soldier ran as a nearby Martian stared at him with greedy eyes. The creature skipped quickly toward him and pounced on his back. It wrestled the struggling man to the ground and grasped hold of his helmet and tugged hard. The locking mechanisms on the helmet failed and, with a rush of bubbles, the helmet was ripped away. The man's eyes told of his terror as blood tinged water rushed into his mouth and on to his lungs. He feebly pounded at the Martian that straddled his chest with his fists until, after a moment, he moved no more. Then a crack appeared in the visor of the Martian's helmet as a nearby soldier took aim and fired at it. The stricken creature let go of its prey and span off, tentacles waving frantically, into the murk.

Hand to hand struggles ensued everywhere as the distance between the opposing forces lessened. Tentacles effortlessly pulled off flailing limbs and human blades stabbed at thick Martian skin. More blood made the murky water darker still.

There were many losses on both sides now as the struggle continued. Bodies of man and Martian alike drifted, limbs waving slowly, in the current.

The Martians, despite heavy losses, had the sheer force of numbers on their side. It was amazing to me that so many of them had survived the death that had overcome so many on land, even allowing for their curious method of reproduction. It was becoming plainly obvious to all the spectators of this vicious struggle that, unless something was done, the Martians would be triumphant and the whole mission would have been in vain.

On the bridge of *Nautilus*, another, quite different, struggle had begun.

'Cavendish,' I shouted pointing and accusing finger. 'Did you know there would be this many of them?'

'How could I?' the rotund man replied. 'I can assure you I had no idea this would happen.'

'Either way, you have shown no regard for the life of your fellow man. All you wish for is the Martian machines to use for your own ends. You would happily let those men out there die for that.'

'For the good of the country, Smith,' Cavendish said soothingly. 'How much better a world will we have with what we can learn from them?'

'All the Martian machines have brought is misery and death. We must help those men out there and if we have to destroy the cylinder to do it, so be it!'

'I rather think it is too late for them,' Cavendish answered coldly.

The battle raged on and the Martians slowly pushed the remnant of our force closer together. Soon only a fraction of our men were left and they were, it was revealed in their frantic radio calls, running dangerously low on ammunition.

Churchill, frustrated and purple with anger, slammed a hand down on his console. His battle experience, planning and sense of discipline had come to nought in this unexpected battle and he drew from the last dregs of soldierly professionalism he possessed.

'Fall back!' he screamed uselessly into the radio. 'For God's sake get back to the ship! Can anyone hear me?'

The only answer was the scratchy and eerily disjointed screams of the panicked and dying.

Suddenly deflated and powerless, Churchill sank back into his chair and fell into a shocked silence. I could see him mentally willing those out on the battlefield to make their way back to us. To safety.

Outside, all that remained now of the force that had seemed so impressive before, was a small knot of men huddled together, perhaps thirty in number, their weapons swinging wildly around at the multiple creatures that edged toward them.

All they could do now was fire the occasional shot to keep the circling Martians at bay.

The human machines were all standing still or destroyed, bodies of men littered the sea floor and floated in the current.

Many Martians had also paid with their lives or lay twitching in the sand. Of the Remote Walkers, only a few remained and they stood watching silently, their heads cocked curiously, as the Martians slowly advanced.

Finally, the human weapons were useless as the ammunition ran out. The weapons were discarded and, somewhat hopefully knowing the brutal disregard of human life that the Martians had shown time and time again, the men all raised their hands in surrender. The Martians moved in and led them away.

On the bridge, the Captain stepped forward.

'This has gone far enough. I will end this once and for all.'

We turned to see him picking up a device and his voice was projected around the vessel.

'Now hear this. This is your Captain speaking. Abandon ship. I repeat, abandon ship.'

'What are you d-?' Cavendish began to ask turning to face him, but was silenced by the sight of the revolver that the Captain now held in an unwavering hand. It was aimed squarely between Cavendish's eyes.

CHAPTER 34
Desperation

Cavendish stared at the Captain, his face pale. His mouth flapped like that of a fish drowning in the air.

I stepped forward carefully and spoke as soothingly as my ragged nerves would allow. 'Captain, what is this? We can still destroy the cylinder even if the men are lost.'

'Look through the window, Smith,' the Captain replied quietly. 'See them come.'

There were Martian machines, accompanied by yet more scores of the Martians in their helmets, cautiously approaching the Submersible.

'It's time to end this and end it now,' the Captain said.

'But–' Cavendish began, eyes never wavering from the barrel of the gun levelled at him.

'You will all leave this vessel now,' the Captain said finally. A strange calm passed over his face and I knew that he was quite insane.

Cavendish and I started to back away but suddenly Churchill darted forward and grabbed at the Captain. A struggle ensued and the two men wrestled for the control of the revolver. A shot rang out and a bullet embedded itself in the sonar console, sparks and smoke emitting from the damaged device. I started forward but the Captain gave a great roar and threw Churchill away from him and to the floor. Churchill made to get up but was stopped by the sight of the revolver being pointed directly at him.

'No, Lieutenant,' the Captain said breathing heavily. 'If you wish to take your chance with the others, you may do so. But try to stop me again and I will shoot you like a dog.'

'What do you plan to do?' I asked.

'Finish the task my brother failed to complete. Now go. All of you.' The Captain said no more but just waved us away with the revolver.

Grabbing Cavendish by the arm I backed away toward the bridge door. As we reached it, I saw that the Martians were getting bolder and moved closer by the second.

It seemed that the sailors had done immediately as they were ordered and *Nautilus* was almost deserted. Just a few panicked sailors rushed here and there.

'What do we do?' I asked Churchill.

'We leave the vessel,' the Lieutenant answered. 'Quickly, I think. I have an idea what the Captain has planned.'

We hurried through corridors and eventually reached a large room that was lined with many cabinets. Churchill opened one and I saw that it contained an underwater suit. I groaned.

I had to open a few cabinets before I found a suit, it seemed many had already been taken. As I started to put the heavy suit on, I saw Cavendish move as if in a trance to another Cabinet in the corner and open it with a small key on a ring he held.

The suit inside was more suited to Cavendish's girth and had obviously been tailored for him. He picked the suit up then dropped it suddenly. He hurried out of the room.

'Cavendish! Where are you going?' I shouted. I made to follow him but a thought occurred to me and I instead resolved to let Cavendish chase his errands if he must. I had remembered his callous lack of regard for human life and was finished with him.

Churchill and I helped each other into our suits as quickly as we were able and I was fastening Churchill's brass helmet when Cavendish reappeared clutching a box. It was the box that contained the Crystal Egg.

Cavendish smiled nervously. 'We can't go without this now, can we?'

Despite the revulsion for Cavendish that Churchill and I shared, we helped him squeeze into his suit and we were soon all ready.

Suddenly, there was a muffled bang and the vessel shook a little. With renewed urgency, we hurried through another door to be faced with a wall. There was a sign that had been placed there, by human hands I assumed, that said simply 'Air Lock'.

Churchill pushed at a sunken switch and a door that I could not see before appeared and started to slide back with a slight hissing sound.

Churchill clicked a switch on his suit and motioned for me to do the same. The Lieutenants gruff voice rang around my helmet. 'Are you ready?'

I took a deep breath then answered. 'Yes. At least as ready as I will ever be.'

Churchill nodded slightly behind his visor. 'Then let's go.'

We stepped through the door into a small chamber with another door at the other side. Cavendish followed meekly behind clutching his box like a child clutches its favourite toy.

The door slid behind us and there was a loud hissing. The hissing died down and then I heard a whine and the chamber began to fill with water.

There was another muffled bang and the rising water rippled violently.

As the water rose to neck level, it took a supreme effort for me not to panic. Breathing as evenly as I could, I attempted to imagine that being underwater was perfectly natural. Each time I took a breath, a deep hiss sounded in my ears and despite my thick suit, the water felt very cold. The air that the breathing apparatus provided for me smelled vaguely of rubber.

When the chamber was full of water, the door in the hull opened and the three of us shuffled out into the darkness.

CHAPTER 35
The Captain's War

My eyes, spoilt by the eerie light inside *Nautilus*, took a short while to acclimatise to the darkness.

As I stood squinting in the gloom, a shape with a bright light attached to the end appeared before me.

I couldn't, at first, make out what it was but I then realised with horror than it was a human arm. The hand, still clenched, held a portable electric lamp. It floated gracefully toward my face, then a current caught it and it swirled crazily away again like some grotesque Catherine Wheel.

Panic set in and I started to take quick, panting breaths. Churchill grabbed my arm and steadied me.

'Easy, Smith,' his tinny voice echoed around my head. 'We must move on.'

We started to move cautiously away from the huge vessel. Cavendish stood and stared straight ahead as if in a trance until Churchill grabbed his arm and shook him roughly. The man blinked then followed close behind us. I saw the last of the sailors from *Nautilus* stride off to either side.

Then, there was a disturbance in the water behind us and a cloud of bubbles pushed at me, I turned to look and I saw that *Nautilus* was now lifting herself slowly and gracefully from the seabed. I tapped Churchill's shoulder and he swivelled around to look with me. Cavendish walked along unsteadily a short way then, noticing we were not with him, turned and staggered back.

'What is he going to do?' I wondered aloud.

'I have an idea,' said Churchill, but said no more.

By now the Martians and their machines were at the vessel and some of the creatures sprang lightly at the hull, clamping on to the metal like limpets. One or two of the Remote Walkers fired off missiles that exploded at the behemoths skin. There appeared to be little, if any, damage.

A few Martians grasped and hung on to the ship as it lifted then began to move toward the cylinder.

One of the things groped with its tentacles at an airlock door but a sailor turned from behind me and loosed off a harpoon. The Martians tentacles splayed out around its body as if in surprise as it was hit. It pirouetted away as it was caught and buffeted by the submersibles gathering wake.

Nautilus slowly turned her great head straight toward the cylinder and the water ahead of her rippled. The Captain must have used the sound weapon.

'Take that!' I heard in my ears. The Captain must have left the radio channel open!

'Captain!' I shouted. 'If you can hear me, please, stop this madness! I know we must destroy the cylinder but you need us! We can help you!'

There was silence for a moment apart from the hissing of my breathing apparatus.

'This is something I must do alone,' the Captain said finally.

I turned to look at Cavendish. His small eyes were red and his mouth flapped with frustration.

So, the sound weapon had been unleashed. Yet, the cylinder still stood.

Nautilus fired off more weapons, great missiles that resembled enormous black sharks. They exited tubes at the nose of our former home and travelled at an amazing speed toward the Martian cylinder.

As they approached, the Remote Walkers fired at them but all missed.

We watched with baited breath for the explosions. When they came, I let out a small whoop of delight. Perhaps now, our task had been completed and we could go home. A huge bubble obscured the view for a moment then I saw, to my dismay, that the base had barely been scratched. The Martians gathered nearby it that hadn't been obliterated in the explosions, danced crazily around on the tips of their tentacles.

'Blast it!' the Captain's angry voice rang around my head.

'You have to come back and pick us up,' I said into my device. 'We can regroup and–'

'No!' the Captain howled. 'It ends now! They want their damn vessel back, they shall have it!'

Cavendish's eyes widened at this and Churchill looked grimmer than ever before as her engines were pushed into full power.

Nautilus hung for a moment in the dark water then there was another cloud of furious bubbles from behind her.

'We have to get as far away as we can!' Churchill shouted. I caught his meaning now and knew what the Captain intended to do. We began to run as fast as we could against the water.

Nautilus sped forward. Martians and wreckage alike in her path were knocked spinning out of the way. Nearer and nearer to the cylinder she went, faster and faster.

I saw Martians near the huge Martian machine scatter, panicking, as they understood what was happening. Again, a few Remote Walkers fired their weapons uselessly at the vessel.

We reached a rocky part of the seabed and crouched down behind it. I peered over the top just as the huge speeding bulk of *Nautilus* rammed the cylinder squarely on its side. A short, mad laugh from the Captain rang around the inside of my helmet but was abruptly cut off as *Nautilus* exploded.

CHAPTER 36
Fish Out of Water

Nautilus' death throes turned our world upside down.

She was travelling at such a tremendous speed at impact that her collision with the cylinder must have crumpled her hull like paper. Again much of what happened next was obscured from our view from a great cloud of bubbles but I assume that something within her gave and exploded because there was a bright light and the water was agitated into a frenzy of bubbles and debris.

A great force moved outward from the impact area and we were knocked completely off our feet. On our backs, we were buffeted around, involuntarily waving our limbs as if in imitation of so many upturned crabs. Some sailors nearer to the site of the explosion were blown clear away from it, helpless in the raging water. The cries of the disorientated men rang around my helmet.

I tried to right myself as other, smaller, explosions rocked the great vessel all along its length. Pieces of metal flew in all directions as *Nautilus* tore herself apart.

Gradually, the explosions stopped and grew lesser in vehemence and what was left of the wounded submersible sank slowly to the seabed. I struggled to see what had occurred at the impact point but, for a while, my view was obscured by tumbling wreckage and air bubbles. I stood up, with some effort, and found that Churchill had made his way to my side.

'My God,' I said breathlessly. 'Why did he do that?'

'I cannot say,' the Lieutenant replied. 'Let us hope it was not in vain.'

The water near the cylinder finally cleared and I could see the result of the Captain's sacrifice. A great rent had appeared in the side of the cylinder and air poured out of it in many places. I could see a few stunned Martians staggering around nearby and a Remote Walker stalked jerkily around, headless.

'Look!' I exclaimed. 'I do believe it worked!'

'Indeed,' Churchill nodded grimly.

A quiet sobbing sounded in my ears and I looked around for the source. Nearby, Cavendish sat rocking slowly. On getting closer to him, I saw that tears streaked his chubby cheeks. On our approach, he looked up like a sad puppy.

'Nautilus is gone,' he quietly uttered.

'But the cylinder is damaged badly,' I answered offering the man a hand. He grabbed at it and pulled himself up.

'We can build another, can't we?' Cavendish said hopefully, like a child that has had its favourite toy broken by some mishap. 'Another Nautilus?'

'Yes. Yes we can,' I said in as comforting manner as I could, although I still felt less than charitable to him. What concerned me was that we make good our escape in case there were further Martians lurking somewhere and, if we had to take this man with us, it should be sooner rather than later.

Churchill spoke up.

'We must leave here. There are Martians around and they are still dangerous.'

'Yes,' I agreed. 'Can you walk, Cavendish?'

'I can,' the Knight asserted, brightening a little. With some obvious effort, he made to put on his old demeanour and he soon appeared to be as the old Cavendish we knew. A slight twitch in his eye gave away the fact that all was still not well with this man. Then he gasped, remembering something, and looked quickly around.

'The egg!' he shouted. 'Where is the egg?'

The box in which the egg rested was nearby, laying on its side on a rock. We walked forward to fetch it.

Cavendish picked up his prize and beamed happily. I made to join him but was brought up short by a sudden, intense pain in my head.

My head felt as if it was being ripped open and I let out an involuntary whimper. I felt probing in my head again, just like I had several times before and pictures came to me. I saw the scene inside the cylinder, water flooding in, dead Martians lay around here and there and smoke was pouring from damaged machinery. Then, another scene came. Martians were taking up weapons in another area that appeared not to be damaged. Human beings stood cowed in some sort of holding area. Where was this? Was it an undamaged part of the cylinder, perhaps? The probing abruptly stopped.

Churchill was staring at me with concern.

'What is it?' he asked.

'The Martians were–' I did not finished the sentence as my eyes had now cleared and I saw the scene before me.

Cavendish stood near the rock, oblivious and clutching his box. Behind him stood a small troop of Martians, weapons raised.

'Cavendish, behind you!' I shouted.

The Knight spun around in panic and groaned.

'Don't make any sudden moves,' Churchill warned in a low voice.

Cavendish dropped his box and raised his hands. Churchill and I slowly raised our hands too. I wondered vaguely if the Martians would understand, or even acknowledge, this human sign of surrender.

The Martians moved forward menacingly.

CHAPTER 37
Out of the Frying Pan …

Having come so far and seen so much, it seemed to me a measure of the way fate had twisted and turned since the war that we were now prisoners of the very creatures we had set out, with such determination and hope, to destroy once and for all.

Behind us, the wreckage of the great and immensely powerful *Nautilus* lay wreathed in a dark cloud of bubbles and her innards lay scattered around her. Beyond that huge, dead bulk sat the ruptured cylinder, its life-blood also pouring out of it and rising swiftly to the surface far above us.

The fact that the Martian base of operations had seemingly been damaged beyond repair appeared not to deter our captors in the slightest. They made it plain, by pointing with their tentacles, that we were to go with them, to where I did not know.

We did not move for a moment. Cavendish stood, his mouth flapping in that way he adopted when things were beyond him and Churchill threw grim glances my way.

Again I felt a probing in my head. There were no pictures this time, just a sort of vague pulling at my mind. The pulling grew stronger and stronger and my head was suddenly pierced by red agony. Through near blinded eyes, I dimly saw the Martians regarding me curiously.

The pain stopped again, as rapidly as it had started, and one of the creatures emphatically resumed its pointing.

'They wish us to follow,' I said, gasping, to Churchill.

'That much I had gathered,' the Lieutenant answered dryly. 'Perhaps we are lucky they do not shoot us where we stand.'

'Perhaps not,' I said, knowing full well what fate met prisoners of the Martians.

One of the Martians moved toward Cavendish's prized egg box and Cavendish, with startling speed for a man of his size and especially one encumbered in a heavy suit and underwater, darted for the box at the same time. The Martian made it first and snatched it up triumphantly, and, at the same time, waved its weapon meaningfully at the man as if to berate him for his stupidity. Cavendish stopped short violently and stood still again, gnashing his teeth and glaring at the creature.

'It's mine,' he mumbled.

'Cavendish,' I said as calmly and quietly as I could. The man continued to stare balefully at the Martian and did not acknowledge my presence.

'Cavendish!' I repeated more harshly. The man looked slowly around, his eyes burned like fire.

'We must go with them, we have no choice.'

Cavendish's anger visibly subsided and we slowly began to move in the direction that had been indicated to us.

The landscape beneath the sea is not much understood by humanity. Perhaps, in some distant time, mankind will make its home underwater and enjoy the riches that lie under the waves. In the future, perhaps, great vessels not unlike *Nautilus* will prowl the depths and travelling through what is now largely unknown will become as commonplace as a walk in the countryside.

As it was, weighed down by the water in my heavy suit and being fed rubber-tinged air, I felt that we might as well have been on some distant planet rather than our own Mother Earth. This illusion was heightened by the dim darkness, the fish that darted here and there before us and by our monstrous captors who skipped along on their tentacles beside us as we walked.

The exertion of walking through the water soon began to tire me and my breaths came shorter and more laboured. The suit, despite the cool water temperature, made me feel progressively more hot and uncomfortable and the feeling of claustrophobia became near unbearable. The unceasing hissing of the breathing mechanism was like some torturous, diabolic sound specifically designed to drive one mad. Periodically, I had to fight illogical urges to tear my suit off and try to swim for the surface. Churchill marched purposefully along beside me but Cavendish fell behind from time to time. When he lagged behind too much, a Martian would prod him sharply with a weapon and the man would try to pick up the pace but the strain was obviously more for him in his condition than it was for me. I felt some pity for him then, despite what I knew of him.

On through this alien landscape we travelled. Here and there Martians skipped about carrying pieces of wreckage or at other tasks.

I wondered why they did not appear disenchanted at the destruction of the cylinder. It seemed to make not the slightest difference to their sense of purpose and they carried on as if all was well with them. What a hardy race they must be, I thought, they are beaten time and again and yet they continue as if their time as rulers of our world was imminent. I did not find this of any comfort in my predicament.

To my dismay, I soon found out the reason for their confidence.

After what seemed like hours of walking, but could only have been minutes, we came across a tall rocky outcrop. More Martians were gathered here bearing weapons, along with a few Remote Walkers, and, after some tenticular gestures between the two Martian parties, we were allowed to pass.

What I saw next made my blood run cold.

As we passed the rocks we came upon a huge construction. Dark, black and squat.

Like a huge spider, the thing crouched there. Martians and machines swarmed around this strange new thing.

We had destroyed the cylinder, but we had made a terrible mistake.

The real Martian base was very much intact.

CHAPTER 38
... Into the Fire

I am not ashamed to say that this latest horrible revelation nearly made me faint dead away. I thrust out a gloved hand and steadied myself on a nearby rocky outcrop.

All our efforts had been for naught and the greatest weapon we had, the submersible *Nautilus,* in which so much hope had rested, lay, a shattered ruin, on the seabed.

We had expended men and machines in our quest to destroy the Martians and, all along, they had sat smug and secure in this new monstrous edifice. Perhaps they had watched with what passed for them as amusement whilst many of our men died trying to destroy what was essentially an empty shell. I imagine that they hooted with glee as *Nautilus* was rammed into that shell whilst they viewed events from a safe distance.

I made a solemn oath to myself then that, if my fate was to die here, I would do anything I could before I met my maker to take at least some of those interlopers on our planet with me.

Shaking the cobwebs from my mind, I eyed one of the Martian weapons greedily but one soft word; 'No', crackling in my ears made me glance up.

Churchill was shaking his head slowly. The Lieutenant was, I realised, an amazing judge of his fellow man. He had seen the look on my face and immediately understood my intention. I could imagine him having a stellar career in politics under different circumstances.

I still lusted for revenge against the Martians, but something in Churchill's steady gaze made me see sense.

For now, I promised myself, I would go meekly with our captors but should chance smile upon me and an opportunity arise, I would seize it and do as much damage as I could.

So, what of this new horror?

As our party were escorted closer to this thing by our triumphant captors, I saw that it was indeed spider-like in general shape. Thick legs splayed out from around the distended black body of the machine. Green lights ringed the body and ran down the length of the legs. At what I took to be the front, a great green window could be seen.

To say the machine was big does not, by any amount, give it full justice. I imagined many hundreds of Martians could be housed quite comfortably within it. I hoped that there were not many hundreds of the monsters to crew it. I did not know, then, if this machine could actually move like its much smaller cousins, but it looked as if the legs could be mobilised. Great joints were visible and huge cables hung here and there. The legs themselves appeared to be much larger and sturdier versions of those on the Fighting Machines.

Movement for this thing would make sense, though and again I cursed these creatures for their ingenuity. A mobile base would make a formidable weapon indeed.

Soon we were underneath the machine and I wondered how we were to be transported into it. As we stood, a long tube extended out from a point underneath its huge belly and thrust down at speed into the sand. The Martians gestured that we were to go into this tube and we entered through a portal in one side. The tube seemed to be made of glass of some kind, or perhaps some other transparent material and I reached forward curiously and my glove touched the surface.

Small blue sparks danced around my glove and I recoiled immediately, although I felt nothing. I looked curiously at my hand as if it were alien to me. Cavendish stood nearby, looking up and around himself as well as his helmet would allow, his jaw open in wonder.

'My God!' he breathed.

When we were all gathered together, there was a sudden vague feeling of movement and I saw that the floor we stood upon was rising up the inside of the tube. I looked out through the clear walls and saw the ground seem to fall away. Feeling rather giddy, I set my eyes upwards and watched the bottom of the machine coming to meet us.

The journey took a very little time and, just as it seemed that we would be dashed against the metal above, a door slid aside, our platform moved past it and we came smoothly to a halt.

The inside of the machine was more impressive still than the outside.

We were ushered out of the tube by the accompanying Martians and into a large round room that I sensed was the very hub of this construction. Smooth walls lit with that eerie green glow surrounded us but set in at different points of them were doors leading to other areas.

Martians scurried here around and machines, not unlike Remote Walkers but with grappling arms and other unknown instruments attached, carried containers and machinery here and there.

A Martian, tapping me with a tentacle, distracted me from my observations. I looked at it sharply.

The creature gestured at my head. I did not understand its meaning and simply glared at it.

'Your helmet, Smith,' Churchill said. 'You can take it off. We are no longer in water.'

Of course. I had been so in awe of my situation that I had not noticed that we had come into a space full of air. I wondered how the water had been pumped out of the tube along the way but could not fathom it.

I saw that the Lieutenant was already starting to unfasten his helmet, so I fumbled at the clasps at my neck. Cavendish looked on as if we were quite mad.

'Come on, Cavendish,' I assured him. 'It's no trick.'

He stared a while longer then tentatively raised a glove toward his helmet. I started forward to help him but he waved me away.

I finished unfastening my own headgear and, lifting it off, took deep, gulping breaths of clean air, untainted by that interminable rubber smell, until my head began to spin.

The Martians gestured at us and we were on the move once more. Down many corridors we walked, goaded and prodded by our monstrous guards, until we reached another large room. I felt sure that I could not traverse these corridors alone as they all looked very much the same. I was reminded of the underground laboratories in London by this fact.

There were many doors set in the walls here, one was opened and we were prodded again until we entered.

In this room sat, by my count, twenty humans. All were soldiers and sailors from *Nautilus*. A few of them recognised us and glum faces brightened a little at seeing more familiar faces.

The door to the prison cell slid quietly closed behind us.

CHAPTER 39
Imprisoned

Our prison consisted of bare walls lined with benches that jutted out from them. Further inspection revealed that these benches were not so much attached to the walls but actually seemed to be part of them. I could perceive no visible joins and no means of support. It was if the whole room had been moulded, benches and all, at the same time and in one piece.

Sitting on one, I found that it actually seemed to give somewhat and mould itself to my shape. It was very comfortable but the feeling was strange. Where it touched my body, I felt warmth as if the thing was gently heated.

With the guards gone, one or two of the men already here began to question us about events outside. It seemed they had been taken prisoner early on in the battle in the sea and knew nothing of the demise of *Nautilus*. Their faces, eager for news, dropped at this revelation and several muttered that we were finished. A general feeling of gloom now hung over the assemblage.

It transpired, also, that the men in this room were not the only ones taken prisoner by the Martians. I was told that the other cells were also in this holding area and were served by the other doors I had seen outside.

The men told us, in hushed tones, of the fact that there had been others placed in this cell but some had been taken away, one by one, and had never returned. The reason for this was unknown, but I guessed that we would never see these poor souls again.

Churchill listened carefully to these conversations and asked questions here and there. Cavendish sat silently on a bench, eyes downcast and hands clasped in his lap. He showed no signs of registering anything he heard.

After a few hours, a buzzer sounded and the cell door slid open to allow entrance to a Martian pushing before it a long flat platform. This strange cart had no wheels, for, as my friend Wells has intimated in his novel based on my Wartime experiences, the Martians had not invented this most simple, to man at least, of innovations. The wheel, in fact, was as alien to them as their technology was to us. Instead, the trolley appeared to float a few inches above the floor and slid smoothly along when pushed. On the top surface of this contraption were large pans loaded with some sort of steaming, thick pink gruel that the attending Martian scooped, with a ladle, into metallic looking bowls. This food, for that was obviously what it was, was handed unceremoniously to all present in the cell. This task completed, the cell door slid open again and the Martian left, hooting softly.

I have found out since, on the investigations of our scientists, that this gruel we were fed seems to have been made from the dreaded red weed that covers the surface of Mars and very nearly covered our own. The Martians did not deem it suitable for themselves, it would appear, as blood met their needs better, but perhaps they had developed it, back on Mars, in experimentation on their own bipeds that they themselves used as food. It appears that the bipeds have a similar physiology to us, in many ways, and this gruel was found to cover our nutritional needs as well as theirs.

I sniffed at it carefully but could detect no smell. The others in the room, asides from Churchill, Cavendish and myself, had begun to take the food into their mouths greedily with a kind of thick metal tube that was attached to the side of the bowls and one of the men bid us follow his actions.

'Once you get used to the taste, it's really all right,' a soldier said. 'It fills you as good as a Sunday roast and you don't feel peckish until the next mealtime.'

I slowly took hold of the tube at the side of my bowl and pulled. It appeared to be stuck there by magnetism and came away easily. I pushed one end of the tube onto the unappealing looking slop in the bowl, gingerly put my mouth to the tube and sucked gently. Some of the gruel, after some suction had been applied, entered my mouth and slid slimily onto my tongue. I took the mouth away from the straw. The gruel had an odd bittersweet taste and I resisted the impulse to spit it out there and then. I swallowed.

After a few more mouthfuls, I grew accustomed to the taste and ate, or perhaps I should say drank, all that was in the bowl. My belly felt full and I lay back on my bench.

The rigors of the day and a full belly took their toll and I fell quickly asleep.

I awoke later, I know not how long had passed, disorientated and feeling vaguely nauseous.

Cavendish, I saw, was curled up silent and unmoving, like an overgrown child, on a bench with his back to us. I could not tell if he was asleep or not. A barely touched bowl of gruel lay discarded, upside down, on the floor beside him.

Churchill was speaking in low tones to a Corporal in a corner and they joined me as I sat up. Churchill informed me that, whilst I slept, another sailor had been taken away by the Martians. I had not stirred, it seemed, through all his imprecations, pleas and final calls for help that had punctuated his rough exit from the room. I thought then that perhaps the gruel was drugged in order to keep us captives docile. I certainly felt light headed and the slight nausea took some time to fade.

There was a plan being formulated, I was next told. Almost at a whisper, Churchill postulated that we could perhaps attempt an escape when the next meal was brought to us. It had been agreed, generally, that this was better than sitting here in this cell waiting for our turn to be taken away like the others. Churchill had somehow stirred within these men an arousal from the general feeling of inevitability of their fate. I hoped sincerely that the Martians did not have listening devices planted in the cell sophisticated enough to hear of this plan but agreed immediately that an attempt to escape may be our only hope.

The plan was simple, as sometimes the best plans are. When the door opened, several men would wait either side and attack the Martian as it entered. As there was no sign of any other Martians with it on previous visits, the men would grab its weapon and kill it quickly to stop it raising the alarm. Then we would attempt to fight our way out, hopefully gaining more weapons along the way. It was a desperate plan, to be sure, but better than sitting and waiting to be dragged away for God alone knew what foul purpose.

The plan settled, as best as it could be, we all returned to our benches and waited.

Later, Cavendish sat up blinking.

'Are you alright?' I asked.

'Yes fine,' he replied levelly, flashing an unconvincing smile at me. He got up and walked toward the door.

'Where are you going?' I asked, but Cavendish did not reply.

Reaching the door, the Knight of the Realm began knocking on the smooth door with all his might.

'I demand to be let out!' he screamed, suddenly red faced.

'Cavendish, no!' Churchill shouted.

'I am a representative of His Majesty's Government and demand that I am set free!' Cavendish continued, then fell silent and stared purposefully at the door before him.

After a few moments, the door slid open and a Martian appeared clutching a weapon. It waved the gun outwards and Cavendish moved forwards. The door slid shut again behind him.

'What the hell does he think he's doing?' a sailor asked. 'They'll kill him for sure!'

I could do no more than shake my head sadly.

CHAPTER 40
The Great Escape

Cavendish's departure and almost certain death did nothing to lighten the atmosphere in the cell.

Some of the men sat around in small groups muttering and cursing under their breath. Others tossed and turned fitfully on their benches.

A general air of hopelessness had settled over the group and I sat staring at the unmoving door.

Churchill tried to rally the men, moving around the cell readying the men for the attempt to escape that was planned. He gave me a reassuring smile and told me that this action gave us hope. Surely it was better, should the plan fail, to go down fighting rather than be slaughtered alone like an animal, he reasoned.

I had enough hatred left in my heart for the Martians for these words to inspire me and I nodded.

The wait drew on.

Later, the buzzer sounded and some men jumped from their bunks and stationed themselves rapidly on either side of the door, tensed like coiled springs. The rest of us sat, trying to look as despondent and cowed as possible, spread around the room in an attempt to allay any suspicions at the reduced numbers the Martian entering may have.

The platform laden with steaming pans appeared and we waited with baited breath. The attendant Martian entered and its saucer eyes widened in surprise as it was grabbed, none too gently, by the men at the door and it squealed as it was shoved bodily into the room.

The pans flew off the floating trolley as it was pushed aside and hit the wall with a crash. A small tide of pink steaming gruel spread over the floor.

The Martian dropped its weapon as it tried to right itself but went after it with lightning speed. Men followed and grabbed at its tentacles and pulled.

A furious battle ensued.

The Martian was immensely strong, like all its kind, and shook a man off with ease. The man careered backwards and hit his head, with a sickening crack, on the trolley. He collapsed like a rag-doll into the pool of gruel on the floor. A small puddle of blood spread out from his head and mingled with the pink mess that surrounded him.

Two other men pulled, with all their might and in opposite directions, at the creature's tentacles. The Martian squeaked in pain. One of the men pulling slipped in the spreading food on the floor and fell over on his back losing his grip on the Martian. The Martian snatched its limb back and used it to flick a sailor deftly away from the weapon that lay nearby.

I, suddenly filled with some kind of primal rage as I have never before or since felt, grabbed the ladle, that was to be used to dispense the food, from the floor and rushed at the Martian bellowing and brandishing the tool above my head with both hands. The Martian looked around and hooted with surprise but I was already upon it. I, without thinking, thrust the handle of the ladle, with all the force I could muster, deep into one of the creature's great black eyes. I fell to the floor, gasping.

Dark liquid jetted in a stream out from the Martian's damaged organ and it squealed sharply again. In its agony, the thing thrashed around wildly flinging the men grappling with it away.

Picking themselves up, the other men made to attack the creature again but Churchill shouted a quick command to cease. He carefully skirted the agonised monster and picked up the weapon, training it on the thing's head.

It seemed that my aim had been true and the Martian was mortally wounded, for soon its frantic movement slowed and it fell to the floor with a wet thump.

Its one intact eye glared at me accusingly, its tentacles waved and slapped around feebly, and, after a great shiver ran through its body, it lay still.

'Right men,' Churchill said, nodding with approval at me. 'Are we ready?'

The men, as one, answered to the affirmative.

The door was still open and, as a group we made for it with Churchill at the lead brandishing the Martian weapon.

As we got outside we stopped dead.

A large group of Martians stood in a tight semi-circle, pointing weapons at us.

This was not the only shock we had in store.

'You should not have done that, you know,' a familiar voice said from behind the group of Martians. 'I had to tell them you might try something like that.'

I gaped at an equally shocked Churchill. The Lieutenant's expression slowly turned to barely suppressed rage at this latest development.

We had been betrayed by one of our own kind.

Cavendish stood, grinning, very much alive and if he were back in charge of things.

CHAPTER 41
Treachery

All I could do was gape disbelievingly at the beaming Cavendish.

I had seen that he was capable of much deviousness and had seemed, of late at least, only to have his own interests at heart, despite his grand protestations that what he did was for the good of England. This new act was too much to take.

Anger surged up within me like a hot river of bitter bile.

'You dog!' I spat. 'You have betrayed your fellow men and for what?'

I moved toward Cavendish fists raised and hot faced but Churchill, despite his own obvious anger, leaped forward and held me back. I struggled against the unyielding Lieutenant's hold on me for a moment but eventually sagged and consoled myself with staring white hot daggers at the man, the many Martian weapons pointed at my head deciding the matter.

'Why?' was all I could manage to utter.

'You would not understand, Smith,' the Knight replied from within the safety of his newly recruited bodyguard. 'There are bigger things afoot here than anyone knows. Even I am just a pawn in a greater game, albeit a more well placed one.'

'You fool!' Churchill hissed. 'Do you really imagine that your new friends will think more highly off you because you have the ear of the Government? I'll wager that all the Martians see in you is a bigger meal!'

Cavendish's grin fell at this and his plump cheeks reddened several shades darker than was normal.

'I will not waste time bandying words with a mere Lieutenant,' he said disdainfully. He turned to me and struggled to affect a reasonable tone.

'Smith, you must see! You are a reasonable man! This is the best solution for us all. We must make peace with the Martians and I am the man to initiate such a historic peace. The British Empire will prosper as a result and we will be the survivors when the next invasion begins. Make no mistake, the Martians will return and in greater numbers. I can help you; join me in this effort I undertake for the good of our world '

'I will not be a mere pet of those things,' I answered as levelly as I could, staring straight into his beady eyes. 'I would rather die than assist you in this monstrous plan.'

Cavendish eyed me for a moment as if waiting for me to change my mind, then, seeing that my resolution was unbowed, he shrugged.

'You may come to regret those words,' he said, shaking his head sadly, and stalked away down a corridor flanked by two of the Martians. One of the creatures left facing us motioned for our unhappy group to return to the cell. Angry, but with no choice in the matter, we went back in.

So, our imprisonment continued but for how long I cannot say.

Churchill seemed to think we were in the cell for only two days, for me it felt no less than a week.

The feeding of the pink gruel continued but the Martians came to dispense it, in force now, emphatically waving weapons at us at the slightest movement from one of our group.

More men were taken away, as time passed, until our group in this cell numbered only ten.

Sometimes we shuddered as we heard the desperate struggles of those being removed as they fought for their lives, in vain I think, outside.

We did not see Cavendish again.

I tried to imagine how someone could do what this man had done, betrayed his own kind so that he could prosper. I was not fool enough to imagine that some humans were not capable of the most heinous act. I knew that many horrendous acts of barbarism by man against fellow man had been perpetrated, over the course of our race's history, in the name of greed, religion; or even both. Sometimes such acts were perpetrated purely for the enjoyment of it. Still I could not fathom the justification of the handing of all of humanity on a platter to a race of monsters for any reason. Such treachery was unheard of in the history of mankind. Did he imagine that he would become a Prince among men at the behest of those awful, heartless beings from so far away? King of the World, perhaps? Did he dream of sitting on some gilded throne, casually ordering the slavery or deaths of millions? What kind of Brave New World was this he envisaged?

In the quiet of what I took to be night, the time when all others in the cell were sleeping fitfully, I mourned for all mankind.

Sounds of a scuffle outside the cell awoke me from a restless dozing. At first, I thought it was just the sound of the Martians gathering outside and readying themselves to bring us our dreary rations. Then there was the unmistakable sound of gunshots, a muted explosion, and a bloodcurdling shriek, like that of a wounded animal. A, very much human, cheer followed this awful sound.

The door alarm buzzed.

The other men in the cell and I sat up. Now what was happening?

The door opened to reveal a familiar face.

'Hullo, mates!' the Sergeant said brightly, grinning from ear to ear.

CHAPTER 42
The Sergeant's Tale (i)

In our predicament and in my dismay, I had completely forgotten about my friend, the Sergeant and his brave commandos.

If I had, in my much-strained state, found the time to ponder his whereabouts, I should have thought him lost in the battle outside the cylinder with so many of his comrades. Or perhaps, I might have, with a glimmer of hope, considered him a prisoner somewhere else in this monstrous new base that we were currently captive within. Either way, the outlook for him would not, I am sure I would have imagined, been good. Perhaps as bad, if not worse in that cold unknown outside, as ours seemed to be in fact.

I did not find out the full story of what fate had had in store for my friend up to this latest meeting until much later. The Sergeant visited me at my home for what he called a 'jolly reunion of old chums'. Wells came, at my invitation, to this meeting as well; he could not resist meeting the man whose character he had written of in his own version of my experiences. The Sergeant and my literary friend were, to my surprise I admit, as old friends from the off. The Sergeant, though not being much of a bookish man had, however, read Wells' account of my story and had evidently not taken the least offence at his depiction within it.

We three sat by the fire, after a marvellous dinner prepared by my wife, sipping champagne, of course, and toasting old comrades.

It is then that I asked the Sergeant about events before he came to free us.

I made copious notes as he recounted his tale, as I knew I was to begin this work my esteemed reader now holds and I felt that his story may make an interesting addition to it. Wells sat quietly as the Sergeant spoke, but his eyes twinkled and his face bore a faint smile throughout, as if in appreciation of a story well told.

I feel that now is, at this point in my work, as good a place as any to recount the Sergeant's adventures in his own words.

'Well, my friends.' The soldier said settling back into his leather armchair and sucking on a fat cigar with relish. 'Where to start? I can't say I really had much in the way of schoolin' but I guess Smith at least knows I can tell a yarn and that is what I'll have to do.'

'Please,' I prompted. 'Just tell us what happened, no more, no less.'

'Well then, this is how it was.'

'We left Nautilus ready to fight and full of get up and go. Vim and vigour, even, my boys were straining at the leash to get back at the Martians and I didn't intend to hold 'em back, I can tell you.

We hadn't gotten far when all merry hell broke loose. The Martian buggers were everywhere and we saw that they had engaged our comrades near the cylinder.

Never in battle have I seen so much chaos and I doubt I will see its like again in my lifetime. It wasn't helped, I know, by our being underwater and those blessed suits we were forced to wear out there. It was like being in an oven after a little effort and breathing was tough. My boys bore it like the troopers they were, though, and I decided we should make a run for it around the side of the scuffle. If you remember, our mission was to blow the cylinder to blazes and, even though we hated to leave mates in peril, we didn't intend to be cut down before we could do it.

So, off we went as fast as we could, dodging and diving, watching out for Martians all the way.

It's funny, men were dyin' out there but one thing sticks in my mind. You know Glenn, quite the wag he is. Well, he started humming 'My old man said follow the van'. You must know it, that Music Hall ditty that everyone likes to sing along to.

Anyway, I thought, for a bit at least, it was quite the song for the occasion and some of the boys started to whistle or sing along with it. Quite what came over us I can't rightly say. I'm sure if Wayne had his accordion with him we could have led the Martians, should we have met any there, in a right merry dance. A soldier's humour can be rough, as I'm sure you know, but the life can be much rougher and we find that the fun we make for ourselves helps keep some of the demons away, if you get my meaning. Some might accuse us of 'gallows humour', but we sees things in our work that a bloke ought not to and we have to lighten the load somehow or we should all end up in Bedlam being laughed at by the Toffs for a few pence.

Anyway, I soon thought better of it and told them best be quiet, as we didn't want to draw attention to ourselves if the Martians could listen in on us. Besides, even to us, it didn't seem right singin' what with what was goin' on out there and all.

We went around behind some rocks and watched the battle for a while and looking for a good route to our objective. One or two of the men wanted to take pot-shots at the enemy, to help our mates out, but I told them to hold fire in case we got spotted.

Then I heard the order to withdraw on my radio device and saw the men out on the battlefield try to get back to Nautilus. The poor blighters couldn't go anywhere as, by this time, the creatures were all around them. But they fought bravely to man, to that I can testify.

I saw the Martians round the survivors up like sheep and start to move them away.

Jameson was all for rushing out there and trying to rescue them for all the good it would do and he made no bones about it. Even though he knew, deep down, that the sensible thing to do was just what we were doing. We had to get to the cylinder and do our job. To try and help our comrades would have been nothing less than suicide and every man jack with me knew that. But a soldier's instincts are strong, my friends. We never leave a man behind unless there is no other choice. In this case there was none and we could do no more than sit and grit our teeth.

Then, just as we were about to move off to see what could be done, we were amazed to see Nautilus start to up and move. She sat there in the water for a bit, then moved quicker and quicker and slammed – Bam! – right into the cylinder. We ducked down behind our rocks as she blew to smithereens. We didn't know what to think. What was goin' on?

When things had calmed down a bit, we looked up and saw that the cylinder had a huge hole in it and we cheered and clapped each other, hard work underwater, on the backs. It looked like we wouldn't need to do our work after all.

Then Glenn said "Sarge?"

I looked around and saw a grim look on his face. He pointed slowly behind us.

One of the Remote Walkers, as that cur Cavendish –
oh yes, I knew all about him and his new friends – called
them, was just stood there behind us. Just lookin' at us with
them strange metal eyes they have.

I figured then that we were sunk.'

CHAPTER 43
The Sergeant's Tale (ii)

My friend stopped telling his story for a moment. For effect, I have no doubt. As I have intimated before, the Sergeant was the sort who never tired of telling of his exploits, much, I found, to the delight of any audience he spoke before. I did not wonder that his orating skills led to many a free drink in the Hostelries he frequented. Wells and I waited for him to resume his tale whilst he grinned at us.

The soldier casually waved his empty glass at me and I took the hint, pouring him more champagne. He swallowed some of the effervescent, pale yellow liquid and smacked his lips with relish. Then, eyes bright, he took a puff of his cigar and continued on with his story.

'Well now, I'm sure you wonder how we got out of that pretty pickle. I can say it was by sheer luck and I don't mind admitting that. Sometimes even the best soldier can be scuppered by an 'appenin' and it was all I could do but stare at the machine, for a moment, as it carried on eyeing us up.

I was surprised, you can bet, when Dawson walked out from behind a rock just past the thing. Where he had been, I don't know, as I thought he was with us, but he stopped short and backed off a bit. The thing didn't know he was there but just stared some more at us.

I managed to catch Dawson's eye and tried to give him the idea he was to be ready. The soldier's mind is always at work, friends, and I hoped that Dawson would catch my drift. I saw him begin to creep towards the thing as quiet as a mouse would. I stepped forward a bit with my hands raised and motioned for the others with me to do the same. The thing jumped back a bit on those skinny legs they 'ave and I saw its weapon pop out from its head. We stopped dead and it started to move forward. Dawson took his chance and jumped on it, pushing against the water as hard as he could. There was a struggle, the thing was thrashing about with my mate Dawson clinging on for dear life. The machine let off a shot, then another. The first shot narrowly missed Dawson, the other hit a rock, blowing it to tiny pieces. Some pieces of rock rattled off the helmet of my suit.

We jumped forward as one, I got my weapon and started beating the thing with the butt and the others copied me. We barely dented it.

Glenn grabbed a leg and pulled with all his might. The thing started to topple, all unbalanced already with the weight on its back. Dawson jumped clear before the thing hit the ground and we set to it, kicking and beatin' it with our weapons.

Then, I spied a sort of door in the back of its head and I started to beat at it with my gun. It wasn't easy, what with the thing wrigglin' around and all.

The panel flew off after a bit of work and my weapon butt went straight into the thing's head. Well, here was another surprise!

Some liquid came out of the head and the thing stopped wrigglin' just like that! It just lay there like some curious dead chicken in the butcher's shop.

"What the-?" Glenn said.

"It doesn't matter now," I told him. "The thing is dead. We must be off, lads, before some of its mates come lookin' for it."

We went off into the rocks as quickly as we could.

We found what looked like a quiet spot and took stock. Our mission couldn't be carried out and our way home was in a million pieces all over the seabed. So, what to do?

Then a thought marched into me head. The Martians had prisoners, lots of our mates that they were taking away. But where were they taking them to? The cylinder had been blown to smithereens, so where then?

"Here's a plan, boys," I said. "What say you for a spot of reconnaissance?"

"What do you mean, Sarge?" Glenn asked.

"Let's follow the blighters and see where they are taking our mates. Their cylinder is a mess so I don't think they'll be going there. So I say we find out if we can lend our pals a helpin' hand, eh?"

The lads all agreed in a wink so it was settled. We moved off in what we hoped was the right direction.

It didn't take long before we saw the last stragglers ahead of us. We rounded another set of rocks and watched as the Martians pushed the soldier and sailor prisoners onwards. We were going away from the cylinder now and we wondered just what was goin' on. We soon found out, all right!

We hung back a bit as we saw the massive machine the Martians had built as their new base. We watched the prisoners being herded into that weird tube and get sucked up into the belly of that horrible new thing. It was an uncanny sight; it looked like the men were floatin' up into the air, or should I say water, from where we crouched.

The base, as you know, looked like an oversized Handlin' Machine, as the boffins call 'em. After all the men had been taken aboard, we saw that the thing began movin'! Slowly, it went, its legs goin' up and down and carryin' the thing forward like some giant insect. I saw that there were little machines, no more than lights really, darting around it like crows flyin' around a dead animal. I didn't know if they had Martians in 'em or not but they moved at a fair clip and weaved about between the big things legs. It was a mesmerisin' sight.

The main body of the machine seemed to hardly move at all, so I suppose it had some sort of devices to keep it steady. Maybe it worked a bit like the suspension on a motor car, but that sort of thing leaves me baffled, as a rule, so I didn't take much notice of how it could have worked. I expect Cavendish's boffins would have had a field day. It would have been like Christmas for them!

The thing started to pick up speed a little and it was starting to get out of sight. It was time for us to do something! We needed a plan."

CHAPTER 44
The Sergeant's Tale (iii)

The Sergeant paused in his recollections once more. He waved his, empty, champagne glass meaningfully again with that usual mischievous twinkle in his eye. I sighed, as his seemingly unquenchable thirst meant I would have to leave the warmth of my drawing room (it was now November and the cold nights were drawing in) and venture down into the cold cellar for more 'essential' supplies.

As I passed the big leaded window in the hall I spied the moon, hanging pale and bloated in the clear, cloudless sky, amongst a glittering carpet of stars. I shuddered as I pondered the possibility that, on a distant red planet far away, somewhere amongst those friendly looking stars, monstrous beings may still be plotting another attempt to take our world from us.

When I had secured another bottle of champagne, I returned to the drawing room to find my two friends in deep and earnest conversation. All talk stopped at my approach, though, and my friends merely smiled at me as if nothing of importance had taken place. I did not, in the end, feel justified in asking the subject of their discussion, even though I felt sure that something had happened. I was not to find out the importance of that short exchange until years later, but that, perhaps, is for another time.

When all glasses had been refilled and fresh cigars lit, the Sergeant cleared his throat grandly and recommenced the story of how he had come to our rescue on the Martian base.

'Well, as I said before, we stood behind the rock watchin' the Martian base lumbering away from us. The only thing we could do was to follow it, so that's precisely what we did. Not much of a plan. I know, friends, but we were only five men and so we had to look for an opportunity. It moved quickly but we could move quickly too and we managed to keep close, but not so close as the little things flying around it could see us. Or so we hoped.

Wayne then told us the bad news. He only had an hour's air left in his tank. In all the excitement, we realised that none of us had checked the meters on our suits. The rest of us checked our supplies and found that we didn't have much more. That forced our hands a bit, as I'll bet you can imagine. We had two choices now,

We could get on board the base somehow or get to the surface and try and get more oxygen and maybe some friends to help us out.

We had a bit of a chat then and decided it would be easier to try and get on board the thing. Besides, all our mates were prisoners and we didn't think they could wait. It galled us to think of what could be happenin' to you all on board that thing, I can tell you.

Glenn, good, brave lad that he is, then suggested we just start firing at the thing in the hopes of enticing the tube down so we could get on board. Sometimes the most simple plans are the best, as any commander will tell you, so that's just what we did.

Nothing seemed to happen for a bit after the first volley of shots we fired so we loosed off more explosive harpoons at the belly of the thing. Then, the machine slowed and came to a halt.

We saw the elevatin' tube begin to come down. We could see there were about ten Martians in it and all we could do now was pray that we were quicker than them. As soon as the platform in the tube hit the seabed the Martians started to spill out and we picked them off through the door of the tube like rats in a barrel. Never have I seen a battle so short, one or two of the things were slippery and dodged about a bit, but my sharp-eyed boys took them down anyway. The last one managed to get a shot off which narrowly missed Thomas, but Glenn got him right through the glass in its helmet and it flopped over dead as a dodo.

We rushed onto the platform in the tube just before it started to go up again.

Now was the nervous part. We didn't know how much the things up there knew and whether there would be a welcoming party but by God we were going to have at them or die tryin'.

The trip up the tube seemed to take forever. We checked our weapons and smiled at each other even though we knew we could be marchin' straight into an awful death. But, if death was on the cards, a soldier's death it would be, gun in hand and with the smell of our enemy's blood in our nostrils. That was how fired up we now were.

The platform reached the top. Two Martians stood behind a console and one barely had time to squeak in surprise before I shot its eye out. The other didn't make a sound. We looked around quickly to see if there were any more but there weren't. I don't think I'll ever figure the Martian mind. Why there were not hundreds of the things waiting for us, I'll never know. Perhaps God was on our side after all.

We were in air now so we took of our helmets and stripped off our suits.

Now it was time to see what could be done.'

CHAPTER 45
The Sergeant's Tale (iv)

'So, there we were, well behind enemy lines and ready to fight,' the Sergeant continued. A log popped in the fire and we started a little in our comfortable chairs. The Sergeant stared into the crackling flames for a moment, then carried on with his tale.

'The entrance room was big and we saw that there were passageways leading off every which way. We didn't hang about for fear that we may lose any element of surprise we might have got. We picked the first passage we fancied and went off up it, weapons ready. A little group of Martians appeared out of a room and we engaged them. We were low on harpoons for our guns now and so we took great care with our aim. We still seemed to have surprise on or side and they all fell quickly, bar one that skittered off on like a scared rat. Thomas wanted to give chase but I stopped him. It was best, I thought, to stay together in this strange place. We couldn't afford, nor did we want, to lose a single man.

We knew now we didn't have much time. The thing that had ran off could warn its pals at any moment so we had to work quickly.

We picked up the weapons from the foes we had beaten, discarded our own, and set off again.

We started to search rooms along the way. Most were quiet and just contained machinery of one sort or another.

In another a Martian was feeding. I don't need to tell you what that means. It looked around just in time to get hit by the weapon I held. I was surprised to find that this was a weapon I hadn't seen before. No beam came from it – that I could see anyway. I pointed the gun, pulled the trigger and the Martian squeaked and exploded in a mess of green guts. There's another toy to give the boffins happy dreams, I'll warrant.

We checked quickly if the poor man the thing had been feedin' off could be helped but he was beyond even God's benevolent hand. Too much of his blood had been supped and he was pale and fading fast.

"Where is everybody else, mate?" I asked him as gently as I could.

"Down the next passageway. Big room with doors with red switches," he answered with no little effort.

"Thanks, mate. We'll come back for you," I said, knowin' full well that this poor bugger had had it.

That poor young bloke even managed a smile at us before the last of his blood dripped out and he passed on to wherever good, brave sailors go.

"Come on, boys," I said to my men. "Time to get our pals out, eh?"

As we left that room, another small unit of Martians were walkin' by and we painted the walls green with their innards. They didn't even have time to get one shot off in reply.

I still couldn't believe that we hadn't been spotted and there weren't hundreds of them at us. Could our luck hold out? We couldn't take any chances and we were watchful.

We went into the next passage, the one, that sailor had told us of, and carefully approached the area where the prison was meant to be.

The door led to a big room, as you will remember, Smith. There were a lot of doors and all had a red switch on to the right of it.

Then, from around a corner at the end of the room came another load of Martians. We ducked behind some kind of machine that stood to one side just in time for some shots to sail over our heads. Some of these Martians were using Heat-ray rifles, whilst the others used the new kind, and a few black marks appeared on the walls above us.

We took it in turns to lean around the side of the machine and fire off volleys at the things as they dodged about this way and that. Drawing a bead on them was tough, I can tell you. Those blighters can move when they want to. One or two of them fell, though but one shot from the one carrying the Heat-ray narrowly missed Dawson leaving a great black burn on his arm. His flesh sizzled like bacon in a pan and he cried out, as well he might. He fell back behind the machine and let the rest of us carry on the fight.

I leaned around the machine again and took aim at the Martian with the Heat-ray. As I loosed off a shot it moved a bit, but not far enough.

The strangest, but luckiest I suppose, thing happened. My shot must have hit the Martian's weapon as it exploded with a bright flash. The Martian just had time to scream horribly as it and all its comrades were torn to pieces.

We could not resist letting off a little cheer then but common sense prevailed. We had no idea when there would be more of those fiends about, so we quickly got back to work.

We hurried to the first door and pushed the switch. A buzzer sounded and the door opened.

And that, my friends, is how we came upon my friend Smith."

The Sergeant sat back, satisfied, in his armchair and Wells nodded approvingly.

'A ripping tale indeed,' Wells said in his thin Cockney accent. 'One worthy, perhaps, of one of my novels, eh?'

We laughed long and hearty at this and spent the rest of the evening in talk of other, happier, things not concerning Martians or death.

CHAPTER 46
A Shocking Discovery

So, here we were, liberated from our prison on board the Martian base by the grinning commandos. The Sergeant stepped forward and clapped me heartily on the back.

'It's good to see you, my friend,' he said. 'Good to see you all alive and well!'

The men in the cell cheered our rescuers with great gusto.

'Shh! Come on, we have to move it," the Sergeant said his facing becoming serious for a moment. "I doubt we'll be left in peace for long.'

Surprised and thankful that we in the cell were, those words reminded us we weren't out of the woods yet. Churchill jumped up and growled.

'You heard the man. Let's move!'

The rest of us got to our feet and made ready to follow the grinning men at the door. Even Dawson, obviously in pain and gingerly holding his burnt arm, seemed of good cheer. Why, still very much in who knew how much peril, we could be so light of heart I cannot say. The commandos' disposition and devil-may-care attitude, I think, must have been infectious.

'What weapons do you have?' Churchill asked the Sergeant.

'Just these odd things," the man answered pointing to the rifle he carried. 'There will be a few scattered around this room that may work and we shall have to find more along the way for you boys.'

'What about the other rooms?' I asked. 'There may be others'

'Next stop,' the Sergeant winked.

We left the cell and went to the other doors. Sadly, there were no more than ten men to be found in those other rooms. The Martians had been taking men away from those cells just like they had from ours, we were told.

A few of the men picked up the Martian weapons that lay here and there about the room. Greetings were quickly exchanged and Churchill tried to get the men into some semblance of order.

'We may now have a fight on our hands, men,' he said. 'Our friends here report that they did not come up against as much resistance as they expected and that does not bode well. We can expect to meet many Martians before we leave this machine and it may not be an easy fight. That we have gotten this far, though, gives me hope and says much about the British spirit. We will do what we must to bring this monstrous machine, and the Martians that cower within it, to its end and if we can survive, so much the better. I say we must not allow the Martians to escape with this weapon and we must prevail!'

The motley gathering of men were visibly stirred by these words, and I include myself in that number. We moved off with a new sense of purpose.

The first passageway we came across was empty of Martians. The interior of the base could be, as I intimated earlier in this text, quite disorientating to move around. No signs, nothing on the smooth, glowing walls to give us any indication of where we could be in this place. We walked around, in silence and on guard, for a while trying to get our bearings. Those with weapons walked at the front and the rear in an effort to cover those who could not defend themselves.

We entered any rooms we found in the hope of finding any of our fellow humans who had been taken away but may still survive.

Most rooms contained strange machinery or were empty. One or two had solitary or small groups of Martians in them that were quickly despatched before they could raise the alarm.

In one large room, we finally discovered what had happened to some of those poor souls who had been taken away from the cells and it was more horrible than I could ever have dreamed.

As we entered, two Martians looked up curiously from a long bench they were bent over. Each was quickly sent to their doom with a well-placed shot from the invisible beam weapons and we could see the work they had been engaged in.

On the bench, a Remote Walker lay prone. Beyond that, an unmoving man was strapped down, his mouth open wide in a silent scream of terror. The worst realisation was yet to come.

The panel at the back of the Remote Walkers head was open. The man beyond had had the top of his skull sliced cleanly off and, instead of seeing the expected brain exposed, there was nothing but a red gaping hole. Blood dripped from that awful wound and fell to the floor with a slow pitter-patter.

It took no more than a second, and the sight of the blood smears around the rear panel in the Remote Walkers glittering head, to understand the implications of this scene.

A man behind me bent over and vomited noisily as he came to the same conclusions as I and, doubtless, the others who stood open-mouthed and suddenly pale in the doorway.

The Martians, with supreme and diabolic ingenuity, were using the brains of men to somehow control the Remote Walkers. Like cattle, we were not only being used as a source of nutrition, but the Martians could also turn other parts of us to equally good use. Man was being used as a weapon against his fellow man.

As we stood shocked, the legs of the thing moved a little and it tried to right itself. Slowly, painfully, it got to its feet and faced us. Did I detect an air of horror in that terrible thing's stance? Did it know what it was? Had it not been given it's instructions and still retained some part of its humanity? It began to clunk and clatter unsteadily toward us then stopped and merely stared with blank eyes, it's head cocked at an angle.

The matter was decided by Glenn who, face full of horror and pity, went quietly behind it. It did not even attempt to move or defend itself as Glenn smashed the butt of his weapon into the open panel in its head.

The Remote Walker's legs instantly folded and it fell to the ground with a crash, splashing small gobbets of gore onto the pristine, shining floor.

Utterly disgusted, our party quickly left the room.

CHAPTER 47
A Fitting End?

I tried, as we headed on through the Martian base, to forget the horrible sight that had greeted us in the Remote Walker room. I could think of nothing more terrible than to end up as a disembodied earthly brain imprisoned within an unearthly machine, forced, by some unknown means, to destroy any man that came upon it on sight. I did not want to contemplate the thought that these human brains may know full well what they were being forced to do, and were tormented by it, utterly compelled to carry out their evil orders regardless of their human emotions. Better to imagine, perhaps, that all humanity left the mind at the removal of the brain making the organic matter within the walkers nothing more than a form of complicated calculating machine. Either way, there was no time to dwell on this in our current predicament, but the idea of this awful thing happening to me haunts my dreams to this day.

Through more corridors we ran at a steady trot. The exertion was beginning to tell on me and, after a strange, inadequate diet and lack of proper sleep, my breath came in short gasps, I perspired as if standing in the hot summer sun in a winter coat and the muscles in my legs ached and complained with the stress forced upon them.

'Come on, mate,' the Sergeant quietly, said keeping pace beside me. 'We will be out of here soon. Keep it up!'

I noticed that, as a man in the peak of fitness, despite his leisure habits, he showed barely more signs of fatigue than if he was engaged in a leisurely stroll through the park.

'Get down!' shouted Churchill suddenly and we, to a man, scattered and fell to the floor with military speed. Guns were raised and fired by those that had them as a troop of Martians skipped lightly toward us down the corridor, dodging left and right with dizzying speed and firing their own weapons.

The beam from a weapon narrowly missed my head and I thrust my terrified face to the floor as a man behind me was splashed over an area twice his size. Some Martians fell twitching but another man near me died with a scream that chilled me to the bone. I looked up in time to see a Martian turning and casting its saucer eyes in my direction. I frantically groped behind me and my hand grasped the barrel of a weapon as the Martian raised its own. Just when I thought it was too late and I was to join the unfortunate dead, the Martian squeaked as a shot from Glenn's weapon severed most of its tentacles. The creature fell to the floor with a wet thump and I saw its eyes widen and heard it squeak again as it was instantly set upon, using fists and feet, by some of those who were without a weapon. Desperation can make even unarmed humans dangerous and the Martian's mewlings soon ended.

There were now two Martians left. One was despatched with a deadly accurate shot from Churchill, the other skittered away crazily, weaving left and right with deadly beams following in its wake, and hooting excitedly. A black mark appeared on the wall an inch above its head as it rounded a corner in the corridor and was gone.

The Sergeant breathed an oath. 'I think we'll have company soon, boys. We must pick up the pace!' The desperate search for an exit continued.

More rooms were quickly searched. One was a feeding room, not unlike the room we had seen in the cylinder on Horsell Common. Instead of Martian biped bodies lying discarded haphazardly and unceremoniously here, there were pale human figures lying motionless and drained of all life fluid.

As in the cylinder, the smell of corruption in this room made the bile rise in the throat. One or two men crossed themselves and muttered a short prayer for these poor lost souls and we quickly moved on.

The next room bore more than a cursory inspection.

In the centre of this large room was a long metal table like that we had seen in the Remote Walker assembly room. Machines that had flashing green lights and beeped and whirred surrounded the table at one end. From the machines, a complicated array of tubes exuded, they twisted and turned this way and that until they terminated in the thing that lay on the gleaming surface of the table. Some of the tubes contained a green fluid that seemed to be being pumped into the man that lay there.

Cavendish.

The Knight lay unmoving and appeared to be devoid of life. Tubes pierced his throat, his arms and several ended in the flesh of his bare legs.

The normal ruddy colour in his puffy cheeks had been replaced by a pale yellow hue. His heavily lidded eyes were firmly shut and his mouth hung open.

Cavendish was completely naked and his arms lay motionless at his side. The reason for his apparent death was brought to my horrified eyes as I saw his chest.

The flesh there had been cut cleanly and peeled back and was held open by large clamps. His ribcage had been broken open and his innards had been, it seemed, pulled out, as an untidy pile of glistening red offal had been placed in a metal dish that stood on a small table to one side.

I remembered Wiggin's talk of the devastation that had been committed on the prostitute Mary Kelly's body by the unknown killer, whom the press had named 'Jack the Ripper', fifteen or so years before, and this sprang instantly to mind as my eyes took in this terrible sight. But this was no senseless slaughter or some unfathomable blood lust. This was science at its most diabolical and inhuman. I had no doubt, though, that our own scientists had committed the same indignities to the corpses of Martians we had found in our laboratories after the war. Cavendish had probably overseen such butchery and was likely getting a bitter, posthumous taste of his own medicine.

Still, although my feelings on the subject of Cavendish had run hot of late, I thought that this was no way for any man to die, no matter what his crimes against common decency and humanity may be. I remembered suddenly that I had seen this type of procedure before. When the Martian in the Kensington base had touched my mind.

I moved closer to Cavendish's tortured corpse.

'Poor deluded man,' I muttered. 'I hope the end was quick for you.'

One of the men behind me, I did not see who, snorted at this but Churchill snapped at him to be quiet.

I lightly touched Cavendish's arm and opened my mouth to say a final farewell. His flesh felt cool and doughy.

I was about to speak when his eyes flew wide open and his mouth opened wider to let out a terrified gurgling scream.

CHAPTER 48
The Knight of the Living Dead

The scream that came from Cavendish's pain-wracked face tailed off into a strangled gasp and then he finally lapsed into quick, shallow panting. He struck me as alike a man drowning, every attempt at drawing air into the ghosts of his excised lungs causing him unimaginable pain and his eyes watered unceasingly as he stared wildly around him as if in search of some sort of redemption. Somehow, with all of his vital organs missing from his mutilated body, Cavendish was alive!

The group of men behind me stood shocked, and I turned to see horror on every face. No one appeared to know what to do and I doubted that anyone would find himself able to step forward to assist if they did.

Cavendish's pale arm shot up and grasped mine with a steel grip. I became strangely fascinated by the visible progress of the green fluid that was being pumped through the tubes into this poor man's body.

Was this fluid keeping Cavendish alive? Was it some sort of embalming fluid that gave life where there should be none? Did the Martians wish to wake the dead for some diabolic purpose, just as they had used our brains in their deadly machines?

Cavendish's head turning toward me prodded me from my reverie. The watering, bloodshot eyes locked onto mine and I again fancied that I felt for myself the excruciating pain this man must be enduring.

The mouth opened and a hiss emitted from it sounding, at first, like the rustle of leaves on a tree in a brisk breeze, but somehow I had the distinct impression that Cavendish was trying to speak. Stooping, whilst fighting the urge to turn and run from this horrible thing before me, I placed my ear closer to the Knight's mouth and tried to listen. The man's breath was heavily tainted with the sour odour of the grave.

'Sssssmiiiittthhh,' I could now hear.

'What is it, Cavendish?' I asked, as I could think of little else to say.

'You. Musssst. Lisssten,' he replied with what seemed like an almost superhuman effort. Between every word he took an instinctive attempt at a breath. How he could even attempt to speak, I do not know and yet speak he did.

'Tell me. I'm listening' I assured him.

His mouth was obviously dry but we had no water to give him and so we could only look on as he licked his cracked lips in an attempt to moisten them.

'I did not mean for things to end this way,' he finally managed. 'I was assigned to negotiate a peace for the empire. I had orderssssssss.'

His head fell back and his dry eyes gazed at the ceiling of this charnel house.

'Orders? From whom?' I asked as gently as I could.

'The Prime Minister,' he finally managed to gasp. 'He knew we would likely be destroyed if there were another attack from Mars … and it was decided … by the cabinet … that we should try … to ensure our survival in such an … event.' He stopped for a moment as the effort of speech obviously tired him greatly. His throat made strange gurgling sounds and he began gasping for breath for a moment as if in a panic. Finally, the noises subsided and he, with great effort, turned his face, his hair in disarray and framing his head like some untidy white halo, toward me.

'I did not agree with what I had to do ... but I am a ... a ... patriot and un ... ashamed to admit it,' he finally continued, foam flecking his mouth. 'I love my country and I would do ... anything to protect her, no matter how the methods I need to adopt may ... appal me. The old que ... queen ... once told me–'

The Knight suddenly stopped his dialogue and turned his face upwards, a beatific smile touching his face for a moment, as if some happy memory now occupied all of his thoughts.

'Cavendish, we will get you out of here,' I decided. I motioned for some men to come and help me, although I had not the slightest idea what to do.

'No!' Cavendish turned toward me again, the smile dropping like a discarded mask. 'I cannot leave here ... now. Detach me from the machines and I will die as surely and as quickly ...as ... as if you had thrust a ... d ... a dagger ... through my heart. I am ... f ... finished. You must escape ... this place and warn them ... the Government. The Martians intend to use this new base ... for another attack on London and they will build ... more. This cannot ... be allowed to happen.'

'But what of your orders?' I said.

Pain twisted Cavendish's face once more, but he was not finished speaking.

'There cannot be any ... ac ... accord with these monsters. We are as cattle to them and they do not ... not need our help to conquer our fellow man. How they have left me ... shh ... should be warning enough to anyone who tries to ally themselves alongside them. The world must prepare for their coming, for come again ... they will!'

'We will warn the world, Cavendish,' I vowed.

'G … g … good man,' he gasped with great difficulty. His chest shook and he gritted his teeth as another wave of pain thundered through him. 'Now you must end … my torment. Please.'

With grim determination, I grasped the tube in his arm.

'Farewell, Cavendish,' I said in as steady a voice as I could manage.

I held his hand and he gripped it with surprising strength. He gave a small, pain-wracked nod and fixed his eyes steadily on mine.

I yanked at the tube and green fluid spattered out noisily onto the floor.

I grabbed at other tubes and pulled them. More fluid pumped out and lay in glistening pools on the table.

Cavendish's grip on my hand relaxed but his eyes remained locked on mine. It took me a few moments to realise that he had stopped panting and his ordeal was now over. I gently closed his eyelids and turned away.

CHAPTER 49
At the Heart of the Base

Cavendish's horrifying ordeal and merciful demise, at my hand, had had a sobering impact on the men. Much as some, including myself let us not forget, had hated him for betraying us, it was too easy to imagine oneself in that awful state; neither living nor dead, aware of every terrible atrocity that had been visited on your person and knowing, finally and with absolute certainty, that there was no way back to life as you had known it before. I would, as would any sane man I am sure, much rather suffer a burning, but infinitely quicker, death from a Heat-ray than endure this monstrous experimentation. I resolved that I would make my capture impossible, should the time come, and force the Martians to slay me instantly rather than have the facility to use me for any of their diabolical science.

A few careful but firm words from Churchill roused us all enough from our morbid thoughts to spur us on with our search for an escape route from this awful place we were trapped within. Weapons were readied once more and we left Cavendish to his final rest.

The corridor was quiet and empty and we made along it quickly but with great care, I trotted along near the front behind Glenn and Jameson, the Sergeant paced me and drove me on, breathing words of encouragement all the way. Being the only non military man present, and therefore not as fit and robust as the others, I felt a little ashamed that I was perhaps slowing the pace, but if this was the case, none of the other men made any mention of it. In fact I felt fully supported by them and, in the way that I was accepted by them, perhaps even as much of a soldier as they.

Our unit, then, trotted along these gleaming, glowing corridors, one after another. I felt thoroughly disorientated but Churchill led the way with a purpose that demanded that we follow.

We saw no Martians for a while, until one unwisely peered out of a door, only to be knocked back squealing by a blast from Churchill's beam rifle.

In the room that the unfortunate Martian had died within, we found many more weapons and were surprised that it was not better guarded such as a similar human armoury would be. Perhaps these unfathomable creatures did not think there could ever be any threat worth guarding against in this, to them, their unassailable lair. To Glenn's obvious delight, we also found his pack that still contained the explosive that was to have been used to incapacitate the cylinder. It had been carelessly discarded in a corner of the room. He opened it and checked through its contents carefully.

'We can make some pretty fireworks with this, eh Sergeant?' he said satisfied, holding up his prize and grinning.

'Indeed we can, mate!' the Sergeant agreed with a smile. 'God willing, before this day is out, we shall put on a display that they will see and hear in the colonies.' He turned to the rest of the group. 'Everyone without a weapon can grab one now, I think. Help yourselves, boys!'

Now a force to be reckoned with, small but determined and every man armed to the teeth and ready for action, we continued on our way.

As the corridor we followed turned sharply to the right, we found ourselves facing a large silver coloured door.

We made ourselves ready with weapons pointing toward the room beyond and Churchill cautiously pushed the switch next to the door. The portal slid aside with a soft hiss.

A sharp squeal and an excited hoot in return alerted us to the presence of a number of our foe within this room and the air crackled with the discharge of weapons as a short but furious battle ensued.

One of our sailors fell decapitated before he had a chance to even cry out but we fought on with grim determination. The five Martians were hopelessly outnumbered and four fell instantly dead whilst the fifth squealed and writhed until, sickened, a man ended its existence with a shot from his weapon.

The huge room we had now secured appeared to be the engine room. It contained similar black machinery I remembered seeing at the rear of the cylinder at Horsell Common.

'Right. This place is as good a launching point for your display, Glenn,' Churchill said.

'Very good, Sir!' Glenn beamed. 'How long shall I set the timers for?'

Churchill pondered this for a moment. The clockwork timing devices on the explosives should theoretically have given us time to get away from this base before the engines, and hopefully the base itself, were blown to Kingdom Come by the high explosives. This, of course, depended on our ability to escape at all.

'Two hours, no more,' Churchill decided finally. 'That gives us a fighting chance at least, but we cannot leave it any longer lest this damned machine reaches its destination, wherever that may be. We have no idea where we are but I'll warrant we are not far from land. Hide the charges well,

Glenn, and ensure that they are placed so as to do as much damage as possible.'

'I don't understand the workings of this engine as well as a human one but I shall do my best, Sir!'

Churchill nodded then turned to the assembled men. 'When Glenn has finished his work we shall see if we can't get off this thing, eh? I want four volunteers to stand guard here to ensure Glenn isn't disturbed. Meanwhile, the rest of the group shall carry on the search. There can't be much we haven't seen now.'

Wayne raised his hand instantly, as did Thomas. Two other men also offered to stay and Glenn set to work.

Churchill checked the corridor, found it devoid of signs of life, and led the rest of us on once more.

CHAPTER 50
The Control Room

At the end of a long corridor further on from the Engine Room we came upon another silver door. This one was open but began to close as we reached it.

'Charge, boys!' the Sergeant cried and we did just that. Another group of Martians, around ten or so, skittered backwards raising their weapons as we did so. Again, incredibly, we had surprise as an advantage and most of the Martians fell with a few well-placed shots from our weaponry.

A few, however, weaved out of and away from the melee and gathered in a small group at a far wall, seemingly refusing to fight. They stood in a tight circle, swaying to and fro, clutching their weapons tightly and pointing them outwards as if defending something.

Churchill shouted for all to cease fire, his eyes fixed on this little band of creatures. The men were confused, but were trained to obey orders and did so.

'What is happening?' I asked.

'I don't know,' Churchill answered. 'But my aim is to find out.'

For a few moments there was a tense standoff. Human beings faced creatures from far beyond our planet and, until recently, our imagination.

Weapons clattered in the hands of both sides and feet shuffled as warriors from both races fought the urge for battle.

I cast my eyes around the room and had an idea that this was the control room of the machine. Complex machinery lined one wall and, at the far end, a huge viewing window was set into another. I could see the undersea landscape passing by through this window, with silvery fish flitting by, and knew that the base was on the move. A large map sat on a platform in the centre of the room. It was there but I could see completely through it and I pondered how this could be. It did not appear to be glass as a soldier near to it was also studying it and pushed a hand forward as if to touch it. To his surprise, his hand went through it as if it were not there. It must have therefore been some form of projected image, although where it was projected from I do not know. Perhaps the platform over which it floated held the key but there were more important considerations suddenly brought to the fore.

The map showed what was unmistakably a photographic image of Southern England. Just off the coast of Brighton a small green light pulsed. If this green light was what I thought it appeared to be, there was no time to lose.

'Churchill!' I hissed.

'Yes, a moment,' he replied tersely, his eyes fixed on the group of Martians.

I held back further comment, for the moment, and looked again at this little group. The Martians were gathered round another Martian. It was similar to them, only some considerable amount larger and its glistening skin had a paler, greyer hue. It perched upon a small silver stool and its tentacles writhed around its great head. I was reminded, by the waving of these appendages, of hearing the tale of the Gorgon, Medusa, in Classics lessons as a boy.

Its great, black, watery eyes locked onto mine and held my gaze.

A piercing pain inside my head warned me that this creature was trying to enter my mind. I must have given out a sharp cry as the pain began as all eyes turned to me.

'Smith?' I distantly heard Churchill ask.

'It ...' I said with difficulty. 'It is trying to communicate.'

Images flashed before my mind's eye now. An opulent building in which this creature, or one similar, sat. Tapestries lined the walls, seemingly showing episodes of Martian history. Smaller Martians attended to this creature's needs as it waved its tentacles emphatically at some form of screen and I had the idea I was looking at how things had been on Mars before the invasion. An arid-looking landscape of red rocks came next, across which a Fighting Machine stalked. Great fields of the Red Weed swaying in the Martian breeze lay beyond that. Finally, I saw, in a huge construction like a zeppelin hangar, the building of a giant cannon and a cylinder being lowered into it. I almost felt the thunderous report as this device was fired and, with a massive spurt of green flame, the cylinder was ejected into space.

I became aware that I was being shaken.

'Smith, don't let it read your mind!' Cavendish was saying. Cavendish?

My vision cleared a little and I saw it was Churchill, not Cavendish who shook me. I have often, since pondered on this illusion but have failed to come up with an explanation.

I tried then, to stop the probing. I built a wall in my mind, brick on brick, with which to close my thoughts off from this creature. As I did so, much to my relief, it appeared to work. The pain faded and my head cleared.

'Are you all right?' Churchill asked concerned. I could see that, beyond him, soldiers were shuffling about nervously. They wanted to kill this creature and its entourage and get away.

'I think I know what this creature is,' I said finally, images and feelings still strong in my mind. 'It is the Supreme Commander of the invasion force. The closest approximation I can come to is that it is named the Overlord.'

'What does this ... Overlord ... want?' Churchill asked.

'It wants to live,' I answered simply.

'I'll bet it does!' the Sergeant said hotly, stalking toward us. 'I say we put it out of its misery and get off this base before it becomes so much scrap metal!'

Churchill simply glanced at him and something in his eyes stopped further words before they left the Sergeant's already open mouth.

'This creature may be useful to us,' Churchill said after a moment.

'Useful how?' the Sergeant asked, his face twisted with frustration. 'The only good Martian is a dead Martian!'

'We have what could be the enemy Commander in our grasp, Sergeant. How can we let this opportunity slip away? If, as Cavendish has said, the Martians plan to invade again, we can learn much about their possible tactics from this creature. It may give us an advantage we may not have without it.'

'I do not agree!' the Sergeant said bitterly. 'We know how tricky these things are. It will try to be away at the first chance it gets! Kill it now and we save ourselves a job later, I say!'

'Kill it now and we are no better than they are. When the time comes, it will be brought to account for its crimes. Besides which, it can perhaps aid our escape. It lives and

237

that is an order. Do you understand?' Churchill's burning eyes bore into the Sergeants, as if daring him to disobey.

There was a tense pause and then the Sergeant nodded, deflated. I had an idea, then, of the greatness in the Lieutenant that would, I was sure, see him rise to bigger things in years to come.

'Sir,' the Sergeant said quietly.

'Right. Men; all eyes on the prisoners. One move to escape and you shoot to kill.'

The men, who had been watching this exchange, nodded their affirmation and levelled their weapons at the Martians.

'Now then,' Churchill said. 'Let's see if we can't stop this thing, eh?'

CHAPTER 51
The Martian Gambit

Churchill took in his surroundings and, after a glance at the map screen, came very quickly to the same conclusion as I. This monstrous machine was headed on a course toward London, presumably across the South of England.

We, and the men not watching the Martian prisoners, gathered in a hurried conference to discuss the next move.

'We appear to be headed toward the South Coast. Why did they just not bring this thing to land at the mouth of the Thames?' I asked, puzzled. 'Surely it would have given them a better chance of surprise, as they would have less distance to go to be in London?'

'Perhaps,' Churchill pondered. 'They mean to sweep away any resistance they find in the South on the way. With a machine like this it would likely take much more firepower to halt than we have in any one area. The terrorist actions have spread our forces a little thinner than I am comfortable with. We were watching for an attack from Mars itself, and we should have, we hoped, had enough warning to prepare for that. What we did not consider was that the Martians had a weapon as potentially powerful as this. In fact, we have no understanding just what capabilities this machine possesses. At any rate, I am supposing that they are banking on the idea that, with resistance in the South crushed, there would only be one major front to cover at the North. With the approach of this thing, there would probably be a mass exodus of people to the North from London, which would hamper any potential attempt at a counter-attack from there. I don't even think the Martians are especially concerned about surprising us. Their aim here and now is to pound London into the ground once again, and I think that this machine is quite capable of that. With London incapacitated again, the United Kingdom would be in turmoil once more.'

'Do you think that our attempt to destroy them has forced them to take this action?' I wondered. Was this a last ditch attempt by the remainder of the invading forces to do our country's infrastructure some serious damage. To soften us up again for the next force who would surely someday come?

'Perhaps,' Churchill nodded slightly. 'Or we could have just sped things along somewhat. All that matters is that we make sure that this plan of theirs does not come to fruition.'

'Amen to that, mate!' the Sergeant said. A glance from Churchill reminded him of his place. 'Sir,' he added quickly.

We inspected the machinery that lined the walls, in hope of finding some way to halt the progress of the base. It would be better that it, God willing, exploded harmlessly out to sea rather than on land where innocent people could be harmed. Even if we could not escape, many lives could be saved if we could stop this thing before it got inland.

A soft hooting made me glance around to where the gaggle of Martians sat watching us curiously. I may have been mistaken, but I could have sworn I saw amusement in some of those saucer-like, glinting eyes.

I did not have the physical symptoms that heralded an attempt at a mind probe from the creatures and, therefore, had no basis for the feeling I got then. The distinct impression I had was that we were wasting our time.

There was another hoot from the Overlord as if to confirm this thought.

Churchill was pushing a lever but there appeared to be no effect. His frown deepened when I addressed him.

'I do not think we can stop it.'

'What? Come on, one of these levers or something must control this thing,' the Sergeant said.

'I think it already has its instructions and it will follow them,' I struggled to put my feelings into words. 'It must have the capability to control itself without intervention from the Martians. I feel that it can think for itself and act on whatever situations it comes across.'

'A self controlling machine?' Churchill asked.

'Yes,' I answered. 'I feel it has a form of brain and a sort of intelligence. To all intents and purposes a living creature made of metal!'

'That's preposterous!' the Sergeant scoffed.

'Look,' I said wearily. 'I don't know how I know this, but I do and that is that. I tell you that I would swear that this thing can move of its own accord and we cannot change its course.'

'Then we must make sure that this ... metal creature ... is incapable of reaching its destination,' Churchill said grimly. 'We must kill it.'

'Surely the explosives my boys are planting, as we speak, will stop its heart,' the Sergeant said confidently.

'I hope it is as simple as that. We must try to warn our forces, though, just in case.'

The green light on the map screen was dangerously close to land now.

CHAPTER 52
A Call to Arms

The seriousness of the situation called for immediate action. As the machine we stood in neared the South Coast, many lives on land were at risk.

'I wonder if this machine has radio equipment of some kind,' Churchill mused.

'Would they need such a thing?' I asked. 'I mean, Cavendish assumed that the Martians communicate generally via telepathy. Then there are the calls we heard from the tripod machines during the invasion. Cavendish, I remember, once likened them a language in itself. He thought that imperceptible, to us, differences in the calls could mean that many messages could be transferred between machines.' An image of Cavendish's ravaged body flickered across my mind and I shook my head as if it could physically dislodge the unpleasant thought from my mind.

'We don't know for sure that they do not use radio,' Churchill answered. 'Our technicians, I know, scanned the frequencies we can operate within to listen for any anomalous signals when the terrorist actions began, but they may have more sophisticated equipment than we do which could explain why we found nothing. But I have to admit, I cannot see anything that look remotely like the sort of thing we need.'

I cast my eyes across the identical looking pieces of machinery at the wall. Nothing looked anything like radio equipment I have ever seen, either. 'So what do we do?'

'We could use our own radio,' Churchill flashed a rare smile. He called a sailor over who was carrying a bulky pack on his back. He must have picked this up in the armoury where the explosives were recovered.

'Is that equipment working?' the Lieutenant asked the sailor.

'Seems to be, Sir!' the fresh-faced lad answered after placing his pack on the floor and flicking nimble fingers expertly over some dials and switches. The harsh hiss of static echoed around the room.

'Excellent! Get to work. See if you can't raise some sort of human contact outside of this infernal machine, if you please!'

'Aye, Sir!' The grinning sailor flicked an exaggerated salute at Churchill and resumed his ministrations on the radio.

For a few minutes there was the disorienting hiss of static and little else. The sailor plugged a headset into the device and the sound of static was cut short.

The Sergeant paced to back and forth like a restless tiger in a cage, casting the occasional glare at our Martian prisoners. Churchill stood staring out of the viewing window, hands clenched behind his back. From time to time he rocked forward on his toes.

The door to the control room opened suddenly with a swish and many guns flicked quickly toward it. A grinning Glenn entered with the soldiers who had stayed with him.

'All done, Sir! Timers set and ... hullo!' He was staring at the Martian Overlord and his would-be guards.

The Sergeant shook his head slightly as if to stop the red-haired soldier asking any more questions.

'Erm … yes. Sorry for the delay. Got into a bit of a scuffle back there with some of those fellas,' he nodded towards the Martians. 'Seems there still a few of 'em about but the ones we met didn't have a hope.'

'Good job, mate!' the Sergeant said. 'How long we got?'

'About an hour, or thereabouts. Hid the charges pretty well, I think. Even if they get to know about them, I set some little surprises for anyone who wants to mess with my work.'

'That may not be enough time,' I said looking out of the viewing window. 'Look!'

Through the window, we could all now see that the window, and therefore the top of the base, was leaving the water. We were coming onto the land!

'Radio?' Churchill snapped.

The sailor was crouched on the floor with the headset on, his tongue flicking around his mouth with concentration.

'Yes!' he said finally. 'I have something … HMS Cavor, stand by for a communication from Lieutenant Churchill of the expeditionary force. What? Yes, there are still some of us alive. No time to explain. Lieutenant?'

Churchill snatched the headset from the sailor and clamped one earpiece to his ear. He took up the microphone and spoke.

'This is Lieutenant Winston Spencer Churchill of the expeditionary mission which began aboard Nautilus.' He listened for a moment. 'Nautilus was destroyed; some of the force still remain.' He listened impatiently again. Finally he snapped. 'Look, much as I would be pleased, under less urgent circumstances, to give an official debrief, the situation is not over and there is no time! Well, if you would care to contact land perhaps you could ask them to look out to sea off Brighton. They will, no doubt see an enormous machine emerging from the sea. I am aboard that machine! No, I really doubt they could miss it, it's very big and looks very odd. YOU can see it, now? You thought it was Nautilus and followed it toward land? Well, let me put this simply, this object must be stopped at all costs. If you are able, begin bombardment immediately and warn any land forces that can be mustered. Thank you.'

Churchill let out a deep breath and handed the headset to the sailor. He looked round the expectant faces of the men.

'You gentlemen might want to brace yourselves,' he said finally.

At that, an explosion rocked the base.

CHAPTER 53
A Way Out

The control room shook in the blast from *Cavor's* guns, throwing the unprepared, despite Churchill's warning, to the floor. If the base had not taken a direct hit, the aim of the gunners, for the first salvo, was close enough to the mark to make them proud of their deadly work.

As the base continued to rock with the force of the bombardment, I glanced at the Martians and saw them skittering around clumsily like overexcited dogs on a highly polished stone floor. The Overlord grabbed, with some of its tentacles, at the stool it perched upon to steady itself.

The Sergeant grabbed onto the nearest machine and clung on, managing to keep on his feet. Churchill seemed, like an old oak in a light breeze, to be barely moved. One sailor, as he fell, hit his head, with a sickening crack, on another machine and fell to the floor moaning.

I had, on some primitive impulse, thrown myself to the floor at Churchill's warning and only found myself sliding a little across the shiny surface on my rear.

'I think perhaps we should make good our escape now, if we can,' Churchill grumbled. 'I shouldn't like to be on board when she goes, eh?'

The men picked themselves up and grabbed for weapons.

'What about them?' The Sergeant nodded slightly toward the Martians.

'They are coming with us, as we discussed before,' Churchill told him, his face allowing no further disagreement.

'Sir!' the Sergeant said simply and stalked toward our unwelcome, and now weaponless, guests. As he reached them he affected a strange pigeon English of the type an Englishman abroad might use on a local man he met whilst in a foreign territory. I was aware that this could have appeared comical in other circumstances.

'Okay you boys come with us, yes?' he said slowly. 'Any mess with us and we bang-bang!' He pretended to fire his gun at them and they backed away, eyes wide. 'You be good Squids, we no bang-bang, ok?'

Squids. This was, I had heard, supposed to be an entirely derogatory term dreamt up by some wag to describe the Martians, in a similar way that natives of other countries under our Empire had nicknames given to them. It is unknown where this term stemmed from but the general populace were catching on to it, even some of the lower illustrated dailies, after the invasion, had begun to refer to the Martians in such a way. It is, I have found, so typically human for one race to mock another in this way, perhaps as a way to help banish any mystique they may have about them. I feel, however, that I shall leave further musings on such things to commentators on the human condition much more qualified than I.

The Martians watched the Sergeant with great curiosity as he paraded around miming that they were to go with us and behave. At the end of this absurd and untimely pantomime, the Overlord let out a soft little hoot. The Sergeant assumed that this meant that they would behave and appeared satisfied.

'See!' he grinned, turning to me and tapping his head with a calloused finger. 'They can understand all right! No need for them to poke around in the old noggin, eh?'

247

Churchill cast his eyes heavenwards and then mustered the men.

'Come! We must be off!'

So, a strange procession left the control room, the Sergeant and his commandos at the front, the Martians, who seemed to have understood the Sergeant's mimes after all, in the middle. Then came Churchill, myself, some more of the men. The man who had hit his head was supported by one of his comrades and, with a few others, took up the rear.

Another explosion rocked the base but we were ready this time and no one fell. Sparks flew from somewhere within the door mechanism and it closed shut, jerkily and emitting a high-pitched screech, behind us. The search for freedom continued.

We travelled another corridor, so like the others we had already passed through. This corridor appeared, though, to head dead straight through the base and I wondered where it led too.

The Martians wobbled along with us but occasionally received a sharp jab from a human-held weapon for no apparent reason. When they invariably turned to look at their tormentors with wide eyes, they were generally rewarded with angelic smiles that hid evil intentions. Still, they received far better treatment than we would at their hands and they should, perhaps, have been thankful for that.

The corridor seemed endless but finally and totally unopposed, came back to where we had started in the base initially. The tube room! I realised that we could have found the control room much earlier had we used the correct corridor! The thought did not have long to linger in my head.

As we entered the tube room, another fight began.

CHAPTER 54
Of Fight and Flight

The waiting group of Martians fired instantly as we entered, killing three men instantly.

Our group scattered every which way and men found whatever cover they could.

The air crackled as energy laced the air as we battled for survival. Our Martian prisoners made their escape, bunched together around the Overlord and hooting shrilly. They headed toward a group of their comrades at the other end of the room.

'Get back here, you damned Squids!' the Sergeant yelled, letting off a few quick volleys with his weapon. One of the Overlord's guards fell limply to the floor, like a deflated balloon, but the others hurried on. The Sergeant took aim again at the fleeing enemy, but a dark patch appeared on the wall close to his head and he ducked down cursing.

Another missile blast shook the base and men and Martians alike staggered here and there. A few weapons clattered on the ground but were quickly snatched up and aimed and fired at the wielder's foes once more.

When the shaking of the base had abated, I saw the Overlord and his entourage disappear from sight behind a group of other Martians. Churchill grunted angrily but soon gathered himself back together.

'We have to find a way off this infernal machine!' he shouted above the noise of battle. 'Keep fighting, but keep your eyes peeled for something we can use.'

The tube, I saw, was surrounded by more Martians who were calmly taking shots at us. To go that way and try to escape down the tube would be suicide. We needed another way.

More Martians fell to our weapons but it seemed that more simply appeared from nowhere to take their place. Worse still, two Remote Walkers suddenly materialised and also took up the fight. I remembered all too well that these were once human beings but I roughly pushed that awful thought aside and tried to hit one with my weapon.

'Here!' Thomas shouted. He pointed towards a row of doors at one wall.

'What is it?' I asked.

'I think they may be just what we need,' the soldier replied, ducking as a shot crackled over his head.

'How so?' said Churchill, making his way, crouching to avoid a shot in the back, over to the young soldier.

'I saw the head Martian and his cronies leg it into one of these things, Sir!' Thomas pointed now to similar doors at the other end of the huge room. 'I didn't see them come out again.'

Churchill frowned. 'Well, they could lead anywhere. But I don't know if we have a choice. We are outnumbered and our escape is blocked.'

He thought, only for a split second, then came to a decision. 'Let's see what's what then. Fall back!'

The remaining men fell back as ordered, firing all the way and cutting down Martian after Martian. I dashed along, too set on survival to be afraid, with them.

The doors were all closed but each had a switch next to it. Churchill, still crouched, experimentally pushed the switch next to the closest door. The door swished open.

Beyond the door was a large space. It reminded me, instantly, of the back of a troop carrying carriage, as I had seen some of these at Holy Loch.

The inside glowed with that same eerie light that the Martians always seemed to utilise in their décor. The room was lined with what I could only assume, from their appearance, to be seats of some kind. These 'seats' were deep and reminiscent of half of a scooped out melon. A viewing window, darkened, was set into the far end of this room and in the centre of the room a bank of machinery sat.

'What is this?' Glenn breathed from behind me.

'The way out,' Churchill said and glanced at me. I nodded as I had a sudden inkling that Churchill was correct.

The Sergeant looked a little puzzled but, despite that, barked orders to our comrades who were, still crouched and fighting for their lives, nearby.

'Come on you lot, get yourselves in here!'

The Sergeant stood to one side inside the door, Churchill on the other.

'Covering fire!' the Sergeant yelled and, as the men desperately tried to make their way towards us fired his weapon in short accurate bursts at any Martian he could see. I skipped into the room and attempted to help, although my aim was far less true than my friend's. Nevertheless, I managed to disable or kill a few of the creatures. Our enemy began to surge forward, firing wildly toward us as if they guessed our intentions.

'Come on, boys!' the Sergeant yelled. 'Get in here and I'll be buying the beers in the pub tonight!'

More men entered, Glenn, supporting the sailor who had been injured in the control room, entered and, dumping his charge unceremoniously in one of the seats, joined us at the door, weapon raised. Soon most of the men were inside with us now, only two men remained outside; Dawson and a sailor who's name I did not know.

'Let's go!' the Sergeant yelled.

The sailor stood and quickly made his way toward us. Dawson also stood and, firing off one last shot turned toward us and began to run. The fair-haired man made it halfway to relative safety before a Remote Walker stalked out from behind some machinery and regarded him curiously.

'No! Run, mate!' Glenn shouted a warning.

As if time had been slowed down, we saw the young soldier glance quickly behind him. His face full of horror, he tried to pick up speed, dropping his weapon in the process.

The walker followed his progress with its blank eyes for a heartbeat or two more, and there was a whoosh and Dawson was dead before his charred body hit the ground.

Before anyone could retaliate, the door slid quickly shut.

'Will the door hold them off?' the Sergeant asked whilst laying a hand gently on Glenn's shoulder.

The soldier fired at the switch with his weapon and was rewarded with a shower of sparks. The green light next to the switch blinked once or twice, then went dark.

'I think it will now,' he said bitterly, a lone tear for the loss of his friend quivering at the corner of his eye.

'Get into a seat,' Churchill said. Then, gently: 'There will be time to grieve for our comrades later. These creatures will soon get their comeuppance.'

We sat down gingerly in the seats and settled back.

Churchill was still standing and looking at the bank of machinery in the centre of the room.

'If I am right ...' he said brushing his fingertips over the switches. 'There!'

There was a low hum that seemed to fill the room and Churchill went quickly to a nearby seat.

Men glanced around in alarm as straps emerged from out of the fabric seats and, snakelike and as if with a mind of their own, encircled each man snugly. A soldier let out a small shriek then sheepishly looked around at his comrades.

I tried to move but found myself securely fastened with only my head mobile.

'What?' someone said simply, as the hum rose in pitch.

There was a rattle, a vague thump and then a building sense of movement.

I looked toward the viewing window and saw lights outside flash past at seemingly breakneck speed.

There was a sudden sinking feeling in my stomach as the escape room was ejected out of the base and into the open air.

CHAPTER 55
Down to Earth

The escape room rocked wildly on its axis as another shell from *Cavor* must have burst nearby.

'Hang on!' yelled the Sergeant.

One did not heed his words, and, as the explosion tossed the escape room around, there was a sharp crack that reverberated around the room followed by a strangled cry. I saw the sound came from a man opposite me and, as I looked, his face turned pale. His eyes rolled back in their sockets until only bloodshot white showed and his tongue lolled out of his mouth. A thin trail of silver drool trickled slowly onto his chest. Whilst the seats we were secured into would give ample support and comfort to their intended Martian occupants, the design obviously did not allow for human physiology and left the head unsupported.

In the shock from the blast, the poor man's neck had snapped back and broken and it had been the end of him. That the man had come so near to freedom and had died so needlessly was so typically and bitterly ironic that, once again, I wondered if we were nothing but playthings in the hands of some malevolent god.

The room settled and seemed to fly straight for a short while. Through the viewing window, I saw a darkened sky pinpointed by tiny stars. Along what I took to be the horizon, I noticed lights of an earthly, rather than stellar, variety in the distance. This could only mean we were headed toward land.

'Where is this thing going?' someone asked.

Churchill shook his head, 'I have to admit, I cannot say.'

'We are in a strange Martian craft and we don't know where it is going?' I asked incredulously, turning my head toward the Lieutenant whilst being careful to keep it as straight upright as I could.

'Escape was the best option, I thought, given our predicament,' he replied with a trace of annoyance in his voice. 'I did not anticipate being held prisoner in a blessed chair!'

'Then we really are in the hands of the gods,' I said under my breath.

Soon, the craft slowed and I felt a vague sense of falling. There was a slight bump and we appeared to have landed.

'Well we appear to be down in one-,' the Sergeant began, when there was a rattling noise as something was loudly pitter-pattering against the outside shell of the room.

'It's raining?' I said, but a quick glance at the viewing window appeared to contradict this. The noise stopped.

There was silence for a moment then the straps that fastened us to the chairs suddenly and quickly snapped back and we were able to move once more. The man who had succumbed to a broken neck slumped deeper into his chair and his head flopped forward. He looked as if only asleep.

Churchill went to the door at the rear of the room and pressed the door switch. It, to my surprise, began to open a little but, thanks to Glenn's, then timely, shot at the switch, would not open all of the way.

The door snapped closed, but started to jerkily open again. The pitter-pattering from outside started once more and something zipped past my head and hit the far wall. Men ducked as they realised what was happening.

Churchill dashed to the gap in the slightly open door.

'Dammit! Whoever's out there cease fire!' he shouted angrily. 'This is Lieutenant Churchill! Stop firing at once!"

The pitter-pattering stopped abruptly.

'Now, for the love of God, come and help us with this door!'

After some organisation, a party of the men outside brought crowbars and levered the door open so that we could exit our strange conveyance.

I found myself on solid ground for what had felt like weeks. I took in air tinged with the slight tang of salt and savoured every breath as if it were the finest wine.

Beneath my feet was sand and it transpired our craft had landed on the seafront.

Disorientation set in for a short while. After the events and locations of the previous days, standing quietly on this earthly beach with a soft, salty breeze ruffling my hair felt quite surreal. The cries of gulls soaring above my head sounded alien and the noise of the nearby waves breaking was like the roar of some mythological beast.

A soldier came and touched my shoulder gently.

'Ok, mate?' He asked kindly.

'Yes,' I said, mentally shaking the cobwebs from my brain. 'Yes, I am very well.'

'Sorry about the welcome and all,' he said apologetically. 'We thought you was Squids in that contraption.'

I smiled at him to let him know that all was forgiven and glanced around.

Churchill was talking animatedly to another officer nearby. The Sergeant stood, arms crossed, with them.

Soldiers milled around looking out to sea, pointing. Nearby, a gun crew attended to their weapon that was pointing the way we had come. As I watched, the gun boomed, the muzzle flashed and a shell flew out over the waves. More soldiers marched quickly over the dunes toward us in a steady stream.

I looked out to sea. I gasped as I saw the base, towering above the waves like some great black cloud. The green lights along its length pulsed and flashed and the smaller lights we had seen below the surface danced around it. Just beyond, a ship sailed at full speed toward it, guns blazing. The shell from the gun on the beach exploded harmlessly in the air between them. The base had, it appeared, broken off from its course to engage *Cavor*.

The small lights flew, like a swarm of angry bees, at *Cavor* and fired off some sort of light weapons, the dark sky now became criss-crossed with green beams. On the ship sped, but small fires sprung up from areas all over the deck. Tracer rounds reached out from the ship and some of the small lights dropped from the sky as they were touched.

'God help all who sail in her,' the Sergeant breathed beside me. Together, we watched the conflict in awe, like small boys at a firework display.

The base stopped moving for a moment, its great front end pointing toward the ship that threatened it. *Cavor* fired off another round and an explosion made the base appear to waver for a moment. Then, a great, wide beam of red light, more terrible and powerful than anything I had ever seen, flew from the nose of the machine and *Cavor* was vaporised instantly, leaving nothing but a great cloud of hissing water. It was if she had never been there.

A few cries of dismay came from the assembled men.

'Did you see that?' the Sergeant said. 'My God!'

The enormous machine stood still for a moment, as if admiring its handy work and an almost deafening cry, louder by far than any I had ever heard, reverberated through the air and shook the ground at my feet.

'ULLLAAA!!'

Men around me clamped their hands to their assaulted ears. Truly, this sound was almost as terrifying a weapon as any the Martians had ever brandished before.

The machine, having shown it's earthshaking pleasure with its handy work, slowly turned and began lumbering toward us again. Towards land. Towards London. Waves crashed around its great legs in dazzling white spray.

'Everybody get ready,' the officer who had been talking to Churchill said. 'Here it comes!'

CHAPTER 56
'We Shall Fight Them on the Beaches ...'

With the passing of the plucky ship *Cavor*, the huge Martian base continued its slow, methodical progress towards its objective.

There was frenzied activity on the beach as more soldiers spilled over the dunes and took up their places.

The officer approached his horse that was placidly grazing on a tuft of grass at the edge of the sand and mounted. The horse whinnied and tossed its mane as if annoyed at being disturbed at its repast, but obediently set off down the lines at a trot. The officer clung on with one arm and pointed out to sea with the other, shouting orders as he went.

There was the sound of motors from beyond the dunes and soon two Heat-ray cannons were wheeled onto the beach by teams of soldiers who sweated with the exertion, despite the cool night air.

Next, a unit of five human Fighting Machines wheezed, clanked and thudded into sight. A small gaggle of white-coated scientists followed nervously behind these clumsy machines watching them closely. It seemed that this new technology was still not trusted enough for it to be allowed to operate in the field without the attendance of these oddest of chaperones. The scientists were, quite obviously from the way they fidgeted and mopped their brows, wishing they were safely in the company of their blackboards and test tubes. When they spotted the base stomping relentlessly toward us, though, their jaws dropped and hurried discussions took place. The allure of new scientific wonders was strong, as it had been to the late George Cavendish, and, temporarily at least, compelled them to forget their fear. They shuffled forward slowly, like a flock of chattering white geese, to gain a better view.

'We have to delay it,' Churchill said loudly, trying to make himself heard over the noise of the general activity and the periodic booming reports from the guns that now lined the beach. 'It will not be long now until the charges do their work and, with luck, stop this thing once and for all. It is imperative that this machine does not get inland. God be with us all!'

One or two soldiers crossed themselves and muttered prayers to their makers. Weapons were shouldered and aim was taken. The beach guns fell silent, waiting for their target to come nearer. A deathly quiet settled over the scene, broken only by the clatter of nervously hefted rifles and the occasional nervous whinny of officers' horses.

'Wait for the order!' Churchill barked. By previous arrangement, it seemed, this honour had been bestowed upon him only.

As we stood silently, the base drew silently nearer. In the light of a pale moon I could see more white spray kicked up as its huge, thick black legs propelled it through the water.

The small flying machines, which had disappeared somewhere into the base after the demise of *Cavor*, re-emerged from behind it and headed towards the waiting men.

Churchill saw this and yelled: 'Fire at will!'

Rifle shots sounded from along the human lines like the pops and crackles of logs on a fire.

The small light machines swooped down from the sky, firing their beams at targets in their path. A beach gun took a direct hit and exploded in a ball of fire, flinging the men surrounding it, like broken, smouldering rag dolls, in all directions.

A man staggered away from the scene, screaming and aflame, until some of his comrades threw him down and rolled him in the sand.

The Heat-ray cannons were hurriedly brought to bear and the air in front of them wavered as their deadly beams reached for our attackers. One, two then three of these machines were caught in the blasts and fell from the sky, showering men below not quick enough to flee with white hot shards of metal.

The base was now emerging onto the beach and towered ominously above us. An enormous metal foot came down and smashed a small cluster of gaily-painted bathing huts near the water's edge to splinters.

The huge machine halted suddenly as if pondering its next move.

The beach guns spoke again and again and puffs of smoke erupted around the bottom of the base. They seemed to have little or no effect.

The small machines continued their assault and men were struck down all around by their weapons.

Then, the glass tube emerged quickly from the bottom of the base and planted itself with an enormous thud in the sand.

'They are coming out!' the Sergeant shouted from nearby.

Through the tube we could see a large troupe of Martians descending, clutching weapons. The platform reached the sand and the creatures spilled out as soldiers surged forward, shouting battle cries and firing wildly, to meet them.

So began The Battle of Brighton.

CHAPTER 57
Blood, Toil, Tears and Sweat

The opposing forces, rushed, the men bellowing and the Martians hooting, head long toward each other and met with an audible crash.

Too close for rifles or other such weapons to be used, a vicious hand to hand battle began in the moonlight on that small area of beach beneath the dark looming shadow of the base.

Humans brandished bayonets and used them to deadly effect, stabbing at saucer eyes and slashing at groping tentacles. The Martians utilised their brute strength and long knives with sharp, wavy blades that glinted in the light from the pale moon. I had never seen them use these weapons before but they used them to deadly effect.

This was no ordered battle with a definite plan. This was an undisciplined melee, a desperate struggle for supremacy and survival on this sandy, damp battlefield.

The cries and squeals of the wounded and dying from both sides rang across the night air as we stood and watched this horrendous spectacle from a little way up the beach. The smell and sight of blood awakened something primitive within me and I, despite myself, wanted to be part of this conflict. I wanted to assist in the destruction of these interlopers who dared to sully our land once more with the stench of their very existence. I wanted to rip and tear at these creatures and send them to whatever hell they went to after they expired.

The Sergeant must have seen me fighting with these instincts as he gently laid a hand on my arm.

'Your chance may yet come,' he said quietly. The feelings dissipated somewhat at this, but bitter bile lurked at the back of my throat.

The battle raged on, limbs and extremities thudding to the sand at regular intervals. Gruesome set pieces flashed across my eyes as this carnage continued.

At the edge of the conflict, a Martian tried to crawl away with four of its tentacles missing. A small group of men followed it then, like a pack of cats toying with a mouse, stabbed at it as it tried to escape. They, mad-eyed, slashed and stabbed until it moved no more.

A man was grasped by two Martians and pulled, screaming pitifully, literally in half, his innards falling to the floor in a wet heap. Another had his head twisted off by thick, rope-like tentacles as if the creature was unscrewing the lid of a jar. A fountain of blood, black and glistening in the darkness, gushed into the air and the man's limp body was flung unceremoniously to one side.

Another charging soldier was set upon by three hooting Martians and his limbs were sliced cleanly off by the weapons they held. The man's twitching torso lay flopping about on the surf and his pitiful cries floated through the air toward me.

A Martian had its eyes stabbed out by a man already covered in green blood and fell away squealing.

Whilst this horrendous battle on the sand was fought, the beach guns kept up their salvos and the Heat-ray cannons took shots at the base. Very little damage appeared to be done by this but, like a great beast annoyed by the constant attentions of mosquitoes, the machine finally showed its displeasure.

The great red beam lanced out from the front of the machine, suddenly and without warning, and sent a trio of guns to oblivion. The sand on the beach was turned to scorched glass at its touch and men and weaponry simply disappeared in a great cloud of smoke.

'Fall back!' Churchill shouted.

The remaining forces began to retreat a little, still firing, but two of the human Fighting Machines clanked forward, belching smoke from their exhausts and began to shoot their Heat-rays at the base.

'What are they doing?' I cried.

'Buying us some time,' the Sergeant replied. 'Look!'

A platform was descending within the tube and, swaying excitedly on it, was another large group of Martians.

The Fighting Machines concentrated fire on the tube and it shifted slightly from its position. Something must have broken within it as the platform fell to the ground too quickly and the Martians, unsupported now, squealed as they fell. One or two attempted, I could see, to cling onto the smooth walls of the tube but it was to no avail.

The glass inside the tube was painted sickly green with their blood as they hit the sand at tremendous speed and a few broken bodies spilled out of the portal.

'Yes!' cried Glenn. His smile dropped, however, when the base's deadly beam reached out, like a thunderbolt sent from a malevolent god, again and wiped the Fighting Machines cleanly from existence.

The Sergeant gathered his men, Thomas, Wayne and Glenn together.

'We need to delay this thing a bit longer, eh boys?' he said. The men nodded as one.

'Smith, you will stay here!' the Sergeant said. 'Glenn, you stay with him.'

'But-!' I began. I wanted desperately to be part of whatever they had planned.

'No!' he reiterated. 'Look, mate. Things aren't going to well. We are just going to keep this thing busy for a bit. As I said, you may yet get your chance. But for now, stay out of it. Someone will have to tell the world about this fight and you should be that man. Stay here and, if you can, survive!'

I nodded but still wished for a part in this plan, whatever it was.

'Good man!' the soldier said and gave me a friendly clap on the arm. He chanted his now familiar mantra: 'When all this is over, I'll see you in the pub for drinks, my friend! Oh, and you're buying!' With that, he turned away.

The men turned and ran over to where the remaining human Fighting Machines were crouched, unmoving on the beach. A quick discussion took place and the scientists in attendance showed their dissent with red faces and waving arms.

The Sergeant prodded one in the chest with a finger and shouted something in his face. Finally, the man shook his head, resigned and in no position to argue, and waved at the machines drivers to dismount.

The three commandos hopped quickly into the cabins, the glass canopies slid shut and the engines roared into life.

In a cloud of smoke and fumes, the three machines clattered and stomped down the beach toward the base.

'Don't worry mate! They'll be fine,' Glenn said at my side. But he could not hide the concern in his eyes.

CHAPTER 58
Their Finest Hour

During the skirmish on the beach, the small flying machines had taken many losses but had wrought havoc among the human forces. They soared above the battlefield at a blinding speed, stopping briefly and suddenly to take a shot at this or that human soldier or beach gun and then, when satisfied at the results, zipping away again to find another target. They were, however, easy to disable with a single rifle shot, I gather this was because of the lightness of the armour required to facilitate the high speeds they could maintain. But, despite heavy losses, they were still a major contributing factor to the severe depletion of the human forces we now faced.

A little way down the beach I saw one following the officer who had been with us earlier. His horse's mouth was flecked with foam and its eyes were wide with terror as it galloped madly toward us, the officer clinging desperately to its back.

The machine buzzed around them as they went, the small beams that lanced out from its nose narrowly kicking up puffs of sand around them.

The officer drew his sabre and frantically swiped at the machine, but it was too fast and the horse's course too erratic for him to take effective aim. The metal threat dodged his clumsy attempts at dislodging it from their course.

Finally, a lucky shot from the machine sliced a leg clean off the horse and it tumbled, with a scream that sounded terribly human, head over tail snapping its neck. The officer was thrown clear only to land in a heap of the burning wreckage of a beach gun emplacement.

His cries and writhing as he was turned, in an instant, to a ball of flame, mercifully, did not last long.

The machine that had ended both these lives began to zip away to search for more game, but it was felled by a clean shot from Churchill's rifle.

'We must do something!' I shouted, sickened at the death and destruction around me.

'We are doing all we can!' Churchill replied, grimly. 'We can only delay them now and hope that the explosives do their work.'

Beneath the base, the melee continued. It appeared now that the Martians were gaining the upper hand despite heavy losses to their group.

The men fought bravely but they must have seen that the game was nearly up as some of their number, desperately tired and streaked with blood, tried to retreat. The Martians, seemingly indefatigable, had other ideas and ruthlessly chased them. Some they cut down with their wickedly sharp blades or others they simply tore apart with their tentacles. It seemed there would be no prisoners, on either side, in this conflict.

I followed the Fighting Machines containing the three Commandos as they moved up the beach toward the base.

As they neared the giant machine, they split up and advanced on different paths. When they were within range of the battle, their Heat-rays flashed and cut down some Martians that had scattered at their approach.

The human machines did not join in the struggle beneath the base, however. The battle was so dense that they would have been in too much danger of hitting human comrades as well as our foe. They simply picked off some small groups of Martians that skittered about on the periphery and then concentrated fire at different areas of the underside of the base.

A shot from one machine rocked the top of the access tube and a small explosion was the reward.

The soldiers who stood nearby me shouted with glee as sparks and bits of molten glass and metal rained down from the tube. The Fighting Machines, rather than present sitting targets, clanked to different positions and resumed their attack.

The first sign that the base began to move again was that the tube suddenly leaned over at a crazy angle. It appeared that it could not, because of the damage to it, be retracted and, as the base's mighty legs began to propel it forward once more, the tube was pushed over. It came away in a shower of sparks and fell to the sand, crushing some unfortunate combatants, both man and Martian, who were engaged in a struggle for life nearby.

'It's moving again! We have to stop it!' Churchill shouted and men ran forward brandishing weapons. Soon, only Glenn and I were left as all had surged forward and a last desperate attempt to stop the machine began. I wanted to go forward and do my part, too, but Glenn forcibly held me back.

Suddenly maddened, I punched him squarely on the jaw and he fell back surprised. I ran forward after the rest, the pain in my hand unnoticed in the heat of the moment.

I picked up a discarded weapon on the way and began firing wildly at any target I saw. I felled two Martians in my anger and a light machine that stopped to target me got a bullet for its pains that brought it to the ground.

I halted for a moment, exhausted, and saw the Fighting Machines standing in a wide triangle targeting the gaping hole where the tube had been. More explosions resulted and men and Martians scattered from debris that rained down upon them.

The base moved on and I saw a leg begin to come down. Directly in the path of its descending metal foot was a human Fighting Machine. The driver, Thomas I was close enough to see now, frantically pulled at the control levers and smoke poured from the machine as the engine was gunned. The machine began to jerk forward but it was too late. The last sight I saw was Thomas mouth open wide with terror and his hands thrust out to the glass as if to fend off the enormous foot as it crushed his machine into the sand.

In another machine, I saw the Sergeant's face contort with anger and grief and he fired his Heat-ray, with renewed vigour, at the huge machine.

I heard exultant howls and looked over to see Martians looming over the dead bodies of many men waving their knives and weapons like banners. Then Churchill and the remaining soldiers reached them and, screaming defiance, took up the fight.

Churchill himself blocked blow after blow from a big battle-scarred Martian and stabbed it in the eye. In its death throes, a tentacle from the creature flailed out and knocked him out cold.

Then, as I despairingly saw the last of the men fighting what seemed to be a losing battle, there was an enormous muffled explosion.

The base was now perilously close to the beachfront houses and any civilians who had stopped, at what they thought was a safe distance to watch the battle, ran away screaming.

An ear splitting screech followed the explosion and the base rocked forward on its massive legs. It carried on a little way, a foot smashing a house to a pile of rubble, but there was another explosion and it stopped suddenly, another leg poised mid-air.

Flames and smoke belched out from the tube hole and more, smaller explosions followed. Small flaming shapes fell from the hole and I realised that these were the bodies of Martians caught in the blasts. They fell to the sand and burned merrily.

Another shape shot out from the side of the base. It was an escape room but it was aflame and it streaked, like some erratic comet, straight toward the sea. It hit the surface at a steep angle and broke apart, flinging its howling occupants at tremendous speed to their deaths.

Explosion after explosion rocked the wounded base now and the glass at the viewing window erupted out into the night. More Martians were thrown clear with flames following them.

There was another screech and the base began to topple over.

Glenn had reached me and had begun to remonstrate with me for hitting him when the explosions had started. His harsh words were forgotten and he whooped with joy at each explosion as the base slowly tore itself apart.

'It worked! It worked!' he repeated dancing around like a man possessed. Even I had to smile, exhausted physically and mentally as I was, at this man's joy at the outcome of his work.

The base fell to the ground with a metallic crash crushing more houses over a wide area. Two of its legs came off and more explosions followed, blowing more houses to pieces with their ferocity.

The wreckage burned for four days.

CHAPTER 59
The Tide Turns

As the base crashed to the ground the Flying Machines, as one, dropped to the ground. The base had controlled all of them, through some means and, with that method of control gone, they were nothing but useless hunks of metal.

The remaining men, at seeing this, carried on the fight with renewed vigour. The Martians, for their part, seemed to have had some of the bravado suddenly taken out of them with the destruction of their greatest weapon and some tried to escape the battlefield. One made it to the water's edge but was cut down by the Sergeant's Heat-ray. Through the glass of the machine's cockpit, I saw my friend cast a weary 'thumbs up' in my direction.

The struggle continued for a while but the humans soon began to turn the tide in their favour and the methodical killing of the creatures from Mars began.

Glenn pointed suddenly further down the beach.

'Well lookie there!' he said.

I followed his finger and spotted an escape room lying on its side in the sand.

From it, in the light of flames that billowed out of what had, until recently, been a beach gun nearby, I saw two Martians crawling away. They were heading toward another escape room that was hovering just above the sand a short distance away.

'Come on, Glenn!' I said and ran toward a small group of horses that huddled at the dunes. I had ridden a horse before in my youth and I jumped onto one taking the reins quickly. Glenn jumped up onto another and, nudging the nervous horses with our feet, we galloped off down the beach.

The wind ruffled my already dishevelled hair as we went and sand periodically got in my eyes but I could still see that, at the door of the intact escape room stood the Martian Overlord. It was waving its tentacles at its fallen comrades to hurry towards it. As we approached, I saw its eyes widen and I vaguely heard it squeak. The tentacle waving grew more emphatic, then. This thing evidently wanted to be off.

I let go of the reins, clung onto the horse as well as I could with my knees, and raising my rifle, fired at the creature. Aiming was difficult with the speed of our gallop and some shots pinged harmlessly off the walls of the craft. Glenn took up the shooting too and the Overlord's frantic state became more apparent. It danced and skittered about the entrance, hooting loudly.

We came, then, upon the crawling Martians and my horse reared without warning. As I was flung from its back, the horse stamped and trampled on one of the creatures into a bloody pulp. The wind was knocked out of me by the fall and I lay stunned on the sand for a second or two. Glenn pulled his horse around and came to where I lay.

'Go ... on!' I said desperately trying to catch my breath.

'What?' Glenn said, dismounting and reaching down to help me up.

'That's the Overlord, you fool!' I shouted angrily. 'It's getting away!'

'Oh!' Glenn said simply. His face suddenly took on a look of surprise and his eyes rolled back. A small trickle of blood ran from the corner of his mouth and dripped onto his collar. He fell forward onto his face, a harpoon protruding from his back.

I spun round looking for the source of this missile. A Martian stood nearby trying to reload its weapon. I groped for my weapon and raised it. Just as the Martian got me in its sights, I fired. The Martian dropped to the sand, lifeless.

Again I looked to where the Overlord's craft stood and saw it begin to rise from the sand. The creature's eyes widened as I took aim and fired. The bullet sped toward the creature, then there was a small gout of blood as one eye ruptured. The Overlord fell back squealing. As the door to the craft began to close and it rose higher into the night sky, I saw tentacles drag the wounded monster away from the opening.

There was a clanking behind me and I turned to see a Fighting Machine stalking up the beach. There was a wave of heat above my head as the machine fired at the dark retreating shape of the escape craft. The shot clipped it and it wavered in the air a little. Small pieces of molten metal dropped to the ground as the craft shot suddenly up into the air then moved forward, at amazing speed, away over the land and out of sight.

'No!' I shouted in frustration and fired volley after harmless volley at the thing. The chamber of my rifle clicked empty and I let it fall to the floor. The Overlord, if it still lived, had escaped.

The canopy of the Fighting Machine opened and the Sergeant sprang out.

'Are you alright?' he asked.

'No!' I said angrily. I could say no more and sank, bitter and exhausted, to the soft sand, my head in my hands. I sobbed, then, for all those who had died and for my inability to stop the creature that had directed all the carnage the Martians had wreaked on Earth.

CHAPTER 60
Cleaning Up

The Sergeant waited for a few moments then held a rough hand out to me.

'Come on, friend. It's time to leave,' he said gently.

I took my hands from my face and looked at him for a moment.

'Yes, we must go,' I said wiping my face, wet with tears, with the back of a grubby hand.

As he helped me up, I said: 'Thank you.'

'What for?' he asked, with a puzzled expression.

'For coming to my aid.'

He dismissed this with a wave of his hand. ''S what mates is for!' he said flashing a quick, warm smile. 'Us comrades got to stick together!'

We walked toward the Fighting Machine. Glenn's unmoving body, the harpoon in his back pointing straight up to the heavens, lay nearby and we stood above him for a moment. The Sergeant's face grew grim and he bowed his head and placed a hand on his breast over where his heart lay.

He muttered a quick prayer and, despite my not being the religious sort, I joined him in a quiet 'Amen', when he had finished.

'You were a good man, Glenn, and a good mate. Let's hope you are drinking a toast to us in heaven!'

'Trying to get rid of me already, Sarge?' a muffled voice said.

The man's body twitched and he laboriously turned his face towards us. He cursed with the pain of the movement but spoke again.

'You're not angels,' he said breathlessly. 'I don't see any wings.'

The Sergeant hurriedly knelt down to him and laid a hand gently on his shoulder, a single tear of joy trickled down his face.

'Glenn! Don't move, mate!' he said, his voice a little choked.

'It hurts a bit,' Glenn managed between laboured breaths. 'How's it look?'

The Sergeant regarded the harpoon. 'You're looking like a pole without a flag, but it doesn't look like it's in too deep. You'll be fine!'

Glenn gave a small painful grin. 'Good. Me missus would kill me if I didn't come home.' He chuckled a little, but the effort turned it into a hollow cough.

'Easy, mate!' the Sergeant said. 'This is no time for jokes. Maybe in the pub when you're better!'

The Sergeant stood up and waved his arms at the men down the beach.

'Hey there! Medic needed here! Hurry up!' he shouted loudly enough for the gods to hear.

Three men soon hurried toward us, two carried a stretcher and one had a medical bag slung over his shoulder.

With Glenn checked over and gently laid, face down, on the stretcher, we bid him a quick good-bye and the Sergeant climbed back into his Fighting Machine. The machine was gunned into life again and set off in a cloud of black smoke that nearly choked me.

I found my horse chewing on some grass as if nothing had ever happened to it. The only sign of anything unusual were the gobbets of Martian flesh clinging to its hooves and a small wound down its flank. I stroked its mane calmingly, mounted and we trotted behind the machine back down the beach toward the battlefield.

At the battlefield, Churchill was standing puffing a great cigar. His head was bandaged but he appeared to have suffered no other ill effects.

A little way off, I saw Wayne's Fighting Machine clanking wildly after a fleeing Martian. The creature weaved this way and that but it was only a matter of time and soon it ran no more.

A few men stood, weapons raised before a small group of cowed looking Martians. Things really had turned for the human forces whilst I was in my futile pursuit of the Overlord. More soldiers had come over the dunes to join the fray and soon the enemy had been overpowered.

Now a small band of the creatures were all that was left of the force that seemed about to overwhelm us.

I briefed Churchill on what had happened with the Overlord while he listened attentively.

'What are you going to do with them?' I asked Churchill, meaning the Martian prisoners.

'Classified,' Churchill replied, winking.

'What?' I asked. I had a terrible feeling that I knew the answer. 'You intend to hide them away somewhere, don't you? They are too dangerous! You know what happened before and there already some of them free!'

Just then, an important looking, rotund man fought his way through the gathering crowd of civilians that had gathered at the edge of the beach. This crowd was being held back by a cordon of soldiers, but the man flashed some papers in the face of the officer there and was let through. A small weasely-looking man with bright black eyes kept pace just behind him.

The important man looked so surprisingly like Cavendish that, for a moment, I was lost in thoughts of all that had gone before since I had first met the Knight in my drawing room so long ago. I came back to myself when he approached and I got a closer look at him.

The man had the same red face as Cavendish, the same white moustache draped across his chops. He even dressed in a similar manner.

'Are you Churchill?' he rumbled. The voice was so alike the dead Government man's and to such a startling degree that I began to doubt my sanity.

'I am he,' Churchill said around his cigar.

'I am Sir James Cavendish,' the man huffed. 'My brother was in charge of your operation.'

'May I say what a good job he did of it, too, Sir,' Churchill said, without a trace of irony. 'A great man indeed.'

Cavendish's face coloured a little darker at this but he said nothing else for a moment. Finally, his eyes moved to the huddled band of Martians that stood a little way away, their human guardians watching them like hawks.

'I am here for the prisoners. We have much to learn from them,' the man said.

'You do?' Churchill asked, slowly taking the cigar from his mouth.

'Quite so,' Cavendish said impatiently. 'Your answer?'

Churchill looked at his cigar for a moment and rolled it between his fingers. He looked at me, straight in the eye and barked one word.

'FIRE!'

There was a series of sharp cracks from behind him and the Martian prisoners all fell to the sand. Their executioners moved quickly in and bayoneted them to make quite sure they were dead.

Cavendish's face coloured purple.

'I'll have you court-martialled for this!' he said barely containing his anger. 'Every man jack of you will swing!'

Churchill regarded him as a boy might watch a fat spider crawling across his wall.

'I had orders from the Prime Minister himself!' Cavendish ranted.

'And I had orders from the King!' Churchill retorted. Cavendish's mouth flapped in that gaping fish look that his late brother had often adopted. He gathered himself together, span around and stalked away, nearly knocking his little weasely attendant over in the process.

Churchill turned to me and winked.

'As you said, Smith, they are too dangerous.' He moved off to direct the cleanup operation as the first rays of a new sun began to peek above the horizon.

EPILOGUE

I would like to take this opportunity to bring a sort of closure to this tale, for now at least. Here, my esteemed reader, is a brief summary of events immediately after the Battle of Brighton.

The cleanup operation took many months. The destruction that the Martian base machine, and its attendant Flying Machines, had wrought on the town of Brighton cost many thousands of pounds to put right. Incredibly, despite the loss of hundreds of human soldiers in the fighting, only twenty civilians were killed in this fiercest of battles. Ten of the dead were in a small hotel on the seafront that was directly in the path of the falling base, why they had not been evacuated during the battle is not clear. The cowardly owner of this establishment, who rather cannily *did* make good his escape, leaving those supposedly under his care to their own fates, was brought up on charges of negligence of the most heinous kind and was hanged, to the general approval of the populace, for his trouble.

Many services of thanksgiving were given in churches up and down the land, particularly in the South East and London, the primary targets, that the death toll had been so astonishingly low.

A few Martians had gone to ground in the area but it is thought that all were found in the following days and were despatched on sight. The Martian Overlord's escape craft was, to my chagrin, never discovered but was last seen, careering erratically and trailing smoke and flame, heading North over the Highlands of Scotland. I pray that the thing eventually crashed and the monsters within were obliterated on impact.

Scientists swarmed over the wreckage of the base and tried to salvage what machinery they could. The papers, at the time at least, were told that the explosions had damaged everything too badly to gain anything from what had been found. I, knowing how these things went in my dealings with our leaders, thought that this may not have been too close to the truth.

Events were, as they always have been, toned down in the press. No mention was made of the mission in *Nautilus*, but it was alluded to that Sir George Cavendish had died a hero, in the defence of the realm, leading an attack on a Martian stronghold. Little mention was made of the many brave men who had died with him, although some, including Thomas and Dawson received the Victoria Cross posthumously. Glenn made a full recovery and enjoyed a solid career in the military. The Sergeant marched proudly into the palace, one fine summer day, to receive the DSO from the King himself. He brought it to my house to show me one day and said he felt that I should have received one too. He never tired as before, in his frequent visits to my house, of telling the tall tales of his previous exploits, but sometimes, when the subject of the mission aboard *Nautilus* came up, his face took on a haunted look and the subject was turned to lighter matters. One does not, I have found, face demons and come away unaffected.

As for Churchill, he did not receive any punishment for his disobedience in killing the Martian prisoners. It seems he did, indeed, have the King's blessing for his actions and, instead of a trip to the gallows, was offered a

Knighthood. Churchill politely declined as he felt that such an honour was above him, such a man as he is.

I, for my part, went home as quickly as I was able. My wife's face was all I wished to see now and, a few days later, I fell gratefully into her loving arms.

So it was that, after all the death and destruction I had seen, came my own moment of joy.

I was, one day, tending the roses in our little garden on a warm day, with nary a cloud in sight in the wide blue sky, my wife returned from town after having gone on 'some errand'. She stood at the gate, simply looking at me for a while, her skin pale and her complexion flawless, and I thought I had never seen anyone more beautiful and that my love for her would last forever and, perhaps, past that.

'John, my love,' she said in a clear, gentle voice as she closed the gate behind her. 'I have some news.'

I put down my clippers and went to her.

'What is it?' I asked, concerned. 'Are you all right?'

She looked at me again with watery blue eyes.

'John,' she said steadily. 'I have visited with Doctor Pegg today. He says that you are to be a father.'

'Can it be true?' I asked as a wave of happiness that almost hurt washed over me. Her slight smile and the love that burned in her eyes told me that it was. 'But that's — that's absolutely the best news a man, any man, can have!'

We tearfully embraced then and, when I thought I could bear to let my darling wife go, just for a moment, I took her hand in mine and led her into the house.

Meanwhile, the rumblings of jealousy and resentment over British power grow louder in Europe. The people of the continent yearn for the wealth and power that we enjoy and strikes and rioting are common amongst these disgruntled peoples. Still the foreign governments, that we do not control, do nothing against us but protest in the strongest possible terms.

Across the British Empire, human Fighting Machines and other technologies are increasingly used to crush the growing insurrection amongst the subjects under our care. The more radical papers tell stories of the ruthless brutality and the stony hearts of those who are at the head of this, our new Rome, and there are those organizations within our own society that vocally, but anonymously, abhor such incidents.

Wealth and power are the aphrodisiacs that drive our leaders and they are not afraid to wield either to keep what they have accrued.

It is the fear of the technology that we apply with such vigour that keeps our nearest neighbours in check and us safe and aloof on our small island. For the time being, at least.

Across the wide, cold gulf of space, it is now, as I write these words, certain that the Martians are plotting anew. The Sergeant, on one of his visits, soberly told me that there has been new activity detected on that arid planet. The Crystal Egg had been recovered, its box slightly burned but the Egg itself unharmed, and scientists gaze into its depths constantly. Huge machines now crawl across the arid surface of Mars and the denizens of that eerie red globe hop excitedly about the Egg's line of sight. Our enemies will, I feel sure, make adjustments to their original flawed calculations and turn their brilliant, ruthless minds to a foolproof plan for our destruction. The next time they come, there will be no mistakes.

Our British Empire of Steel, like all great Empires over time can, I am sure, not last forever unopposed. Whether this opposition originates from our envious neighbours on

Earth, or from equally envious creatures from a distant red planet is, ultimately, of no consequence.

One day, I fear, the citizens of this small, green island will once again be routed and the world will, this time, surely follow.

THE END?

BONUS STORY
A Strange Document

Author note: This story was my first short fan-fiction and consists of a snapshot of life on board the HMS Thunder Child during the original 'The War of The Worlds'.

I've included it so you can see how I first started to find my way in the realms of storytelling. Looking at it now, it's a little rough around the edges but I hope you enjoy it.

A STRANGE DOCUMENT

BY TONY WRIGHT

FROM A LETTER TO A WELL KNOWN
INVESTIGATIVE JOURNALIST FROM A SOURCE
AT THE MINISTRY OF DEFENCE.
File Ref – MOD/WOW3/PO24a/HGW/JW

London 18th September 2004

Jeff,

Was just searching through the files we were discussing the other day and I came across this manuscript. I remembered you were researching THAT war and thought you might be interested in this. Perhaps I should draw your attention to Chapter 7, as it directly relates to your current interest. In case you were wondering, the chap responsible for the files at that time slapped an order on it after being tipped off by the publisher. Policy at the time forbade discussion of the subject in any form once things had calmed down, as you will know. So, unfortunately, the poor old bugger never did get his memoirs published. Not the definitive proof you were after alone, maybe, but interesting in the light of recent rumours I referred to in that excellent restaurant the other night. Put it together with the other stuff I gave you and make your own mind up.

I don't need to tell you that I know nothing of this, Cheers!

H.

NEPTUNE'S WARRIOR
by Capt. J.C.B.Smythe (Retd.)

Chapter 7: The Demise of a Brave Ship by One Proud to Serve on Her.

Attentive readers will be aware that, by the turn of the century, I was already familiar with the peculiar things that can happen in the service of this great nation's Navy.

As a young, fresh officer in 1891, and aforementioned in this humble collection of reminiscences, I had served aboard the HMS Scorpion on her voyage to Noble's Isle. There I had seen sights to chill the blood, but, as I have touched upon this subject earlier, I shall say no more.

Nothing, however, could prepare me for the events that occurred a few years into the new reign of His Majesty King Edward. Shortly after these events I saw, in a popular news sheet of the time by the name of 'The Pall Mall Budget' or some such, an account of the war which mentioned in passing the brave stand made by HMS Thunder Child. I then vowed to put forth my own account of this struggle, having been 'in the thick of it' as the popular saying goes. Now I can fulfil that solemn vow.

By the time of my transfer to *Thunder Child*, I had made the rank of 1st Lieutenant and had some considerable experience with men and ships. *Thunder Child* was a queer type of vessel, cigar shaped and low-lying, but her crew were of the most robust and hardy type that I ever had the honour of serving with.

Built in Chatham in 1879, *Thunder Child* was one of only two in the Polyphemus Class designed by the late Admiral of the Fleet Sartorius. Her sister ship, the *Polyphemus,* was the other. Both were Ironclad Torpedo Ram ships of 2,640 tons each, thrust through the water by twin screws at a top speed of 18 knots. They were both initially armed with five torpedo tubes, six Hotchkiss machine guns and, of course, a formidable ram. In 1882 they were both commissioned and served for long stretches in the Mediterranean.

It was shortly before the coming of the Martians that they separated. *Thunder Child* was returned to Chatham for refitting where I joined her, whilst *Polyphemus* remained on active duty for refitting at a later date. *Thunder Child* was fitted with 12 pounder guns, fore and aft, as it was hoped to make her more flexible in battle.

I had been in my new position for a few months when news of the spreading chaos in the South East of England reached us. Rumours were rife as to what was the nature of this new threat. Several times I had to 'calm the fever', as it were. The lack of news and that human malady they call 'curiosity' caused tongues to wag among the lower ranks.

The general feeling in those early days though was that we would crush this new terror like we would crush any other insurrection within the British Empire; swiftly and cleanly, with the minimum of fuss.

After the Surrey defeats and the Martian advance, we hurriedly put to sea to join a small Channel Defence Fleet. There were three other Ironclads that I distinctly remember in this fleet, namely *Miskatonic*, *Carrie* and *Cavor*. I later served aboard *Cavor* as my first command. My extraordinary experiences with the experimental metal cladding the 'boffins' gave her will be laid down in another chapter.

Thunder Child, at any rate, soon lay off the Essex Coast amongst the most extraordinary flotilla of assorted ships and boats which were gathered to carry a seemingly unending stream of humanity across to the continent and safety.

I remember well, as if I could forget that dreadful time, standing on the quarterdeck at the side of the Captain, as the great man muttered darkly under his breath at the seemingly suicidal manoeuvrings of this strange collection of vessels. We watched with baited breath as this fishing smack narrowly avoided that yacht, as people crammed into small boats struggled against the waves, with varying success.

That night, at dinner, we discussed the latest turn of events.

'Apparently, the Army are taking heavy casualties in Surrey,' said the ship's Doctor quietly.

'London will be next, I'll wager,' intoned the Commander toying a wineglass.

There was silence for a moment.

'Dash it all … I'd much rather be at the front line giving those … those … things a taste of British steel. In a matter of days we have been reduced to scurrying rabbits while those bastards stalk about the country on their metal legs … murdering!' exclaimed the Doctor, his unseemly outburst suddenly breaking the hushed atmosphere of the dining room.

The Captain spoke up. 'Our place is here. They have not, so far, made it to the coast. We may yet be the last line of defence, Gentlemen.' He paused to look about the room, savings a special glance for the Doctor.

'I will not hear any more of this, especially in front of the men. We are all chomping at the bit, I am sure, but I am also of the mind that our time will come.' The Captain spoke quietly, that is, as quietly as a bear-like man with a booming voice can speak. He spoke in a calming manner, though, and presently the conversation turned to other things.

I glanced at the Doctor and his thin, red face grinned sheepishly at me, his anger at his perceived inaction abated. Dinner resumed as usual.

I did not join in the forced, but otherwise light, banter. My thoughts were with my wife and daughter at home. Were they safe? I tried to calm my fears in the knowledge that my wife's brother (a dependable fellow if ever there was one) would likely ensure their safety and, soon, I felt a little better. In my bunk later, though, I gazed at their pictures and I am not ashamed to say that I prayed to the Almighty that he would keep them safe from the clutches of evil.

The next day I awoke at dawn to the thump of faraway guns.

Hurriedly, I dressed and headed to the quarterdeck. The Captain was already there. Indeed, despite his usual upright bearing, his huge bearded face gave away the fact that he must have been up all night.

'What's happening, Sir?' I asked.

He turned his great, owl-like visage towards me. 'Looks like our friends are heading this way. Gunfire coming from the coastal gun batteries.' He nodded landwards then returned his gaze to a distant point on the horizon.

Above the land, plumes of smoke rose lazily into the air. At intervals there came distant thumping as the Army guns bravely fought this unseen menace. The chaos in the water around us continued. Foam churned as a myriad of floating transport carried frantic, crying figures over the channel. How long the continent would be safe I did not know. How long before green flashes would be seen above the skies of France, Spain or Germany? Would those in the New World or our Antipodean cousins, perhaps, soon gaze with dread at those ghostly streaks of light tearing up the black blanket of night? Why should the Martians stop here unless we stopped them? I wondered how many other minds had pondered this.

A steward brought in hot black coffee and we sipped it silently as we watched the billowing smoke and tried to imagine the terrible struggle that was taking place on land. It seemed to me that the guns thumped with the regularity of a great beast's heart. The heart of England ... an England fighting for its very life. I'm sure that, like me, every soul on board *Thunder Child* willed that great heart to beat stronger and stronger, to give our England the strength to shake of this dreadful virus that had invaded its body. More than one silent prayer was, I could tell by the rapt faces around me, said in those quiet moments.

It was my practice to take a turn around the ship a few times a day, to 'grease the wheels'. After I had finished my coffee, I made my excuses and did so, shrugging off the melancholy and thinking businesslike thoughts.

In the lower quarters, I noticed a small knot of men standing around talking in low tones.

'Lacking something to do, Gentlemen?' I asked sharply, causing a jolt in one or two of them. Most of them drifted away into the bowels of the ship on some most likely urgent errand. One Able Seaman, however, remained behind.

'What is it, Jenkins?' I peered at him with the beadiest eye I could muster. It was a trick I had seen a Master-At-Arms use early in my career and, after much practice, I found that it always worked most admirably in putting off complainers and malingerers.

The boy, painfully slight and looking barely of age to be in the Service, approached me slowly.

'Well, spit it out, lad,' I said eyeing him again.

The boy stood for a moment wringing his hands as if searching for the right words.

'Sir,' he took a deep breath. 'Sir, me an' the lads was a-wonderin' … wha' with the Marshuns an' all … Well, Sir … wha' chance do we 'ave? We've 'erd terrible things about them … murderin' an' killin' … Big machines we've 'erd about … an' 'orrible guns of fire …'

The boy was obviously terribly afraid and my heart went out to him. Of course, I could not pander to him, that would not have done at all.

'Jenkins, what did you join His Majesty's Navy for?' I asked him sternly.

The boy thought for a moment, then answered. 'Sir, I joined up 'cause I wanted to see the world an' have adventures like my Father an' his Father before 'im.' He looked at me hopefully, wondering if this was what I wanted to hear.

'And adventures you shall have, Jenkins,' I answered. 'Out there no more than a few miles away is adventure. Just think what stories you will be able to tell your children, and your grandchildren. You can tell them that you served on the triumphant *Thunder Child* when she helped drive the Martian invaders clean back to where they came from. You can tell them that you saw those machines fall one by one as we showed them what real British grit can do. You can tell them that you helped to preserve the great British Empire for them and their children.' I waited and watched him.

Presently, a small smile flickered across his boyish face. 'Right you are, Sir! I'll be sure to do jus' that!' Jenkins exclaimed and, flicking a quick salute in my direction scampered off, his oversized uniform flapping on his thin frame.

Smiling, despite myself, I returned the salute to his scrawny back. At that, I returned to my duties.

It seems that perhaps my talk with Jenkins must have had a better effect than I could have hoped, as no more word of dissent or unease reached my ears. Indeed, morale seems to have risen, along with the healthy tension that goes with a wish to get 'stuck in' before a battle.

The ship's company waited with baited breath but, for a time, no sign of the Martian invasion showed, barring the ever increasing palls of smoke and the thump of the guns away to the distance. We had more news; London had fallen and part of His Majesty's Government had retreated to the Midlands to direct operations. The Martians did indeed have huge machines in which they stalked the land, although we had yet to see one. We did not have long to wait.

The morning was taken trying to instil some semblance of order into the general rout that was taking place in our stretch of water. Boat hit boat, we would intervene in the ensuing chaos and get jabbered at for our pains in English, Danish, French or whatever language the Captains of these motley vessels spoke. As the day drew on, the smoke from the coast grew thicker and the thump of the guns more intermittent. I did not think this was a good sign.

Soon after 2 o'clock in the afternoon we saw the first of them. The bright sun glinted at first on a small metallic object on the horizon and, suddenly, the alert rang out.

Coming swiftly down the coast was a Martian Tripod. Even at that distance we could only gape at the immense size of it.

On the quarterdeck, the Captain swore into his beard. At the enemy's approach, some guns to the South began a quick thumping. The game was afoot!

As we watched, two more Martians appeared, single file, as rapidly as the first.

With the slick ease of a greased wheel, *Thunder Child* sprang to life, the Captain barking orders that were obeyed with astonishing speed and precision. Beside him, my heart thudded in my chest as adrenaline surged through my system. My God, nothing we had heard had prepared us for the sight of those monstrous machines that filed towards our strange armada along the coast.

My esteemed reader will doubtless have read descriptions of these diabolical things but I shall attempt my own as descriptions seem to differ to varying degrees.

Each machine was something in the area of 100 feet high. Like a great shining ovoid that perched, somewhat precariously it seemed to me, on three delicate looking legs. For their speed, theirs was not a graceful motion, rather rolling gait, strange to behold and hard to describe. A writer once described it as 'like a milking stool walking' or some such. It was a little like that but also not so. The spindly legs of the machines crawled, spider like, as they propelled the contraptions and little puffs of some kind of green steam or smoke sprayed from the joints as they bent.

The machines had a kind of cabin projecting from the forward part of the ovoid which swayed about, gracefully, on a stalk not unlike a swan's neck. I understand, from information since received, that this 'head' or 'cabin' was where the Martian drivers lurked. From under the 'head' dangled a small forest of metal cables or tentacles that waved about expressively as the thing moved. These loathsome giants periodically emitted an uncanny, wailing howl that I took to be their method of communication. I have since learned that this may not, in fact, be the case, although I do not profess to comprehend the details given later by the scientists.

The first of these machines waded out to sea toward us and our little charges that, with renewed vigour at the sight of these invaders, frantically battled their way toward safety.

The Captain barked more orders and *Thunder Child* headed at full power towards the behemoth that staggered towards the panicking vessels so near to freedom. The twin smoke stacks belched sparks and billowing black clouds as we rushed headlong towards our quarry. The Captain, ashen-faced, but with a clear, calm voice spoke. 'We are not to fire until I give the order.'

'Sir?' I asked, not a little confused.

'We will charge the closest machine first. Wait for my signal.' That said, he turned and stared resolutely at the enemy ahead.

We steamed on. The distance between our ship and the machine closed rapidly. The Martian in his craft was directing a strange beam at some of the small vessels, those that it touched turned to fire instantly or exploded in a fearful fashion. Great clouds of steam and smoke probed the already soot-streaked sky. I fancied that the little white waves that broke against the monster's spindly legs glowed with some unearthly light.

It must have tired quickly of this game, because it swung its 'head' round swiftly as if looking for more worthy prey. Soon enough it alighted on a large steamer that was painfully pulling out to sea behind us, crammed full with people. As it headed towards the overloaded vessel, it suddenly seemed to spot us as we sped towards it. The machine stopped dead and seemed to look with some surprise at the low slung, grey shape that approached it.

'Damn it! On my order!' bellowed the Captain, as if to stay any gunner's itchy fingers. 'Go and keep an eye on those gunners, Smythe.'

'Sir!' I said and rushed out on deck.

Men were there, staring transfixed at the looming shape above us.

'Why doesn't it attack, Sir?' asked a familiar reedy voice. I turned and saw Jenkins at my side, his face a mask of horror at the apparition before us.

'We've got it surprised, Jenkins,' I said, wondering the very same thing.

As I spoke, the Martian raised its head, seemed to look directly into my eyes and fired some form of projectile from a gun it unhitched from its body. The canister glanced harmlessly off the armoured sides of our great ship and span off into the sea, discharging as it went a dense, black smoke. The other Martians approached us now as our nearest adversary raised a large metallic box in one of its repulsive tentacles. As the Martians' terrible Flame Ray pierced the side of *Thunder Child*, throwing great clouds of steam and showers of white hot metal in all directions, the Captain bellowed 'FIRE!' and our forward guns boomed.

The ship lurched alarmingly like a wounded animal but the Gunner's aim was true. The first Martian machine seemed to wheel about on one leg, then crash with a great spray of water into the depths. A whoop of joy issued from the men assembled on the deck and, turning towards the steamer, I could see distant figures jumping on her deck and waving their arms.

Dense black fog and intense heat radiated from the side of our plucky ship but still she sped on, turning a little to confront the second form looming nearby.

'See, Jenkins, your grandchildren will thrill to this yarn!' I said, excited as the rest at our success.

'Reckon as they will, Sir,' breathed the boy.

As she went, her guns spoke again and again. Shells splashed into the water, some even hit other human vessels, but we were oblivious to this, concentrating as we were on the second Martian that was heading toward us at an alarming rate.

A few shells ineffectually burst around the Martian's 'head' as it swung its awful weapon around wildly, trying to strike a bead on us.

Then, that deadly flame leapt out at us and I suddenly found myself thrown, like a child's doll, far up into the air and out to sea. Even as I flew, though, I saw the deck explode into shards of metal and splinters of wood as if at a quarter speed. The blast obliterated the giant spindly tower as *Thunder Child* played her last card. She, outraged, took a terrible revenge against her attacker and scattered it to the four winds. Through the hissing of the superheated water around the shattered ship, I fancied I heard poor, young Jenkins scream as he was torn from his body and sent to the place where all brave sailors go to their final rest.

Of that awful day, there is not much more to relate. As the valiant Ironclad Torpedo Ram *Thunder Child* breathed her last, she had indeed taken with her the one that had melted her brave heart. With her supreme sacrifice and that of her crew, she facilitated the escape of many thousands of terrified, helpless people. For a few brief moments, she showed humankind that there could still be hope, even against the greatest adversity.

As I floated, vulnerable but strangely tranquil, in the seething water, I could swear that I saw a giant flat, metallic shape, not unlike a tea saucer and bigger than the largest dirigible, float slowly overhead. This vision was quickly lost to my burning eyes as it suddenly accelerated towards land.

I was rescued, bleeding, severely burned and half drowned a short time later. My war was over. I recovered eventually, as will be seen, and resumed my career. To this day, though, I often wake in the still of night, soaked with sweat and sobbing. My ears still sometimes ring with the remembrance of the last, agonised scream of the *Thunder Child's* passing.

Of *Thunder Child's* entire crew I, alone, survived to mourn her.

THE STORY CONTINUES

If you have enjoyed this book, watch out for ...

'THE WAR OF THE WORLDS: REMEMBRANCE'

The Martian threat on Earth has been overcome, but the danger to mankind has far from passed.

By 1914, world tension is close to boiling point.

As Europe heads inexorably toward a war that will set man against man, the Martians, having learned from their mistakes, begin their attack plans anew.

Will this war be the war to end all wars?

The War of The Worlds: Remembrance will be an epic alternate history of what becomes man's most desperate struggle for survival yet.

FURTHER READING

For those who can't get enough of The War of The Worlds, I recommend the following:

The War of The Worlds by H.G Wells – The original masterpiece.

Scarlet Traces written by Ian Edginton and illustrated by D'Israeli – an interesting graphic novel that portrays a changed England after The War of The Worlds.

Global Dispatches – The stories of various real historical characters set during the original Martian War.

The Space Machine by Christopher Priest – a story that runs parallel to Wells' work that is set partially on Mars.

www.scifishocks.com – A forum that has a section devoted to discussion of The War of The Worlds in all its forms. Run by the author of this book.

www.thewaroftheworlds.com – the official website of Jeff Wayne's marvelous musical version of the The War of The Worlds story.

www.hgwellsusa.50megs.com – the H G Wells Society

AUTHOR'S BIOGRAPHY

Tony Wright was born in West Sussex, England.

He runs the thriving Science Fiction and Horror related internet Forum, www.SciFiShocks.com and administrates on other The War of The Words related web forums. He also writes song lyrics for the experimental rock music project, 'Playing With Pylons' and likes nothing better than a good (or bad!) horror or Sci-Fi movie.

Tony lives in the beautiful North East of England and Aftermath is his first novel.

You can, if you dare, follow Tony on Twitter: www.twitter.com/scifishocks.